Street Dreams and Nightmares

THE DUOLOGY

AL-SAADIQ BANKS

And Nightmares

BOOK 2

AL-SAADIQ BANKS

TRUE 2 LIFE PUBLICATIONS

This novel is a work of fiction. Any resemblances to real people, living or dead, actual events, establishments, organizations, or locales are intended to give the fiction a sense of reality. Other names, characters, places, and incidents are either products of the author's imagination or are used fictitiously.

Author: Al-Saadiq Banks

Contact Information:
True 2 Life Publications
P. O. Box 8722
Newark, New Jersey 07108

Email: alsaadiqbanks@aol.com
Twitter: @alsaadiq
Instagram: @alsaadiqbanks

www.True2LifeProductions.com

Edited By: True 2 Life Media Conglomerate LLC
Email: alsaadiqbanks@aol.com
P.O. Box 8722
Newark, New Jersey 07108
For Editing, and Typesetting Services

"Most men never think about the end game until the end game is in front of them. They never fully committed to themselves that they were in it for the good or the bad because they never thought far enough into it to see the bad. So, what do they do when they're confronted with the bad that comes with it? They flip like an Olympic Gymnast"

— Lefty

Hall Of Fame Boxing Club

DARRYL DECIDED TO STAY away from the block today. Last night he witnessed a lot of talking to detectives taking place. He hasn't contacted anyone because he isn't trusting them at this point. His curiosity is driving him crazy though. He wonders about Smitty's condition because it determines his fate. Overall he has no regrets but he does know a shooting charge is all he needs to violate his probation. He took the day off from the block, and had nothing else to do but come to the gym.

Darryl stands ringside, watching as Lefty and a pro boxer out of Baltimore are about to spar. The gym is packed, and no one is working. Instead, everyone is crowded around the ring waiting for the show. This sparring match appears to be to Lefty's disadvantage. With the Baltimore fighter 6 feet 6 inches tall, he stands over Lefty like a skyscraper. He's beautifully crafted like an African sculpture with bowling ball shoulders and solid tree trunk legs. For the first time, the gym members are worried about Lefty.

The bell rings, and Lefty walks to the center with his usual sluggish demeanor while the African Tower

1

dances to the center. Upon their introduction, the African Tower flings a quick jab that taps the forehead area of Lefty's headgear. Lefty tries to cut around him, but he throws an even faster jab that pops him in the same spot. Lefty flinches at the African Tower, and he flings another jab. Lefty slips to the right and fires a power-packed right hand to the body. The whole gym sighs, just imagining the pain that right hand must have caused.

The African's face twists with agony. The right hand makes his intestines tremble, and he drops his arm to cradle the pain. Lefty unloads a mouthful of leather from the straight jab, which sends the giant back a few steps. Lefty quickly turns over a right overhand that crashes into the ear of the African man.

The African Tower backpedals to get away, but Lefty jumps right on him. Lefty throws a limp left into the air just as a ploy. When the African man reacts, Lefty fires a right to the man's body again, hitting the same spot. The African man stands with his face scrunched with pain. Lefty plays with his mind by jumping at him and making back-to-back senseless moves to confuse him.

The African man doesn't know what he should protect. He blocks his face, his side his chin, in confusion. Quickly, Lefty fires a straight right to the chin. The African's knees buckle. The look on his face is that of one in a scary movie. The African drops his hands and runs to the corner. He forces the top rope down and hurdles over it. He stands in front of his trainer with his hands high, signaling for the trainer to remove the gloves. He's had enough.

The man's trainers are pissed. They drove 4 hours from Baltimore just for the sparring session to last for a minute before he quits. The trainer removes the gloves, making their way to the locker room angrily.

"I'm the one in there taking that abuse, not y'all. That motherfucker hit like a mule," the African says. He has no regret for quitting whatsoever.

Lefty gets out of the ring, and Darryl daps him up. "Good work."

Lefty stares over Darryl's head into the eyes of Boobie Salaam. "Ay, when you gone give my Baby Boy his money back?" Lefty asks as he points to Darryl. This catches Darryl by surprise. "Took all his money in the ring that day and never even gave him a chance to get it back. Every man deserves the opportunity to get his back, right?"

Boobie Salaam understands this to be a set-up. With all the times Lefty has called him out, and he didn't get in the ring with him, he knows he can't possibly accept this invitation. "In due time, I'm going to give him that opportunity."

"Yeah, alright," Lefty says in an evident brush-off.

One Hour Later

Darryl is dropping Lefty off at home, and he thinks this is the perfect time to proposition him. The proposition isn't for his gain alone, though. This proposition could very well be of benefit for Lefty as well. After thinking long and hard about all that has happened, including last night's shooting, Darryl realizes he can't run at this pace forever. He's gaining more enemies by the day, and the reality is one man can't fight an army alone.

"Yo, I've been thinking," Darryl says, interrupting Lefty's dinner.

Lefty looks up. "About?"

"I think I got a way for you to better your situation." Lefty looks over again with a blank expression. "Last night, I just took the block over. From here on out, I got it to the neck. If you want to come out there, you're

3

more than welcome. It's enough money out there for the both of us."

As much as Darryl would like to see Lefty better his life, he also has his agenda. He's out here alone and feels he needs someone by his side he can trust. "I will front you the work until you can buy your own. And if you find you an apartment, I will put the rent up for the first ninety days."

Lefty laughs. "Nah, Baby Boy," he whispers in his normal low and husky tone. "I don't sell no drugs. That ain't my thing. I appreciate the invite, and I appreciate you wanting to help me and give me a boost," he says gratefully. "But, just like the Muslims say...a man can't change his conditions until he changes the conditions of his heart."

Lefty nods his head up and down slowly. He points at his own chest. "I got a lotta shit in here and here," he says as he taps his temple. "That I have to change before I'm able to change the things around me."

Darryl nods his head as well. As weird as it may sound, Darryl feels him. "I get it."

Lefty chuckles. "Baby Boy, you know, you a good man. A nigga ain't never offered to help me with nothing. All a motherfucker ever wanted to do with me is use me. Even though I can't accept your invitation, I appreciate it."

At the traffic light, they lock eyes. "And that's from the bottom of my motherfucking heart."

"You a good nigga and remind me of a dude who is like a brother to me. Real good nigga, but like I always tell him," he says as she shakes his head from side to side. "Good niggas get used, abused, and walked over." Darryl pulls off, but still, he listens attentively. "One day, I wanna put y'all two in the same room. Two good niggas together, I'm sure, will make greatness."

Darryl parks in front of Penn Station, and Lefty gathers his belongings. He looks over at Darryl without blinking his eye. "If you ever need me for anything outside of selling dope, I'm here for you. Do understand that I have listened to you talk about how you are out here all alone." Lefty smiles. "But trust me, you may think you're alone, but I'm always with you in spirit. And if you ever call on me, I'm gone come running."

The Next Day
The Location

DARRYL GOT THE WORD that Smitty is out of the hospital, lying up in the comfort of his own home. He was shot in the hip and the knee. Apparently, everybody from the block has gone to see him except Darryl of course. To Darryl's surprise, some of the customers and even neighborhood folks have gone to visit Smitty. He didn't realize so many people had love for Smitty. Now he believes that love may have turned into hatred against him. He may have created more enemies with that move and realizes he can't trust anyone at this point. Still, he has no regrets because he feels that move had to be made.

Darryl has been keeping his ears open and no one has uttered a word about them being questioned by the detectives. The fact that no one is mentioning it, to him is confirmation that he can't trust any of them. Gossip has come back to Darryl of what Smitty claims he's going to do in revenge. Darryl is almost sure he's speaking purely off of pride. He's glad to hear that Smitty is claiming to handle their beef on the street instead of letting the authorities handle it for him. In no way does Darryl believe he's ready to do what he claims he's going to do. Although he doesn't believe him, he will take his threat as a promise and keep his eyes open, and his gun cocked at all times.

As far as the rest of the members of the block, they're all ready to fall in line. When Darryl first stepped onto the block this afternoon, they all looked as if they saw a ghost. No one knew what to expect from him. As he stepped onto the side of the street, they were all posted, he saw all of them take their last breath before he got there. With fear, they held that breath until he passed.

He didn't say a word to anyone. He just sat a few feet away from them quietly. His silence made them more uncomfortable. Darryl hates to oppress anyone. The fact that they have an overnight fear of him is unreal to him. He hates when one takes advantage of the weak, but in this case, it's different. He refuses to share money with vulnerable individuals that will not stand up for themselves. Until they are willing to stand up and fend for themselves like men, they will have to follow his rules and protocol.

All this is a bit much for them to digest in just two days. To go from doing their own thing to working for him is an entirely different game. Under any other circumstances, none of them would even entertain the thought. After witnessing what happened to Smitty for putting up a challenge, they all understand he means business.

As hard as it may be for them to look at Darryl in this light, he has given them no choice. Little by little, they have witnessed his transformation without them paying notice. There are so many things he's done over the past months that prove that he's not the same Darryl they've known for years. The money and the streets have changed him.

Smitty claims Darryl shot him out of fear of what he was about to do to him. The others saw it differently. They saw a look in Darryl's eyes they had never seen before. They watched him pull the trigger with ease, not force. They watched him aim at his target before squeezing again. Then they watched as Darryl stood watching with great pleasure as Smitty rolled around on the ground. The look in his eyes showed no compassion.

If this shooting isn't enough to prove to them, he means business; many other situations should support the fact. The times he has taken shots at stick-up kids, and the way he ran down on Fu-Red is more than enough proof to make them believers. As much as they hate to view him in that light, they have no choice. Whether they like it or not, Darryl has become someone not to be played with.

Darryl sits back on the porch peeking from side to side. All the members from the block are huddled around him. He digs his hand in the shopping bag that sits between his feet. He retrieves two bright white pampers from the bag, and he hands them to Zak before he digs his hand inside again. The next two, he passes to Shaka. In total, he gives out ten pampers.

This is quite humiliating for them to be taking work from him. Since none of them are willing to go to the length that he's proven that he's ready to go, they will not go against him. They've watched what he's capable and willing to do, and none of them want to be made another example.

As they stand, awaiting his instructions, he pulls his revolver from his waistband. They stand with nervousness. He lays the pistol on his lap before covering it with a newspaper. He leans back on the porch, laying in the cut. "Now, let's get money."

One Month Later/November 27, 1990

DARRYL IS ON HIS WAY to Spanish Harlem. His operation takeover has been a total success. Everyone on the block plays their part in handling their business as prescribed. On the flip side, Darryl has held up to his bargain of protecting them as he promised.

He doesn't look at it as protecting them. He looks at it more like safeguarding his investment. The word must have spread throughout the city that he's not having the stick-ups on his block because he has only had one encounter with stick-up kids in the past month. That encounter resulted in him blasting two stick-up kids. Since that night, things have been pretty quiet.

With everyone pumping Darryl's work, his flow has increased radically. His twice-a-week trips have expanded to three times a week. Ripping through a kilo every three days gives him a profit of about thirty-thousand dollars a week. This puts him in a financial position he never dreamt of being in.

Darryl and Unk walk beside each other as they approach the building. "Papo, what up?" Unk says as he passes a familiar man.

The man follows behind them. "Uno momento, Poppy," the man says as he takes the lead. They follow him through the small area that separates the two buildings. "Wait, right here," the man demands. He grabs hold of his walkie-talkie and begins to spit a few words of Spanish into it.

In a matter of minutes, a black, tinted car pulls in front of the building. "Get in," the man instructs.

"Huh?" Darryl asks with uncertainty. "Go where?"

"Just go, no worry," the man claims.

Darryl looks at Unk to see what he has to say. Unk looks at the man. "Papo, what's up?"

"Go, go," the man barks. "No problemo."

Unk studies his eyes before looking back at Darryl. "Come on," he says as he starts to walk toward the car. The man follows closely behind, and he takes the lead once they get there and opens the back door for them to enter.

They both slide in and the man slams the door shut. He then runs to the driver's window and says a few words in Spanish to the driver. The driver pulls off and begins speeding through the busy city. "What the fuck you think this is about?" Darryl asks Unk.

Unk shrugs his shoulders. "Beats me."

Darryl observes as the driver goes through blocks he's never been through. Ten minutes later, the driver slows down and stops. Darryl looks around, paying close attention to his surroundings. The area is quite different from the area they just left. The area seems less congested, and the streets are bare. No Dominicans are posted on the corners. There are no signs of drug activity in the area. Darryl looks back at the street signs, which read 194th Street and Audubon.

As they're parked, Darryl notices a short Dominican man walking out of the building they are sitting in front of. As the man gets closer, his face becomes familiar. It's the face of the man he met months ago at the spot. The man they call the Big Boss.

The Big Boss stops at the back door. He waves them on to get out. Unk forces the door open, and they both get out. "Yo," the man says with an inviting smile. He reaches out to shake Darryl's hand.

"What's up?" Darryl asks as he returns the handshake.

"Come on," Big Boss instructs as he leads them into the building. They walk in silence throughout the quiet corridor and take the stairs to the third floor. Once they reach the top of the staircase, Big Boss pulls his keys from his pocket, and he opens the door to the first apartment on the floor. He opens the door and holds it open for them to enter first.

Darryl walks in first. He looks around at the tidy apartment. The sweet aroma of fresh Spanish food cooking seeps through the air. As he's looking around at the rest of the apartment, his attention is snatched by a beautiful young Dominican girl. She walks past them without even looking their way.

Big Boss leads them into a bedroom. "From now on, no go to the spot," he says. "Come here," he adds. "No hot here. Nobody on the street and no policia," he says. "Much better for you is much better for me," he says with a smile. He looks away. "Barbara!" he shouts.

The young Dominican girl walks into the room. "Barbara," he says as he points to Darryl. "This is our friend Dee. Dee, this is Barbara."

They lock eyes. "Hey," the girl whispers with a smile.

"What's up?" Darryl replies. Darryl is shocked that the Big Boss even remembers his name. He feels like such a little fish in the pond that he assumes his name isn't even of importance to him. He also believes he's met so many customers he would never remember him.

Darryl doesn't know that as many customers as he's met, not many come to buy a kilo from him every three days. Because Darryl does, he has made a good and lasting impression on the Big Boss. He's made such an impact on him that he would hate to lose him as a customer. He can't take the risk of Darryl getting locked up down at the hot spot.

"How much you need?" Big Boss asks.

"The same," Darryl replies. "One kilo."

The Big Boss speaks Spanish to the girl, taking off across the room. She stops at the armoire. She opens it and what Darryl sees brings a sparkle to his eyes. He sees at least twenty kilos piled up on the shelves in clear view.

She turns around to them. "Come on," she says. Darryl walks over to her, trying hard to keep his eyes on her and not the beauty on the shelves. He doesn't want to come across as suspicious. "Which one do you buy?" she asks.

"Huh?" Darryl asks with confusion. She holds two separate bags in her hand. Inside one bag Darryl sees bright white cocaine with shiny crystals sparkling. Inside the other bag, Darryl sees cocaine that is not as appealing.

"The good one," she says as she lifts her right hand. "Line for line guaranteed." She then raises her left hand. "Cheapy-choppa," she says with a smile. "Nineteen dollars a gram, or fourteen dollars a gram."

"The good one," Big Boss shouts from another room.

"Ok," she replies as she places the bags back on the shelf. She then grabs a sealed kilo from the top shelf and hands it to him.

The words fourteen a gram stick out in Darryl's head. He looks back at Big Boss. "What's up with the cheapy-choppa? Is it any good?"

The man walks over. "It's good," he replies. "But not the best. No line for line. You cook one gram, maybe seven lines come back. No ten lines," he adds. "One kilo, three hundred grams cut maybe on one kilo," he explains.

The price of fourteen dollars a gram is quite tempting to Darryl. Seven lines doesn't sound half bad to him, especially with his two-for-five operation. He feels his clientele will never be able to tell the difference.

Darryl looks over to Unk. "What you think?"

Unk stands, afraid to answer. He remembers what happened the last time he talked them into buying the cheaper product. "Nah, go with the regular one," he urges.

Darryl debates back and forth in silence. The Big Boss steps up. "You buy regular one," he says. He then speaks a few words of Spanish to the girl, and she begins dumping cocaine from the other bag onto the scale. She bags it up and hands it to the Big Boss.

"Here," he says as he shoves the bag to Darryl. "You take one hundred grams," he says before pausing. "Take it to your customers, check it out. Psst." He sucks his teeth as he waves his hand. This holds no real value to him. "No problem. No, pay me for nothing. Just tell me what you think. Maybe you people like it and you no need to spend nineteen from now on. They like it, you save money and make money," he says with a smile.

"Thanks," Darryl says gratefully. He passes the bag over to Unk, and he wraps it in paper towels. He then unravels a black shopping bag he pulls from his back pocket, and he packs the kilo into the shopping bag.

Big Boss speaks Spanish to the girl once again, and she begins piling rocks onto the digital scale. She bags it up and hands it to Unk. The Big Boss speaks again. "One ounce," he says. "Every time you come, she give you one ounce."

Unk's eyes light up with joy. This is the very first time he's ever felt appreciated in any spot he's ever been to. "Thanks," he smiles. He nods his head up and down. "I like you, Big Boss." He smiles. "Thanks."

"No problem," he replies. "I no you Boss. He is," he says as he points to Darryl with a smile. "I take care of you, and you take care of me. We take care of each other," he adds. "Valuable customer," he says as he points to Darryl.

Darryl stands gloating. He likes the sound of that, and he feels like he has arrived. For the first time in this game, he no longer feels like a mere peon. Today he feels like *The Man*. Oh, what a feeling.

-4-

The Location

THE STORE CLOSED HOURS AGO. With no lights from the store and no light coming from the streetlamps, one can barely see in front of them. A few nights ago, Darryl came up with the idea of blacking the area out. He had all the lamps broken and even shot out two of them. With it pitch black out here, it gives them the advantage against stick-up and police.

Darryl stands posted up against the laundromat while everyone else is on the opposite side of the street. He observes the area. As his eyes scan the block, his attention is caught by a beautiful, 850 BMW cruising the block. "Damn," he mutters to himself as he admires the vehicle.

He keeps his eyes glued on the car as it slowly approaches the intersection. He can't see inside due to the dark tinted windows. He's shocked to see the car slow down just as it gets to Shaka and the rest of the crew. He has no clue who is there and what they could be slowing down for. He automatically becomes alarmed.

He sits down on the stoop of the laundromat, attempting to be as discreet as possible. He slides his hand into his army jacket pocket and grips his revolver. He watches with caution as the car speeds up through the intersection. He peeks through the windows of the vehicle parked in front of him. Through the windows, he sees the BMW pass by him.

Suddenly the brake lights pop on. The car stops, and the reverse lights come on shortly after. The car comes toward him in reverse, slowly. Darryl stands up with his gun gripped tightly in his pocket. "Yo, who this?" he asks as he cuts his eye across the street. He peeks across the street as the car is coming. None of them reply.

The car stops directly in front of Darryl. Darryl has his gun gripped in hand, inside his pocket. The passenger's side window rolls down, slowly exposing the passenger's face. The man's face is unfamiliar to Darryl. Darryl slowly pulls his hand out of his pocket.

"Yo," Darryl hears faintly in the background.

Darryl bends down, peeking into the car. "Who that?"

"It's me, Boobie Salaam," the driver says.

Darryl is shocked to see him. "What's up?" Darryl asks.

"I need to kick it with you. Let me pull over."

Kick it with me, Darryl thinks to himself. For what? About what? He watches as Boobie Salaam gets out of the car and makes his way over to him. The passenger has gotten out as well. As he approaches, he extends his hand for a handshake. Darryl returns the handshake with slight hesitation. "What's going on?" Darryl asks.

"You," Boobie Salaam replies with a smile. "I've been trying to find you. You haven't been in the gym in a minute, huh? You ain't boxing no more?"

"Yeah, I'm still boxing," Darryl whispers. "Just had to put it on the back burner for a minute. Boxing ain't paying the bills."

"I can dig it," Boobie Salaam replies. "That's exactly what I've been looking for you for. I got a way we both can make some paper and pay the bills," he says with a smile.

Oh, Darryl thinks to himself. This is what it's all about. Darryl assumes this meeting is about Boobie Salaam propositioning him to take work from him. *This nigga must don't know who the fuck I am, Darryl thinks to himself. He must think I'm some little ass boy that he can run game on and get me to take work from him.* "Nah, I'm good," Darryl replies with arrogance.

Boobie Salaam smiles. "How you know you good when you don't even know what I got planned for us? You never know, it could be very beneficial for you. As a matter of fact, I'm sure it's beneficial for you."

"I'm sure," Darryl replies. "I'm my own man. I do my own thing," he says as he stares Boobie Salaam directly in the eyes. "Always have been and always will be."

Boobie Salaam smiles again. "I don't doubt that, lil' bruh, and I ain't here trying to get you to give up your independence. Do your thing. You're supposed to do that. I'm just trying to put a little extra bread on the table for the both of us. Before you reject it, just hear me out first. It doesn't cost you nothing to listen, do it?"

Darryl turns his head away from Boobie Salaam. "Go ahead. I'm listening."

"Thanks, lil' bruh," he says with his signature charming smile. "Dig, I've been watching you in the gym. I watched you from the first day I met you. You know the day me, and you moved around." Darryl's heart sinks as he thinks of that day. He lowers his eyes with shame. "I put the pressure on you just to see what you were made of. I found out you got the heart of a lion. I saw it in your eyes that you didn't want to quit, but your body couldn't go any further. I gained a hell of a lot of respect for you that day," he says.

Hearing this lifts Darryl's spirit. It seems like everyone who saw that sparring match all respects him, and it's evident that what they saw was different from what he thought he displayed. He's amazed every time someone tells him this.

"I've been around for a long time," Boobie Salaam says. "When the average cat gets hit with that shit I hit you with, they fold like a chair," he brags. "They run to the corner and never run back out of it. I'm not going to lie to you. I didn't know you had it in you. I judged the book by its cover, just like most are going to do," he whispers.

"And that's why I need you with me. Oh, and not to forget the way you spared my lil' nephew. That showed class I didn't expect you to have. I thought you would take revenge on him. And when you didn't, I fell in love with you as a champion in the making. I need you with me," he repeats once again.

"Need me with you? How?"

"Here it goes," he whispers as he looks around. "I just started this little underground boxing situation, and I got fighters coming from all over the city and even out of town," he informs. "Some niggas alright with the hands, but none are that skilled. They think they can fight better than they actually can. Me," he says as he taps his chest. "They all know me and what I'm capable of. No one in their right mind will get in the ring with me," he brags. "As I said, no one will expect you to be able to fight the way you can. We can put you up in there with these non-fighting mufuckers and take all their money," he says with eyes stretched wide.

"It's big money on the table! Last Saturday, I put twenty on a kid that I thought was a sure shot, and I lost it all," he says with a look of despair. "With you, I will put fifty grand up because I saw your work, and

I saw their work. They don't have nothing on you. Whatever the pot is, we split it down the middle, you and me," he claims. "What you think?"

"I don't know about that," Darryl replies.

"Think about it. Here, take my number and call me on Saturday, and I will come pick you up and take you to the spot. After you see how easy taking their money will be, you will be ready to strap up that night. I bet you! It's easy like taking candy from a baby!"

Boobie Salaam stops short and turns around. "Oh, and bring your man with the one hand if you can. Lots of heavyweight work be in the building too. It's money on the table for everybody."

The Location

IT'S ONLY EIGHT, and it's already pitch dark outside. Heavy rain pours from the sky. The rain is so heavy it's blinding, and it's difficult to see your hand in front of your face. Darryl stands against the wall between Shaka and Zak, and Rashawn stands next to Zak.

A customer turns the corner, walking toward them. "Let me get two," the man shouts.

A short, husky man dressed in army fatigues steps up from the car he was leaning against. "What's up, what's up?" he asks as he bounces from side to side in front of the man anxiously. He opens his hand, flashing a few vials. "Right here. I got you."

"Nah, I'm good," the man says. "I want it from my man right there." He points to Darryl. Darryl shakes his head from side to side sneakily, but the man isn't paying the slightest bit of attention to him.

"Come on, come on," the man demands. "We all got the same thing," he says as he exposes the vials once again. The man is quite hesitant because never before has he seen this dealer. "Look," he says as he shoves the vials into his face. "Check it out."

The man lowers his face closer to the dealer's palm, studying the vials. Just as he gets within three inches of the man's palm, *Smack!* The life is smacked out of him. He backs up in shock. He has no clue what's happening until he's turned around and the cuffs are slapped onto his wrist.

"You dumb motherfucker," the man says as he drags the customer by the handcuffs. The cop escorts the man to the white Cherokee that's parked a few feet away. The hatch of the jeep is snatched open, and the man is shoved into the back.

Darryl looks at Shaka, shaking his head. They all stand in fear. The police have been posing as drug dealers for the past half hour. Some customers sensed something wasn't right and kept it moving. The ones who were not savvy enough to pick up on it are all piled into the unmarked cars parked along the block.

In total, there are five cars out here. The Cherokee is parked right in front of them. A Pathfinder is parked across the street, and so is a small Buick. The two unmarked cars can be spotted from miles away. There's no coincidence they're parked directly in front of the alley they all use to stash their work. Thirteen police occupy those vehicles, and only two are standing with Darryl and the crew. The other eleven are scattered out in the backyard, searching for their stashes that they are sure are back there somewhere.

Darryl manages to play it cool and calm. He realizes there is enough work in that backyard to send all of them to prison for some years. Time creeps by, and finally, Darryl sees an officer come walking out of the alley. Two more follow him. In seconds they all come pouring out of the alley. They're all coming to the side of the street where Darryl and the crew are standing.

Darryl's heart is racing. He looks over to Zak, who has fear in his eyes. Zak shakes his head from side to side, and so does Darryl. They both feel like it's over.

The officer standing in front of Darryl looks to his partner and speaks. "What's up?" Everyone listens with their undivided attention. They all need to know what's in store from this point on.

The officer shakes his head with disappointment. "Nothing. Nothing at all," he whispers.

"Nothing?" the man asks. "Impossible!" he shouts. These officers have been watching from a block away with binoculars and have even had an undercover walk through to figure out the exact house they were running to. "That's the spot they been running back and forth from," he explains. "Y'all ain't look hard enough. Let me go back there. I bet you I will find it."

"Psst," the officer replies. "We've been back there for over an hour. We turned over every can, shook every branch, and tore every piece of aluminum siding down. We did everything except dig a grave back there. It isn't back there, and I'm telling you this for certain. They must be going back there and running into another yard or something," the man says with confusion. "No pressure today, though. It's always next time."

The man turns away from his partner and stares Zak in the eyes. "Okay, gentlemen. The party is over. Y'all got lucky. We didn't find it tonight, but we will find it," he says, nodding up and down. "Y'all get out of here before I come up with a reason to take all of y'all in with those crackheads we got in the car." He gives his partners a head nod, signaling them to head to the cars. "Oh, and tell D-Low we're on his ass."

Darryl knees buckle at the sound of his name. "What," he mumbles to himself as he picks up his step. He leads the pack down the street. They can't get away fast enough. They watch the cops, who are all still standing where they left them. In seconds they've cleared the block and are all out of sight.

One Hour Later

Darryl and the crew step onto the block cautiously. They all peek around, looking for signs of the police. After finding the coast clear, they all dash through the alley with the speed of lightning to the backyard. Darryl stands at the entrance while everyone else scatters. "Here go mines!" Zak shouts as he holds two mud-covered pampers in his hand.

"Mine right here," says Rashawn.

"Got mine," Zak says.

Darryl stands with satisfaction as he stares at his men, all holding dirty, filthy pampers. He looks around. Just as the cop stated, they have torn the entire yard apart. Everything is out of place except for the pampers. Not one of them has been opened or tampered with. They have not even thought of looking inside them, but Darryl completely understands why. It could be a shitty job, so no one wants to do it.

This proves that his stash is fool-proof. He's sure their work will never be found. He realizes that is only half of his battle. The other half of the battle is staying out of the way of the police. Them knowing his name causes him concern. He wonders how they became aware of him. He also wonders how they know his name without knowing his face. Whatever the case is, he must keep it like that.

-6-

Days Later

ASIA RIDES SHOTGUN in the Honda Civic while her best friend Tammy drives. Asia is home for Christmas break, and she hasn't been back for twenty minutes, and they're already on the road. Tammy missed Asia so much that she couldn't wait for Asia to return to Jersey. She was so anxious to see Asia that she sat in Asia's room for over two hours, awaiting her arrival.

Tammy and Darryl are the two people in the world that Asia missed the most. Asia missed the two of them even more than she missed her mother. While away, Asia spoke to Tammy and Darryl three to four times a day, but still, that wasn't enough for her. She longed for the day she could stand face to face with the both of them again.

For Darryl, she doesn't just want to talk to him or see his face. She longs for his touch. The little sexual experience that took place before she left was just enough to make her desire more. All the months she has been away, she's been dreaming of all types of things she wants to do with him. Now that she's finally here, she hopes she has the heart to live out those dreams.

"Turn right here," Asia says as she points to her left. "He's going to be so surprised to see me."

"Oh, he doesn't know you're coming?" Tammy asks.

"No," she replies. "I just talked to him an hour ago, and I lied, telling him that I won't be leaving until tomorrow morning. You should have heard him whining like a baby." She laughs. "I can't wait to see the look on his face when he sees me pull up," she says with a bright-eyed smile. "Park right here," she says as she points to the empty parking space.

Tammy does as she is instructed. "That's his car right there, right?"

"Yep," Asia says as she flips the sun visor down. She quickly applies lip gloss to her lips. She puckers her lips together, trying to dull down the shine. She closes the visor. "I'm so nervous," she says as she takes a deep breath.

"Nervous. Why?" Tammy asks.

"I haven't seen him in over three months. What if our chemistry isn't the same? What if he doesn't love me the same? What if he is displeased with my appearance?" she says as she looks down at her protruding gut. "You know I have put on ten pounds," she says with a smile. "I can pinch way more than an inch. I'm a cheeseburger away from being fat," she says sadly.

"Girl, please. Three months ain't nothing. I'm sure he will love you the same."

"I hope so," she says as she forces the door open. "Well, here it is," she says as she gets out. "Wish me luck," she says before slamming the door shut.

Severe anxiety fills Asia's gut. She walks as fast as she can, but still, she can't seem to get to the corner fast enough. Her heart is racing, and her palms are sweating.   She's so nervous that her lips are even trembling.   Finally, she makes it to the corner.   She stops to adjust her clothes and make sure everything is flowing correctly.   She inhales a deep breath and steps around the corner.

Darryl looks to the corner and can't believe his eyes. He does a double-take hoping his eyes are deceiving him.   He and Asia lock eyes without either of them saying a word. Asia melts right before his very eyes.

Her face turns cherry red with humiliation.   It takes her all the strength in the world to muster up enough energy to move.   She turns around and runs full speed around the corner.

Darryl unloosens his arms from around Sunday's neck.   Instead of Sunday backing away, she wraps her arms tighter around his waist.   She pulls him closer. "Huh? So are you going to give me the money or not?" she asks.

Darryl stands with a dumbfounded expression on his face. *This can't be happening, he thinks to himself. Please, God, I know this didn't just happen. Please tell me I'm dreaming.*   He backs away from Sunday in a trance-like state.   He leans on the car behind him.   Tammy's car bends the corner, confirming this is real and not a dream.

He peeks out of the corner of his eye as the Honda approaches slowly.   As the car is about to pass, Sunday lays her body against Darryl's.   "What's the matter, baby? You just went from hot to cold on me."

Darryl looks Sunday in the eyes.   They say what happens in the dark always comes to light.   He never truly understood that statement until now.   As he stands there, he tries to find an excuse for what Asia just saw, but nothing comes to mind.   This was never supposed to happen like this.   Sunday was all a point to prove, and now it has backfired on him. He fears that he may have just blown his relationship with Asia all for nothing.

Sunday speaks again. "Did I miss something? Fill me in. What just happened?"

Darryl stares Sunday in the eyes. He shakes his head from side to side. "You would never understand."

-7-

Two Days Later

ASIA LIES IN HER BED, tossing and turning. She's locked herself in her room for the past two days. The dark cloud above her has her smothered. She lies in a fetal position cradling the love-sickness she feels in her belly. She's been lying in bed, yet she hasn't gotten a wink of sleep. Every time she closes her eyes, the vision of Darryl hugged up in another woman's arms pops up in her mind. She tries to shake away the image, but it won't disappear.

She sings along with singer Rose Royce's voice which seeps through the speakers of her stereo system. "Just a vacancy," she cries. "Love don't live here anymore." She shakes her head from side to side as the tears drip from her swollen eyes.

She hasn't eaten since but the emptiness in her belly is not from hunger. It's love pains. The emptiness she feels in her stomach is nothing compared to the emptiness she feels in her heart. This is a feeling she never knew existed. She's never been so sad in her life. Before this, she never knew the feeling of pain, and her jolly life never called for this feeling. This situation has turned the rose-colored glasses she's worn through life to be dark and tinted, and it's placed a burden on her soul that she can't bear.

Darryl meant the world to her and still does, but she could never forgive him for what he's done to her. This has put a damper on her self-esteem as well. Seeing the beautiful girl with the hourglass figure makes her feel like she lost Darryl because of her physical appearance. For the first time in her life, she feels less than beautiful.

A million unanswered questions ran through her mind. How did she come in and destroy what took them two years to build? What didn't she do that the woman has done? Was it sex? Was it the fact that she made him wait so long? Was it that she was inexperienced, and he desired and wanted more? Was it the time and space they have had apart the past few months?

Only one person can honestly answer these questions, and that is Darryl. The answer she will never know because she refuses to answer his calls. He's called a zillion times, and she has yet to respond. Nor does she plan to answer. She's so disgusted with him that she doesn't even want to hear the sound of his voice. No answer he can give her will justify what he's done to her. "Love, don't live here anymore!"

* * * * *

It feels like the end of the world for Darryl. He wishes he could turn back the hands of time, and if he could do it all differently, he would. He wishes he could go back to the very first day he ever said a word to Sunday and never say a word to her. He never imagined it going like this. For one, he never even pictured himself in a situation with Sunday, let alone did he imagine getting caught with her. He wishes he would have just cut all dealings weeks ago when he planned to. If he had, he wouldn't be going through this now, and he didn't, and now he's stuck with only himself to blame.

Every time he envisions Asia's look on her face, it brings tears to his eyes. He can't shake that vision from his mind. To know he hurt her hurts him even more. For nothing in the world would he intentionally hurt Asia.

For the past two days, he's been calling her with hopes of her answering so he can explain. The fact that she won't at least hear him out pains him even more. He has so many things he wants to say to her, and he would instead look her in the eyes as he tells her those things, but he would settle for over the phone if she gave him no other choice.

Darryl stands on Asia's porch. He rang the bell and is now awaiting an answer. He refuses to give up on her, and there's no way he's going to lose the love of his life without putting up a fight. The door opens, and Asia's mother sticks her head from behind it.

"Hello, Ma," he whispers in an attempt to find a soft spot in her heart for him.

She rolls her eyes with disgust. She looks over his shoulder as if he isn't even standing there. "May I help you?"

"Ma, can I please come in? I need to speak with Asia, please."

"I don't think that would be a good idea. She's not in much of a talking mood. She's been in her room for two days now, and she hasn't eaten or even spoken to me. So I know she doesn't want to talk."

"Well, she doesn't have to talk. I just need her to listen. Please, Miss Davis? I'm begging you," he says with his eyes filled with tears. "I can't leave without speaking to her."

Miss Davis shakes her head, very annoyed. "Give me a second, and let me see what she has to say," she says before slamming the door in his face. Darryl paces circles around the porch.

Five long minutes pass, and the door finally opens. Darryl walks toward the door expecting Miss Davis to open it for him to enter. Instead, she extends her arm through the narrow opening. From her hand dangles a plastic shopping bag. "Here are your belongings you left here over time," she says. "Asia says there's nothing to talk about."

"Huh?" Darryl asks. "But, Miss Davis."

"Darryl, there's nothing I can do. I don't know what the two of you are going through. She hasn't said a word to me about it, and I just know that she's heartbroken. I've never seen her like this before," she claims. "I don't know what to say. Maybe just give her some time and let her get over whatever it is that she's feeling. Maybe then she will have a change of heart," she says with pity on her face. "Until then, I don't know what to tell you."

"But," Darryl blurts out before she cuts him off.

"I gotta go now," she interjects. "Give her some time alone," she says as she closes the door gently in his face. Darryl stands for minutes, just staring at the door. The ease to his heartache and suffering lies behind that door, just a few feet away, and still, he can't get to it.

Five Minutes Later

Darryl stands posted up on the block. He leans against the phone booth while holding the receiver tightly in his hand. His stomach bubbles as he listens to the phone ring for what seems like an eternity. Suddenly a clicking noise gives him some hope. The line is silent. "Hello, hello!" he shouts. "Hello."

"You abandoned me," singer Rose Royce sings in a sweet but depressing tone. "Love don't live here anymore." Hearing these words on her answering machine brings tears to his eyes. Right after that verse, a loud beep sounds.

Darryl hesitates before speaking. He's trying to choose the right words. A half a minute goes by before he finally gets it together. "Hmm, mmm." He clears his throat before swallowing the lump of nervousness. "A, you know that's not true," he whispers.

His voice trembles with nervousness. "I didn't abandon you. I would never abandon you." He clears his throat again, trying to clear away the tremor in his voice. "Asia, I feel crazy talking to this answering machine, but I know you don't want to see my face right now. If this is what I have to do to get you to hear me out, then here it is. I know what it looked like, but I'm telling you it wasn't that. It was nothing," he claims. "She's nothing. Asia, you gotta believe me when I tell you that girl means nothing to me."

The tears are now pouring from his eyes. He lowers his head to keep people on the block from seeing him cry. "The only person in this world that means something to me is you, and you know that I love you more than life," he says before sniffing.

"Asia, I never meant for this to happen, but it's this game," he cries. "I got caught up in it. I don't know how I let myself get caught up. It started out just you and me. Every move I made, I had you in mind and still do. She's not even my type. You're my type," he says before sniffing again. "You're clean and wholesome, and you're all about me. These money-grubbing gold diggers don't care about nobody but themselves."

Darryl pauses before speaking. He can't believe he's somewhat admitting to cheating on her with Sunday.

He feels he's already gotten caught in the act, so there's no reason to lie. He hopes that coming clean will make her respect his honesty and help her to forgive him.

"I know I fucked up, but whatever I can do to fix this, I will. Just say it." He sniffs. "Asia, I love you, and you're my world. I hope we can get past this, and you will forgive me because I can't live without you."

He sobs like a baby for a few seconds before he catches himself. "Asia, dig deep in your heart and try to forgive me. Please," he begs. "I promise you this will never happen again. I made a mistake, and I learned my lesson. Trust me. I'm paying for this mistake. To know that I caused you pain rips me apart. Please, Asia," he begs.

"If you truly love me, you will give me another chance. Don't let a bitch that means nothing to me destroy what we have. My heart is in your hands," he cries. "Forgive me, please," he begs. "Please," he says before slamming the phone down hanging it up.

Darryl leans back against the wall. He flings his head back and stares into the air. He pinches the top of his nose, placing his fingertips into the corners of his eyes. He's attempting to stop the tears from flowing, but still, they flood his eyelids. "Damn," he mumbles. "How the fuck did I get here?"

As he lowers his head, he notices a pack of ten Newark Police officers walking around the corner. "Not right now," he mumbles to himself. He's not in the mood right now to be fooling around with them. He's sure an encounter with them will bring the worse out of him, and he knows where that will get him.

The lead cop Darryl is quite familiar with. It's the cop who took his money from him. He quickly walks toward Darryl, and the other officers follow at his heels. Darryl looks at the cops, and they all appear about his age. He assumes them to be a bunch of young rookies straight out of the academy. All of them are clean-shaven, and none of them even have the cop edge in their eyes yet.

The lead officer stops feet away from Darryl. "This right here is D-Lowe," the cop says. "Whatever y'all do, don't ever invite D-Lowe to a fair one. D-Lowe is a professional boxer, and he's nice with his hands. My old partner made the mistake of inviting him to a fight, and it didn't go in his favor. Don't be like my old partner," he says as he looks at all of them with a smile.

The cop looks to Darryl. "D-Lowe, don't you go putting your hands on my rookies. You gone treat them with some respect when they come through here. If not, you will have bigger problems than you can ever imagine. Understood?"

"I respect everybody until they disrespect me."

The cop steps up face to face with Darryl. "My police will do police work, and I guess you will do whatever you call this out here," he says only loud enough for Darryl to hear. "We all have to coexist. They have a job to do, and they will do it. I'm not here to tell you to say no to drugs or none of that politically correct shit. I was only one mistake away from being right here with you, so I understand the struggle," he says before shrugging his shoulders arrogantly.

"But because I'm not out here with you and I'm dressed in blue, I can't sympathize with you. What I will tell you is this," he says before he looks to his left, then his right. "Your name is ringing from here on down to the precinct. We know that everybody out here is working for you. We also know that any gun goes off out here, that gun was in your hands."

Darryl keeps the same face on as if the cop hasn't said anything but his mind is racing. He stares the cop square in the eyes. "Streets always gone talk. I fight. I'm a boxer, and that's all these hands do," he says as he clenches his fist at his waist. "All the rest of that I don't know nothing about."

The cop shrugs him off with disbelief. "Fine and well," he says calmly. "I said all that to say to you, if you may have ever thought about pulling out before it's too late, now would be that perfect time," he says as he turns around and walks away. "You're throwing rocks at the penitentiary."

He walks off, and his rookies follow. "Now everybody say good day to D-Lowe." He looks back at Darryl. "None of us know what tomorrow will bring."

-8-

Two Days Later
Hall of Fame Boxing Club

DARRYL WALKS INTO THE GYM locker room with his head hanging low. He knew he should've never jumped in the ring today, with his mind as cloudy as it was. He let his pride and ego make him go against his better judgment. A group of fighters from out of Dover came through for sparring work, and Darryl was called out.

He only came to the gym today to relieve his frustration and maybe help get Asia off his mind for a couple of hours. Never did he expect to be in the ring sparring. He isn't even in sparring shape. He hasn't been running, and he hasn't been coming to the gym consistently. Still, he let his ego take over.

All three rounds went against him. Nothing he tried worked. No combination he attempted to put together actually came together. And no punch he slipped, missed him. He moved around like he was in the twilight zone for three rounds. The only thing he did was build the confidence of the new and young boxer he was sparring with. Because he handled Darryl, the fighter now has newfound confidence in himself.

Darryl couldn't shake Asia from his mind. Until now, he'd been in the house, sick in bed for two days. He called Asia over and over again, getting no answer. Despite what her mom told him, he continued reaching out to her.

He realizes her mom is right about needing time to get over the situation. He understands she could possibly get past it in due time, but he doesn't want to take that risk. He's afraid if he leaves her alone long enough, she will never come back to him. Because of that, he plans to continue to reach out to her for as long as it takes.

Lefty walks into the locker room. "You looked a mess out there," he says as he passes Darryl.

"Yeah, I know," Darryl replies. "My head wasn't in the game."

"Then why were you in the game?" Lefty asks. Lefty takes a seat next to Darryl on the bench. "What's going on, though?"

"Long story," Darryl replies. "I'm just going to give you the short version. My childhood sweetheart comes home from college and catches me with another chick, and now she ain't answering my calls or nothing."

Lefty stands up, showing that he's uninterested in the topic. "Baby Boy, let me share something with you." Darryl sighs silently. He's not in the mood for Lefty's life lessons and preaching right now. All he needs is an ear to hear him out. "One thing I hate is for a man to complain after receiving the consequences for his actions. You knew she was your childhood sweetheart and what she meant to you when you entertained the other girl, right?"

"Yeah," Darryl shamefully admits.

"You know the problem with most people?" Lefty asks. "People think for the moment and never think about the end game. Main man has a successful run in the dope game, living for the moment. Never once thinking about the end game until the end game is in front of him. Then there he is sitting in the interrogation room with *Federales* all around him. You know why he snitches?"

Darryl shrugs his shoulders. "Nah."

"Because he never pictured himself in that room. Had he pictured himself there before he got there, he would've known that he wasn't built for it," he says with emphasis. "He never fully committed that he was in it for the good or the bad because he never thought far enough into it to see the bad. So, what does he do when he gets confronted with the bad that comes with it? He flips like an Olympic Gymnast. And then him and his loved ones expect you to sympathize with him, but I can't," he says with his face covered with disgust.

Lefty shrugs. "He got what his hands called for. Just like I can't sympathize with you right now. You knew you loved that girl and still decided to cheat on her. If you would've thought about the end game and realized the possibility that she could find out, then maybe you wouldn't have cheated on her." Lefty pauses just to check Darryl's pulse. Darryl has nothing to say for himself. The truth is he never looked at the end game, never picturing it to end like this.

"If you really looked at the possible end game, you would've understood that you could either get away with it or not get away with it. If you would've considered the possibility that the end game could be this right here, you sitting here hurting," he says pointing at Darryl. "Then you would've known you weren't built for the end game, and maybe you wouldn't have cheated."

Darryl nods his head, recognizing every word as truth. As Lefty has stated, he truly wishes he would've thought of the possibility, and he wouldn't be sitting here going through this. "You're right," Darryl agrees.

"But if by chance you would've understood how it can end up and still you moved on with your cheating, then you committed to it and can't cry about it in the end. You got what your hands called for. You made the mistake of not thinking about the end game. Women make mistakes. Men don't have the luxury of making mistakes."

Lefty raises his nub in the air. "Shot my own hand off. I did it to myself." Darryl listens closer. He's finally gotten an answer to one of his questions after all this time. "When I chose to put a gun in my hand, not knowing how to use it properly, I never thought about the end game," he says as he rubs his hand over his nub. He cradles his nub.

"When I shot my hand off, I got what my hands called for. I lived most of my life with what most would consider a handicap. I had to learn to write with my other hand. Barely able to carry certain things. Can barely tie my shoes. I can't do anything that requires two hands. As talented and vicious as I am as a boxer, I can't fight professionally because I only got one hand. I shot the other one off. Me, I did it. And guess what?"

"What?" Darryl questions. He wants to hear this.

"Not one time have I ever complained or cried about it. Know why?"

"Why?" Darryl asks.

"Because I did it to myself. I got what my hands called for. I never felt sorry for myself or even sympathized with me because I did it to me. So, how the hell could I ever sympathize with you for what you've done to yourself?" Darryl sits sulking in the truth. It's a tough pill to swallow, but it's what he needed to hear right now.

-9-

Hours Later/9:30 P.M.

THE CONVERSATION WITH LEFTY earlier helped Darryl put things into their proper perspective. It didn't stop the pain, but it helped him to stop sitting around feeling sorry for himself. He compared his situation with Lefty's and figured if Lefty could get over his obstacle, there's no way he should be sitting around like this. He loves Asia, and he hopes she can one day get over it, but for right now, he has to get up and get back on track.

The block has been dry for a whole day. Darryl is allowing this situation to affect his money. He couldn't pull himself together yesterday to go to New York to re-up. He thought about the evident reality that the customers would not stop getting high because he has no work. They will simply go elsewhere. And even that didn't push him to get up and get it together.

He came to his senses after talking to Lefty. He knew he had to make a move, but he knew his head was still cloudy. As he got into his car and prepared to follow Unk over to New York, Lefty's word replayed in his head over and over. *"If your head wasn't in the game, then why were you in the game."*

He saw firsthand what happens when you're distracted and your head isn't in the game. The last thing he wanted to do was go to New York and bust a move without being focused. He only got punished for three rounds when he made that mistake earlier today in the boxing ring. Making a mistake like busting a move with a cloudy mind could cost him more than three rounds. It could possibly cost him a 10-15 year sentence, or even death.

After weighing the options, he decided to stay and let Unk bust the move. He made the call ahead of time as he usually does just to give them the heads up, and he sent Unk off with a bag of money. Knowing how reckless Unk can be, he was on pins and needles the entire time Unk was gone. All he could picture is Unk doing something stupid that draws attention to himself, and the rest would be downhill from there.

He's finally able to breathe again. He arrived here at Unk's brother's house just ten minutes ago. Unk sticks his hand inside the plastic bag and hands Darryl the kilo. The work has arrived safe and sound. Now it's time to check and be sure everything is what it's supposed to be.

Darryl quickly rips through the casing. He slits the rubber casing with his car key, and that aroma that he has grown to love seeps into the air. He digs the tip of his car key into the corner of the brick, scooping a hefty chunk. Unk already has his shaker in hand. Darryl dumps the coke into the shaker, and Unk runs off to the sink. Darryl scrutinizes the work. Beautiful scales dance around the interior like a disco.

Unk steps back to Darryl's side. He winds his wrist, and with each twirl, the coke bangs against the shaker, ticking hard enough to break the glass. "Shit rocked up as soon as it hit the water," Unk says as he stops shaking. They both look inside the bottle, and the size of the rock inside blows their mind. "You see this shit right here?" Unk asks in disbelief.

"What the?" Darryl says with astonishment. "Can't be." Darryl looks at the kilo in his hand, and he sees his come-up right before his eyes.

Unk runs to the back porch while Darryl digs his hand inside the bag again. With so much going on, he can't even appreciate the milestone he just reached. Under normal conditions, today would call for a celebration. Today he copped two kilos. As he pulls the second kilo from the bag, he has a moment of joy. His spirits are lifted.

His heart beats rapidly as he tears through the casing. The imprint in the center is an image of the solar system planets. He quickly opens it, and it's the identical twin to the other; the same beautiful interior. There he stands, holding two kilos in his hand. He feels like King of the Jungle right now.

Unk appears with glassy eyes. He gazes at Darryl with his jaws locked. He wants to speak, but the words won't leave his mouth. He can't talk, so he simply nods and throws a 'thumbs up' in the air. A long fart seals the deal.

Darryl knows what this means. He looks to Unk. "You know what this means?" Unk's mouth twitches from side to side like a windshield wiper, still not able to speak. Darryl holds the kilo up to Unk's face, pointing to the imprint of the solar system. "And we're off! To the moon or bust!"

-10-

Six Months Later

I T'S A BEAUTIFUL FALL DAY. With the temperature close to seventy degrees, it feels more like Spring. Darryl leans back against his newest toy. The black-on-black 1991 Acura Legend Coupe, also known as the Big Boy coupe, is the hottest automobile of the year. The unique rounded bubble shape replaces the old squared-off box edition that has been on the streets for the past three years.

He has been the proud owner of the new vehicle for about a month. You would think he would be used to it, but he's not. He still gets butterflies every time he looks at it. He thought he knew all about the attention a car could bring as he drove around in the BMW. That attention is nothing compared to what he now receives when he pulls up in the new Acura. It's a different type of attention. People stared at the BMW, but they gawk when they see the Acura Legend.

He takes great pride in being the first one in the entire city to own one, and Sunday takes great pride in that as well. His primary reason for buying this vehicle was to gain Sunday's approval. He listened to her tell him time after time tell how much she loves the new Acura Legend. With the purchase of this car, he feels that he finally earned her respect.

Sunday seems to treat him a bit differently now. She's even showing jealousy when it comes to him. His name is now ringing in the town, and talk of him has been in the mouths of the other Sunday types of the city. Sunday is aware of this too, which is why she keeps a tight leash on him. After all, she feels like he's her project, and she's part responsible for bringing him up to level. She refuses to have all her hard work be in vain and lose him to another.

Darryl has become the talk in all of the beauty parlors and the barbershops. The 'North Pole' is now one of the city's monumental landmarks. Yes, the block is now nicknamed The North Pole, and not The Location. Someone referred to the block as the North Pole, jokingly because of the amount of snow(cocaine) that's being moved out here. Darryl liked the sound of it and adopted the name. He hated the reputation The Location had and no longer wanted to be attached to that anyway so the new name came in right on time.

This block has become one of Newark tourists spots. Men ride through in amazement as they watch the drug traffic. The addicts scramble around like roaches, in clusters. Women drive through just hoping to get a glance of Darryl and his crew. If they're lucky they will get flagged down by one of them. They all know that D-Low is like the Santa Claus of the North Pole but they will settle for one of his elves if they had to.

Up ahead is like a taste of Germany. A string of European cars are lined up. A candy apple red Maserati, a 325I BMW station wagon, and Mercedes Benz station wagon are all parked back-to-back. The cars belong to the other members of the park. They are having more success working with Darryl than they have ever had working alone.

The picture out here looks a lot bigger than it really is though. With an auto-body and mechanic shop being right here on the set, they have the hometown advantage. The owners of the shop specialize in German cars and go to the auction in search of salvaged high-line automobiles. Those automobiles may have been destroyed due to flooding and because of that they are sold for dirt cheap. The mechanics then revive the cars and sell them for dirt cheap because they can't get the title. With the hustlers of this block being right here and seeing every car that comes on tow truck from the auction they get first dibs.

A block full of European cars makes the block ring out even more. The years of the automobiles may only range from 1985-1989 but they aren't slighted by the spectators throughout the city. Not a single one of these cars were purchased for more than seven-thousand dollars but no one would ever imagine that. Darryl's Acura is the only car that was paid for full price, brand-new from the dealership and still his car can be overshadowed by the others. That's perfect for him though because he blends in and not necessarily stand out. Together, they look like a big deal out here but for those that really know, know that D-Low is the biggest deal, here on The North Pole.

Darryl looks to his left at Sunday, standing right next to him. Agitation covers his face. Ever since he got the vehicle, she begged to drive it. She begs and throws temper tantrums like a small child when he tells her no. The last time she asked for it, he told her no, she didn't speak to him for three whole days. "Why can't you take the BMW?" he whines.

"I don't want to take that ol' raggedy BM," she whines back at him. "You ain't going nowhere. Why can't you just drive that one? You gone be on this block all day, as usual."

"No, I'm not. I got some shit to do," he whines like a baby.

"Come on, please?" she begs.

"Hmph." He sighs. "Where y'all trying to go to anyway?" he questions.

"Nowhere in particular," she replies. "Just chilling."

Darryl doesn't want her to have the car, but he isn't in the mood for arguing and not speaking if he doesn't. He pulls the keys out of his pocket. "Here," he says with attitude as he looks away from her.

Without saying a word to him, she takes off, running to the driver's seat. "Come on, y'all!" she says as she looks at the car full of girls that are double-parked next to them. She waves the keys in the air. "Follow me!"

Darryl walks away from the car, agitated. He leans against the phone booth and looks around at the surrounding area. Crowds and crowds of people swarming the block in search of cocaine cause the look of agitation to vanish, and it's replaced with the look of great satisfaction.

He's appreciative that his newest plan is a success. Just three days ago, the block was looking abandoned. The two for fives ran their course. Blocks all over the city have adopted the two-for-five strategy after seeing his success with it.

Going a few days without reaching his regular quota inspired him to develop another strategy. One sleepless night he came up with a plan. With the rest of the city selling nickels and two-for-fives, he decided to turn the block back into a dime block. They're not just selling the regular dimes, though.

The dimes of cocaine in small iodine jars are something that no one in the city has ever dreamt of doing. That is until now. Even with them now knowing about it, few people can afford to do it. His dimes are equivalent to two and a half dimes of average size.

The jars, which are about, an inch in height and the width of a silver nickel, consume so much cocaine that even he was worried if he could afford it or not. The small profit margin made him question if it was even worth it. After witnessing the drastic increase in the flow over the last two days, he no longer questions it. At the end of yesterday, his team finished off a total of more than 60 pampers. Each pamper is filled with 50 dime jugs. That's more than 3,000 dime jugs which is more than thirty grand gross.

The jugs have brought him a flow with the increase of an additional ten to twelve grand more a day. With just two days in, he's sure this is just the beginning. By the time the word spreads around the city, he's expecting to at least double his earnings. Another one of his bright ideas has taken the block to a higher level. Not many will adopt this method because they won't be able to afford to. This will either make them get down with him or get rolled over by him. This all started as him wanting to take over the block, but now he wants to take over the city.

-11-

2 AM

DARRYL CRUISES ALONG the one-way block. Before he even gets to the middle of the block, he spots what he came in search of. The red BMW sits parked in the alley of the small two-family house. This house is where Sunday's best friend lives.

He looks up to the second floor and finds the light on. He wonders if Sunday is up there. He's been calling Sunday's house and riding past looking for her for the past two hours. The last time he heard from her was when she dropped his car back off to him and told him she was going out with Roselyn. Now that he sees Roselyn's car, he can't help but wonder if Sunday just used her as an alibi.

He has always felt like Sunday could be using her as an alibi but never had a way of proving it until last week. In all the time he's known Sunday, he never knew where Roselyn lived. He doesn't know if Sunday has intentionally kept that from him or not. The only reason he found out where she lived was that Roselyn and the crew were about to go out and didn't have time to go and pick up Sunday. That left her no choice but to ask him to drop her off.

He has to come past here whenever he's looking for Sunday out of pure curiosity. He understands the stalking and suspicion is too much, but he can't help himself. He tells himself he's not going to put up with it any longer, but still, he puts up with it. It's like he's a glutton for punishment.

Every so often, Sunday pulls her little disappearing acts where he doesn't hear from her for hours. When he does hear from her, she has some story she swears by. He never believes the stories she tells him, but he has no actual proof. Also, at that time, he's just grateful that wherever she was, she's no longer there.

His jealousy has become uncontrollable. As much as he tries to keep a grip on it, he can't. The only thing he can think of to solve his jealousy issue is to leave her alone altogether. That's easier said than done, though. Each day he comes up with another reason he should let her go, but he hasn't gotten rid of her yet.

He often wonders if this is God's way of paying him back for what he did to Asia. He sometimes looks at Sunday as punishment for his actions. Not a second of the day goes by that he doesn't wish that none of this ever happened. If he just would have left well enough alone and stayed true to the love of his life, he wouldn't be in the mess he's in with Sunday.

His jealousy has gotten the best of him. It's weird how the attention he once loved now bothers him severely. He can't stand for a man to even look at her, let alone speak to her. Sunday recognizes the change in him and loves every bit of it. The more jealous he becomes, the more she feels he cherishes her.

He has no idea how he even allowed himself to get like this. Not only has he lost the true love of his life, but he's also stuck with a woman who shows him every day that her only use for him is whatever she can get out of him. He wishes he would have cut her off long ago, and he wouldn't be in this mess. He had it all planned out, but when it was time to cut her loose, he realized he couldn't because he had developed feelings for her. He confuses those feelings. What he thinks is love is really just obsession.

He is obsessed with the attention and the praise he receives for having her as his chick. He feels so complete having a woman of her caliber. Her street credibility adds so much to his image. He's so addicted to the sense of power he feels having her by his side that he fears not having her there. Foolishly, he feels privileged to have her.

The attention he gets when he's with her is a source of attention he never got while being with Asia. Sunday has a reputation of only dating guys who have lots of money. Because of that, they automatically assume Darryl must have an abundance of money. Being that they perceive him to have money, they treat him accordingly.

The news has spread through the city like a forest fire in such a short time. Everyone has them labeled as a couple. Men hate him for the simple fact, but they respect him. On the other hand, women have their antennas up in search of the infamous D-Low. They idolize her so much they would do anything to have Darryl and get one up on her. Being with her man would make them feel equal to her.

Darryl continues to stare at the window to see any movement. He has to know if Sunday is up there. Something tells him she's not, but he has no way of proving it. He looks at his watch. "Nah," he says to himself as he thinks of ringing the bell. At least if he rings the bell and finds her not here, there will be no excuse she can give him. Finding out the truth may be what he needs to cut her loose.

Before he realizes it, he's out of the car and standing on the porch ringing the bell. After he presses the bell, the embarrassment kicks in. "I'm playing myself," he mumbles to himself. "Damn, I shouldn't have done that," he says as he tiptoes down the stairs.

"Who?" the voice sounds from the second-floor window.

Damn, Darryl thinks to himself. He looks up with shame. Roselyn hangs out of the window with her headscarf on. "Ay, Roz." There's an awkward silence for seconds. "Sorry for ringing your bell this late, but is Sunday up there? It's important. Sorry."

"Sunday ain't here," she replies as confusion sets on her face. "I haven't seen Sun," she says before shutting her mouth. She realizes she may have given her girlfriend up by saying too much.

"Oh, nah?" Darryl asks with a grin on his face. "She told me she was with you, and y'all was going out." He chuckles as he walks to his car. "Again, Roz, I'm sorry for ringing your bell this late."

Darryl gets into the car and peels off. He's burning up inside. He can't believe she has lied to him. He assumes she has probably been lying to him all the while. "Lying bitch," he utters. "Roselyn ain't even seen her lying ass."

Darryl's thoughts run wild. He wonders where she is and what she's up to. Whatever she's up to, he's sure another man is involved. If not, there would be no need for her to lie. "That's it!" he shouts as he bangs his hand on the steering wheel. "I ain't going through this shit over, no bitch. I'm too smooth for this shit," he says as he tries to psyche himself out. "That bitch is done!"

-12-

The Next Night

AFTER A LONG SLEEPLESS NIGHT, Darryl finally received a beep from Sunday at ten in the morning. Apparently, Roselyn had already warned her because she had her story intact. Her alibi is she never got with Roselyn. Instead, she went out with two other friends he didn't know. Supposedly they got so drunk she ended up crashing on her friend's couch.

He has no way of proving her wrong, so he feels the best way to handle the situation is to leave her alone, point-blank, period. They stood face to face as she cried her eyes out and begged him to believe her. As much as it affected him, he didn't show it. He's gotten so used to her crocodile tears that he no longer believes in them.

He has no plans of taking her back. He said he's done, and there's no turning back. He's sure he will be tempted on those lonely nights, but he must get over it. They say only one thing helps a man get over a woman, and that's another woman.

Darryl stops at the red light on Irvine Turner Boulevard. A few feet up ahead is the sign to Routes 1 & 9. His destination is the Swan Motel. He looks over to the passenger seat of his car, where his ace in the hole sits. He stares at her momentarily while they sit in silence.

Passion looks back at him. "What?" she asks. "Why are you looking at me like that?"

"What. I can't look at you now?"

Before Darryl can reply, his car is bumped from behind. He looks in the rearview. "Stupid motherfucker!" he shouts as he forces the door open. He steps out of the car and takes two steps toward the car behind him—both doors of the Z24 pop open. Two men come running toward him. He spots a shiny chrome object in the hand of the man on the driver's side, and he realizes just what this is.

This is no accident. It's a carjacking. Darryl quickly hops back into the car. As he drops himself onto the seat, he notices another man running in his direction, coming from the vehicle sitting in front of him. Darryl tries to close the door, but the man holds it tightly. Darryl grabs the steering wheel and cuts it to his left as hard as possible. With his free hand, he reaches underneath his seat.

The sound of gunfire rips through the air. Darryl mashes the gas pedal, dragging the man along with him. Two more gunshots sound. *Boom! Boom!* Darryl picks up speed as he crosses the intersection. The man is still holding on for dear life.

"Stop this fucking car," he demands. The man has his arms wrapped through the window

as he screams with fear. "Stop this car." Darryl steers the car with his left hand and fumbles with his gun with his right hand. He manages to squeeze off two clumsy shots. *Boom! Boom!*

"Oh shit," the man screams. He lets the window go and falls to the street.

Darryl watches as the man rolls onto the highway. The Z24 pulls up and rescues the man. Darryl pulls the door closed and steps on the gas, speeding up the highway recklessly. He looks at Passion sitting on the edge of her seat, and he's surprised to see that she hasn't even broken a sweat.

Darryl feels a warm sensation. Moisture on his chest causes him to run his hand over it. He touches his sweater only for his fingers to sink into the wetness. He looks down. "Oh shit! I'm hit!"

-13-

Three Days Later

"**A**NOTHER YOUNG BROTHER HIT.** In my dying bed, half dead. Gangster Lou, bring me a motherfucking head," Darryl sings with Azie, rapper of Mobstyle. As he leans back in the seat, allowing the music to set the tone, he grips two nine millimeters on his lap.

Luckily for Darryl, he only suffered from a mere graze to the chest. His hospital visit was a short one lasting less than two hours. The actual hospital visit lasted less than an hour. The visit from the detectives took up the remainder of the time.

They questioned him over and over about what had happened. They even asked him to pick the culprits out from the mug shots. Darryl admitted it was a carjacking situation, but he didn't pick any pictures out of the mug shots. He has no face to pick out. Even if he did recognize them, he wouldn't identify them. His motto is: what happens on the street stays on the street.

After doing some research, he found out there are only three Z24s in the entire city, one is sky blue, and the other two are red. He narrowed down his search by the rims of one of the cars. He later found out the car without the rims belonged to a man from this block.

"Yo, I need protection," Darryl sings animated-like. "Two bullets in my midsection. Smith and Wesson, teach them motherfuckers a lesson. You take the west side, he'll take the east. I won't sleep until they rest in peace. Gun down the beast and let the brothers feast. They tried to play me, Azzie. Bring me a mother, a brother and smother the little baby. Tonight, just make sure my kids and my wife is alright."

Darryl peeks over as the car passes the group of young men. It's too dark for him to identify anyone, but he doesn't care. He's here to send them a message. "Bend the corner and let me out," he instructs the driver. Once the car is stopped, Darryl draws his hood tight. He hops out of the car with both guns drawn at his waist. He peeks around the corner and sees the men heavily engaged in conversation. He glances to his left and his right before stepping around the building. *Boc! Boc! Boc!* He fires with a vengeance. *Boc! Boc!* The glare from the gunfire illuminates the dark corner.

"Ohhh!" one man screams as he dashes off. The other three take off across the street. Darryl aims at the man who is still in his path. *Boc! Boc!* The man tumbles over, and Darryl switches his focus to the group of three men running across the street. *Boc! Boc! Boc! Boc! Boc! Boc! Boc! Boc! Boc! Boc! Boc! The guns sound off like a round of a 4th of July firework session. Cling, Cling, Cling!*

Darryl looks down at his empty guns and takes off in the other direction. A few feet away, the getaway car is awaiting him. He snatches the passenger's door of his Acura open and dives into the seat. The driver peels off quickly and busts the right turn with perfection and all gas. The Acura speeds down 11th Street, doing more than 80 miles an hour. Darryl pulls the hood off of his head. Just as they reach the Springfield Avenue intersection, he looks behind. To his glory, the coast is clear. There's not a police car or any other car in sight.

He looks over to the driver's seat. "Take it easy. Slow down," he demands. "We good."

Passion slows the Acura down. She turns the car on 18th Avenue and continues nonchalantly down the block. "Did you hit anybody?" she asks.

"I hit a few of them," he replies. "I watched one of them flip over," he says. "I ripped his ass!" he shouts with joy.

A smile covers Passion's face. "Good!" she shouts. "I still think you shouldn't have done it in your car, though. I mean, this is the car you drive every day."

"They busted their move on me while I was in my car. I had no choice but to do it in my car, so they know it came from me."

Passion doesn't put up a bit of defense. "I'm with you, win, lose or draw."

Darryl lays back in the seat and digests it all. He bops his head to the beat as he joins the song. "Young Jamaican, faking, curry goat eating motherfuckers. Let them know, we play rougher!"

-14-

One Week Later

Knock! *Knock! Knock!* Darryl is awakened out of his sleep by a banging on his front door. *Knock! Knock! Knock!* He pops up in the bed, startled. He looks at the clock, and it reads 3:27 a.m. *Ding, dong!* The bell rings before the banging on the door again. *Knock! Knock! Knock!*

His heart is racing with nervousness. Who could be ringing his bell at this hour of the night? He gets out of the bed and tiptoes across the floor. *Knock! Knock! Knock!* The knocking on the window is so loud and hard it sounds like the glass is about to cave in.

He peeks through the peephole and gets a close-up view of his guest. "Pssst." He sighs as he stares into Sunday's face. He hasn't spoken to her since their last beef about lying about going out with Roselyn. He heard her out that morning and never talked to her again. She beeps him numerous times a day, but he never returns her calls.

He doubts she will leave because his car parked in front of the house indicates that he's home. Maybe she will get tired of banging on the door and just leave, he hopes. *Ding, dong! Knock! Knock! Knock!* Something tells him she's not going anywhere.

The last thing he wants to do is bring this type of attention to his new apartment. He's been living here less than a month. With his landlord living upstairs from him, the last thing he needs is for them to think this is the type of company he keeps. "Damn, I have to open the door," he mumbles to himself. "Or she's not going nowhere."

He's been fighting with himself for the past two weeks. Every time she beeps him, he has to refrain from calling her back. He knows she's no good for him, but he can't help himself. He misses her dearly, and he's surprised he's gone this long without giving in.

He's afraid to open the door for her. Deep down inside, he fears that he will not be able to control his feelings if he sees her. "I'm gonna open the door for her just so she will stop causing a scene, but in no way I 'm taking her back," he says to himself. "We are over; done," he says with complete confidence in himself.

Knock! Knock! Knock! He snatches the door open with anger. "What?" he snaps. "Why the fuck are you banging on my door this time of night?" He's bluffing her. In no way is he as mad as he is pretending to be. He's happy to see her, whether he admits it or not. She stands without replying. "Why the fuck you out here banging on my door and causing a scene?"

"Because I miss you," she whispers with sincerity in her eyes. "I need you to hear me out," she says as she peeks back at Roselyn's car, sitting double-parked in front of the house. The car is filled with women, and Darryl assumes they must have just left a party or a club.

His heart is softening as the seconds creep by, but still, he tries to remain strong in his spot. "Why are you missing me?" he asks with attitude. "Don't miss me. Miss whoever the fuck you spent that night with."

"D," she says as she looks into his eyes. "I already told you where I was, but you refuse to believe me."

"And you still gonna lie about it?" he asks with rage. "Later!" he says as he pushes the door in her face.

She wedges herself in between the door and the frame. "Please, please?" she begs. "Don't do this," she cries.

"Watch out."

"No," she replies. "Don't close the door in my face," she barks with venom. "I'm coming in." She slithers her way through the door. She peeks her head out. "Y'all go ahead!" she shouts to Roselyn. "I'm good! I will call you in the morning!"

"You ain't coming in here," he says as he shoves her with very little energy. "You better not let them leave you."

"It's too late already," she replies as Roselyn cruises up the street.

"Psst." Darryl sighs as he walks away from the door.

Sunday slams the door shut. She walks over to him and grabs him from behind. "Damn, I miss you," she whispers in his ear. "You don't miss me?"

"Nah, when you crossed me, you lost me," he replies.

"Crossed you?" she asks as she turns him around. "I never crossed you. I told you that. So, you telling me, he doesn't miss me?" she asks as she grabs his manhood through his boxers. She strokes him gently. "Maybe not," she says. "You probably be giving it to somebody else," she says as she looks into his eyes for an answer.

"Don't worry about who I give it to. Worry about who you giving that to."

"I ain't giving it to nobody. I've been holding it all for you, just waiting for you to stop being mad at me."

He stares into her eyes as he tries to read her. "Tell me where you were that night."

"I already told you," she replies.

"Well, tell me again. A lie you can forget. The truth remains the same. Where was you?"

Sunday stands quietly as she tries to get her story together. Memories of that night play clearly in her mind. *She is on her knees as Sal stands in front of her. He holds her by her chin as he feeds himself to her. He thrusts himself in and out of her mouth slowly as she stares into his eyes. He strokes her hair with his other hand, twirling locks in between his fingers.*

He grabs her by the head and tilts her head back using both hands. He backs away from her teasing her lips with his tip. He grabs her chin again, snatching her mouth open. "Open your mouth," he demands. She unrolls her tongue like the red carpet, and Sal dick lashes her tongue, smacking his manhood on her tongue repeatedly. She sits submissively, just waiting for his following command.

He yanks her hair, gripping it in his fist and with the speed of a jackhammer, he fucks her mouth. Sunday fights to pull away. She gags as he bangs her tonsils. Tears overflow from her eyes while her pussy drips a fountain of pleasure. After seconds of pounding, he pulls back. With one hand, he holds her head, and with the other, he holds himself. He grunts as his buck shots splatter all over her face.

"Eeelk," she says as she backs away from him. She wipes her face off with her panties.

Sal laughs hysterically. "Eeelk what?" he says with a smile on his face.

"Your nasty ass," she says. She smiles as well.

Sunday shakes her head, attempting to shake away the vision. If Darryl could read her mind right now. Guilt covers her face, and she wonders if he can see it.

She shakes her head. "You just refuse to believe me," she says convincingly.

"Swear to God you wasn't with no nigga that night," he says as he stares deep into her eyes. She hesitates before replying to him. "Swear to God," he demands. "Say swear to God I wasn't with no nigga that night."

"I swear to God I wasn't with no nigga," she says with a straight face. "Ok," she asks. "Now you satisfied?"

Hearing this melts his anger away. He now has no choice but to believe her. He wanted to believe her anyway, regardless of if she swore or not. Deep down, his heart can't take the thought of her being with another. It's easier for him to accept whatever answer she gives him than to face the truth.

"You forgive me now?" she asks as she hugs him tightly.

"Nah," he says with a rebellious demeanor.

"What can I do to make you forgive me?" she whispers seductively.

A thought pops into Darryl's mind. He knows exactly what he wants. Although it won't help him forgive her or even forget, it will take his mind off it for a little while. "I know what you can do," he whispers. Embarrassment covers his face. He doesn't know how to say what he's thinking.

"What?" she asks. At this point, she will do almost anything.

"You know," he says as he looks into her eyes. "That," he whispers.

"What?" she asks with no idea of what he's talking about.

"You know," he repeats as he points to her mouth.

Her eyes stretch wide. "What? Suck your thing?" she asks.

Darryl looks away with shame. "Yeah."

"No, boy! I don't do that. I told you that from day one. I don't suck nobody thing."

Darryl looks at her with a blank expression on his face. *It was worth a try, he thinks to himself.* "I never have, and I never will. Hell no," she snaps.

It's all lies, and she does it with a straight face. The truth is every man can't bring the freak out of a woman, but Sal has tapped into the freak in her. On the other hand, Darryl sees no freak in her; therefore, he can't tap into something that he doesn't know is there.

-15-

South Munn Avenue, East Orange

THIS APARTMENT BUILDING at one time was the perfect residence. Today, the front of it is flooded with drug activity. Darryl had to muscle his way through the crowd of dealers just to get inside. The bold look in his eyes saved him from any harassment they wanted to apply.

Darryl stands in the elevator staring straight ahead. To his left and to his right stand two men who are foreign to him. An hour ago, he received a call from one of his customers placing an order. When he got here, he expected to see the man he had grown familiar with. Instead, these two men were waiting for him in the hall.

Upon Darryl's arrival he called and the man told him that his cousin was downstairs waiting for him to arrive. As soon as he stepped into the hall, one of the two men called his name. The whole situation has Darryl quite uncomfortable. He knew he should have refused to see anybody outside of the man he usually deals with, but he continued anyway.

As much as his gut told him not to go with the strangers, he didn't listen. His ego was on the line. He felt if he had backed away, they might have got the feeling he was afraid of them. He feared a rumor like that floating through the city because no one would respect him anymore. A great deal of hard work has been put into building the reputation he now has, and he refuses to let anyone tarnish it.

The two men stare at each other, giving some type of signal to one another. Darryl sees this from the corner of his eye, but still, he stares straight ahead. He pretends he sees nothing, but he's now sure that something isn't right with this whole ordeal. He feels more than uneasy.

In the bag, Darryl holds half a kilo of the cheapy-choppa. He's come here with the hopes of making an easy ten thousand dollars off of this deal which equals a profit of twenty-five hundred dollars for him. Judging by the vibe, this profit isn't going to be as easy to make as he expected it to be.

The elevator stops, and the doors open. The man to Darryl's right steps out first while the other man stands behind him. Darryl's heart skips a beat. "Come on," the man says as he waves Darryl on.

I should back out right now, Darryl thinks to himself. This shit doesn't look right. His ego forces him out of the door. Before he realizes it, he's following the man through the piss-smelling hallway. The man stops short and taps on the door in front of him, and the door is snatched open quickly.

The man steps inside, and Darryl follows hesitantly behind him. As soon as Darryl steps into the apartment, the door is slammed shut behind him. Darryl peeks around and notices three more unfamiliar faces. As he stands, they all come walking in his direction. "You got the work?" the man who led him into the apartment asks.

Darryl swallows the uneasiness in his throat. "Yeah," he replies as he slams the bag on the table. The moment is tense. Darryl peeks up as the men all stand around the table with their eyes glued to his bag.

Darryl drops his hand into the bag. A digital scale appears in his hand. He drops it on the table, and now more tension is in the air. They seem to be eagerly awaiting his next move. They stand like a hungry pack of wolves with him as the prey in their eyes.

Darryl grabs the chunk of work and drops it on the scale. He quickly drops his hand back into the bag. He retracts his hand, with a nine-millimeter gripped tightly. He takes five steps back quickly. *Cling, cling!* The gun sounds off as he slides a bullet into the chamber.

The eyes of all the men stretch open with surprise. "Ten thousand. Let's get it," Darryl says calmly.

"Hold, hold," one man pleads. "Take it easy. We got your money."

"Ok, let's get it then. No disrespect to nobody. Business is business!"

-16-

Hall of Fame Boxing Club

DARRYL AND LEFTY walk out of the gym after a day of hard work. Darryl hasn't been to the gym in a while, so it's like he's starting all over again. He's trying to get back focused, but the money gets in the way. He never believed that boxing could be so far in the back of his mind.

"Listen, Baby Boy," Lefty says as he stops short on the curb. "Look at it like this, you never know what the few hours you spent in the gym could've saved you from. These three hours you just spent in here could've saved you from anything that was meant for you in the last three hours. You could've been making a move at, let's say, five-thirty-three, and in the middle of that move, police could've pulled you over and locked you up. Or you could've gotten shot in that time or shot somebody and killed them in that time."

Darryl listens attentively. He never looked at it like that, but it makes all the sense in the world. "Yeah, I always say the gym makes me miss so much on the block, but I never looked at it from that perspective. Could be missing some bad, too."

"Yeah, Baby Boy, this your balance right here. Your scale of deeds, the good and the bad. Never let the bad deeds outweigh the good deeds. Niggas end up in a fucked up spot when they don't have the balance. Niggas are ripping and running all day long with no balance. You can't run like that forever, Baby Boy. Sometimes even the hamster has to jump off the wheel and take a breather." Lefty walks away, leaving his words to marinate in Darryl's mind.

"You need a ride?" Darryl asks.

"Nah," Lefty says as he points to a raggedy old tow truck that sits parked. He opens the back door and throws his gym bag on the backseat. "My man was short-staffed and needed a car picked up and brought to the shop. That ran into my gym time, so he told me I could use the truck to get to the gym if I did it for him."

Darryl has barely heard a word he said. He's focused on the tow truck. The 'For Sale' sign in the back window sparks his curiosity. "How much?"

"Eight thousand," Lefty replies. "I only know because people have been stopping me all day asking me the price, and I done linked like seven people with my man who say they want to buy it."

Damn, only eight? That's light, Darryl thinks to himself. He quickly thinks of all the money he can make towing cars. Lately, he's been thinking of starting his own legitimate business, and he just had no clue what type of business he wanted to get into. As he thinks about it, he feels as if this truck was sent to him as a sign.

"I want it!"

"You don't tow no cars," Lefty chuckles. "You don't get no dirt under your nails."

"Nah, I'm dead serious. I need this."

Lefty sees the seriousness in his eyes. "For you, I will see if I can talk my man down a little."

"You don't have to talk him down. I got the money for it right here in my bag," Darryl says as he taps his gym bag. "I can follow you over to him, and we can make this deal right now."

"That's what it is then. Follow me. I been wanted you to meet my man anyway. I been told you he somebody you should know. Ain't no better time than now."

"Ok then, lead me to him," Darryl says.

Lefty climbs in the tow truck, and as old and beat up as it looks, it revs up strong like a new engine. Lefty hangs his head out of the window, looking behind him before pulling out of the parking spot. Darryl follows close behind. His stomach bubbles with the same anxiety that he gets every time he makes a new flip. To him, that's a good sign.

Minutes Later

Money Dee stands in the shop as Lefty leads Darryl inside. "Money, this my man D-Lowe I've been telling you about," he says as he looks directly into Money Dee's eyes. "Baby Boy, this my man Money, I've been telling you about," he says as he looks Darryl in his eyes.

"Both of y'all know I don't vouch for many niggas, but in this matter, I vouch for both of y'all. This business is about the tow truck, but I think there may be some other things y'all have in common. I'm in the middle of this meeting, but I don't have to be included in any other meetings y'all may have in the future. I trust that both of y'all will handle each other as if I'm in the middle even when I'm not in the middle."

Lefty steps back so they can step closer to each other. They shake hands firmly. "Glad to finally meet you," Money Dee says genuinely.

Darryl nods his head respectfully. He's heard so much about this man that he knows this is a come-up in the making. Not many have the privilege of shaking his hand and knowing him, but now that he has been granted the privilege, he's sure it's only up from here. As Lefty has mentioned, this is starting as a tow truck purchase, but he's sure there's a bigger opportunity here.

-17-

Two Months Later
Cocaine Alley

WHAT STARTED AS HIGH HOPES and wishful thinking for the tow truck ended up being an upset, a bad investment. Darryl rented a garage to run his tow truck business out of. It's hard to call it a business when he's done not a bit of business in the entire two months that he's been in business. All that he's gotten out of this is discouragement.

He hired Passion to work for him as a dispatcher. With no jobs to dispatch, Passion's only job is to please Darryl sexually throughout the day. They bring pleasure to every dull moment by sexing each other. In the two months they've been hanging out in the garage, they've had so much sex that they've gotten bored with each other.

The garage has turned into no more than a meeting spot where Darryl meets his customers who buy weight off of him. He keeps half of a kilo of the cheapy-choppa in the office. Throughout the day, his customers come through by appointment only. At least the garage has served the purpose of keeping him and his customers safe.

Each day he regretted even wasting his money until he came up with the perfect way to make his money back off the truck. He's found a use for the truck. In just one trip, the truck has already paid for itself. With this being his second trip, he's now ahead of the game.

Sunday speeds up the highway. She mashes the gas pedal like she has lead in her foot. "Slow down!" Darryl shouts furiously.

"That's not me. That's him," Sunday replies as she points to the bright yellow tow truck in front of her.

The brake lights of the truck pop on before the truck slows down. A few feet later, the truck comes to a complete halt. "What the fuck?" Darryl says frantically. Sunday zips around him and drives away slowly. "Hold up, slow down," he demands. He looks back through the side mirror. "Pull over on the shoulder," he commands.

The hazard lights come on before the driver's door swings open. Unk gets out of the truck and runs to the front. Sunday giggles as he lifts the hood and sticks his head under it. "That raggedy shit done broke down," she utters with sarcasm.

"Yo, shut...the...fuck...up, please?" Darryl whines. "Now ain't the time for your negative bullshit." He's sick and tired of her negativity. Ever since he bought the truck, she's been telling him he's wasted his money, and the business will never work out for him. She's done nothing but down him for trying with this just as she downs him and tries to belittle him about everything else. He's gotten to the point that he's tired of her but still not tired enough to send her on her negative ass way.

"Damn!" Darryl shouts. "This shit crazy!"

"What you want me to do, back up?" Sunday questions.

"Hell no!" Darryl shouts as he thinks of all that is in the tow truck. In the middle lane of the highway, the tow truck sits with a week's worth of work inside of it. Darryl has packed five kilos in the truck. Three kilos are the raw, Grade A, and the other two are the cheapy-choppa.

This has to be the worse luck anybody can have. Here they are with the tow truck stuck on what is known as Cocaine Alley with a truck full of work. This area between New York and New Jersey near the George Washington Bridge is known as one of the most prominent drug transporting routes. Bergen County police and D.E.A. and State Police sit back hiding in little pockets, looking for suspicious vehicles passing through.

The joint task force has it down to a science, and most of the time, they are dead on target when they pull a car over. They sit here clocking and recording license plates, and when those license plates come right back, through, it's a dead giveaway. Unk always thinks ahead of the game, and since he knows they clock license plates going into New York, he doesn't take this way going over. He takes the long way in which he calls the Eastern Seaboard way. Even with all of his precautions, he still finds himself at risk right now. This tragedy of him sitting here stuck is like throwing them a freebie, and the police don't have to work for it. A cop can ride by, and miraculously these five kilos will fall onto his lap.

"Damn, I can't leave him back there, though," he whispers. "State Troopers pull up and his ass outta here," he says as he begins to worry. "Back up," he whispers. "Nah, hold up. Fuck that. Ain't no need in both of us getting caught up. That's my man, though. I can't do this to him," he says as fear sets on his face. "Hmmph." he sighs. "Back up."

"For what, though?"

"I gotta help him."

"How are you going to help him? You ain't no fucking mechanic."

"Well, at least I can grab the work and go before the troopers pull up."

"Yeah, and get your stupid ass locked up and me with you," she snaps.

"Get locked up for what? For all they know, I saw him stuck on the highway and gave him a ride."

"Ok, you got it all figured out."

"Just back up. I didn't ask for your advice."

Sunday backs up along the shoulder. The closer she gets to the tow truck, the harder both of their hearts pound. Darryl reaches over and taps the horn to catch Unk's attention. Unk doesn't look up at all. He's busy under the hood.

Unk comes up from under the hood and runs to the driver's side. He gets inside the tow truck. Darryl can hear him attempting to start the engine but to no avail. It clicks twice before starting on the third try.

Unk hops out of the truck and runs to the front of it. He slams the hood shut and gets back inside. With no hesitation, he speeds off. He mashes the gas pedal until his speed exceeds ninety miles an hour.

"Go ahead," Darryl commands as he wipes the sweat from his brow.

Thirty Minutes Later

Miraculously they've made it back to the garage without the truck breaking down again. As Unk is backing the truck into the garage, safe and sound, Darryl has another problem on his hands. "Who the fuck is that?" Sunday shouts furiously.

"Shhh," Darryl says as he shoves her into the garage area.

"Shhh, my ass! Who the fuck is that?"

This is Sunday's first time coming to the garage. She was never interested in coming here because she has no interest in the business whatsoever. She tells Darryl every day that it's a complete waste of time. As much as he's starting to believe her, he wants to prove her wrong, and that's what keeps him opening up the doors every morning.

He initially offered the dispatcher job to Sunday, but of course, she refused. She told him she wanted no parts of his Sanford and Son junk business. Even with him trying to do something positive, she found a way to humiliate him. He figured he would kill two birds with one stone by paying Sunday a few hundred dollars a week for working. This way he would have her locked in all day, knowing her whereabouts. Also, she could make a few dollars for herself and stay out of his pocket, begging for everything.

"You got your lil' bitches over here working for you?"

"Shhh," he says, hoping that Passion doesn't hear her from the next room.

"Fuck that!" she barks. "Fucking go-go dancer looking bitch! With her cheap, busted ass!"

"That's my man Sheed's cousin," he lies. "She needed a gig, so I hired her," he lies once again. "Shit, you didn't want the job."

"And I still don't want it, but that bitch ain't gonna be working here!"

"Could you stop calling her a bitch?" he whispers. "I told you that's my man cousin. She like a cousin to me, too."

"Fuck that like a cousin shit," she says with jealousy in her eyes. "Either you're going to fire the bitch, or I'm going to fire her," she says as she points in his face. "But the bitch is getting fired today. What's it going to be?"

Darryl hesitates before replying. "I hired her. Let me fire her."

-18-

Eleven Months Later/May 7, 1993
194th Street and Audubon

UNK LAYS ON THE GROUND and crawls underneath the small Volkswagen Jetta. He hooks the tow to the undercarriage. After the car is linked to the tow truck, he wiggles from under the car. He gets up and makes his way to the front of the truck.

This may appear to be a normal tow situation, but really it's a drug move. Darryl came up with another one of his bright ideas. He makes purchases of salvage cars just for this. To avoid him having to drive on the turnpike with over a hundred thousand in cash, he loads one salvage car onto the tow truck. In that car, his buy money is packed away safely.

He parks the car in a safe place for the connect to get inside and get the money. The connect then later packs the car with work. It's then that Unk takes the ride back to New York to pick up the vehicle. Darryl has a total of ten junk cars that he keeps in heavy rotation just so no one will continuously see the same cars traveling back and forth.

Unk climbs into the tow truck and pulls off. The truck bounces up and down Audubon Avenue on its merry way. Darryl waits for Unk to reach the corner before he takes off. He's careful not to tail the truck too closely. The last thing he wants to do is bring attention to them. In no way do either of them need any attention.

Underneath the back seat of the Jetta is the end to their freedom if they're caught. Stacked on top of each other are six kilos of raw and four kilos of cheapy-choppa. With the success of his business, this is only enough work to last for the week. One hundred and seventy-thousand dollars spent brings him a profit of approximately 90 grand.

Darryl barely goes to the block. He allows his team to run the business. The only time he goes through is to drop off his load of pampers. He drops a case of pampers in the morning to open up the block. He goes through more pampers in a day than a Day Care. His block rips through a case and a half of pampers every day, over 100 pampers. The block now generates an average of forty-five to fifty grand a day.

Using no cut with the dime jugs, Darryl only gained about $700 profit from every 100 grams. That resulted in him scoring a profit of only $7,000 off every kilo. Thanks to Unk and one of his bright ideas, Darryl could almost double his profit margin. Unk introduced Darryl to procaine, fish-scale cut.

The fish-scale cut looks exactly like the beautiful fish-scale grade. It even comes back line for line, just without the hit. Darryl solely uses it as a filler to pack the jugs and give the illusion that he's giving away so much more than everyone else. Even with the procaine cut, his dime jugs come back like two of everyone else's dimes, and the work is so pure that there's no-hit greater than his.

This method helps him score another $5,000 off every kilo, bringing his profit margin to $12,000 a kilo.

A bird and a half flies through the block every day, granting Darryl close to 20 grand profit a day. He has built himself a cocaine enterprise, bottle by bottle, jug by jug, gram by gram, and kilo by the kilo. His block is an engine, and all he has to do now is oil that engine.

While the block is doing what it does, Darryl's total concentration is on his wholesale business. This has been an overnight success for him, and his clientele broadens more each day. His clientele ranges from customers who buy half ounces to customers who purchase whole kilos. With him being competitive with the prices in New York, he finds himself in a great position.

Paying fourteen a kilo for the cheapy-choppa gives him a profit margin of five grand per kilo. No one has ever complained about the quality of the work. After all, the work they pay top dollar for in New York is of lesser quality than his cheapy-choppa. It all works out for everyone, especially Darryl. He keeps his block ahead of the game by wholesaling the cheapy-choppa and selling the raw Grade A only on his block. There is no competition!

-19-

Two Days Later

THE GYM IS EMPTY. Darryl sits on the edge of the ring, tying his hand-wraps when Boobie Salaam walks in. Boobie Salaam scans the gym. "Just the man I need to see." He walks up to Darryl and reaches for the handshake. "I'm sure you noticed I haven't been around as much as I used to."

Sure did, Darryl thinks to himself. The whole gym has noticed. The word in the gym is Boobie Salaam stopped coming to the gym on the count of Lefty. Everyone believes he's trying to avoid getting in the ring and mixing it up with Lefty.

"Listen," Boobie Salaam says. "I've been working, and I'm back here now because I finally got it all together. All the pieces of the puzzle are laid out except for one, and that piece is you."

"What you talking about?" Darryl asks. "I told you I ain't with that underground boxing thing."

"What I'm talking about is bigger than that. While I was away, I did some real studying about this boxing game. I learned a lot. I'm finally ready to put everything I learned into motion. I'm about to start my own boxing league with a whole commission behind it. I don't know how much you know about me, but I'm a money magnet," he says with arrogance.

"I got a bunch of money niggas behind me, and we going to pump this thing up. Look at it like the semi-pros of boxing. We get this thing booming, and promoters and management teams will be knocking our doors down. I need you with me, though."

"What you need from me?" Darryl assumes this is some slick old head con game, and he's about to ask him for money.

"No, it's more like what you need from me," Boobie Salaam replies with sarcasm. "I got the blueprint," he says with his eyes stretched wide. "Didn't you tell me your dream was to become a pro-fighter?"

"Yeah and?" Darryl asks.

"Well, I'm here to make your dream come true."

"Yeah, right."

"I'm serious, lil' bruh. It's simple. We can go down to Trenton and pay thirty dollars to get your professional license. You'll have your pro license in the cut, and meanwhile, you can be climbing up the ranks in our semi-pro league."

"And then what?" Darryl asks. "Fight for a thousand dollars a fight? I can't live off of that. That's a waste of my time."

"What if I know a way that you can score that same thousand a fight without fighting at all?" he asks.

"What you mean?" Darryl replies.

"I mean, I got the hook up in North Carolina where mufuckers will get knocked out for five hundred dollars. Niggas hurting, and they will take a dive just to put food on the table for the month."

"But what does that do for me? It's still a grand a fight. It cost more to get to North Carolina than I will make off the fight. Anyway, that ain't what I'm about. I'm not into paying my way. I like to earn mine."

"And you will earn yours. When the time is right," he adds. "The more fights you have, the more you make off of a fight. By the time you get eight and O, you will be worth about seven or eight grand a fight."

"And that still ain't worth shit."

"Lil Bruh, you gotta crawl before you walk. What you think you're going to come out the gate making three million a fight? Come on, lil' bruh, you gotta be honest with yourself. Now check the plan. We pay them mufuckers their price to get knocked out for us. All we need is like twenty wins. For less than fifteen grand, you will be twenty and O. That makes you a contender. You then will be ranked across the country. Once you're ranked, you start making a decent penny. But that is when shit gets real. At that point, we start getting the tough fighters coming at us."

Boobie Salaam now has Darryl's full attention. He's all ears as he listens attentively without missing a single word. "I figure we can get you to twenty and O in about a year from now. Like I said, not even fifteen grand out of pocket. But our first fight will at least make a hundred and fifty grand. Fifteen makes you a hundred and fifty. How sweet is that?"

"Real sweet," Darryl agrees. "Too sweet to be true."

"How you figure, Lil bruh? That's how this boxing game goes. The Italians have been doing this forever. They just fucked up and gave me the in. I was knocked off with an Italian boy who broke it all down for me. His father was a big deal fight promoter. He even gave me the connections I need to get it all rolling. All we have to do is follow the blueprint.

Niggas take dive after dive, and meanwhile, we train hard and prepare for that day we really have to fight.

Two years from now, you can be Mike Tyson status for all we know. And this shit out here," he says as he points out of the window onto the street. "Will be all behind you," he says as he stares into Darryl's eyes. "So, what you think?"

"I mean, it sounds good, but..."

"But what? Ain't no buts in it. Everything after but is bullshit. If you truly believe in yourself, then why not invest in yourself? I got five other fighters ready to roll. I'm going to do this with or without you. I just want to bring you in because I believe in you.

See, with them, I'm putting all the cheese up. I'm paying for everything, robes, gym equipment, gym dues and paying for the nigga to take the dive. I'm only giving them a cut of the money when it's made. With you, I know you got your own money, so you will pay for everything yourself. In the end all I want from you is a twenty percent promoter's fee of the purse. Not the lil' bullshit fights. I'm talking about once we get you twenty and O and you make a hundred grand, break me off twenty grand, that's all."

It's all sounding sweeter and sweeter by the second to Darryl, but still, he doesn't believe in it totally. "If it's that simple, then why isn't everyone Mike Tyson status?"

"Simple, Lil Bruh," he whispers. "Cause everybody ain't made to be on top. Some mufuckers are scared to be on top. It's a different kind of air up top, Lil bruh. The air is so thin up top that it suffocates some mufuckers. They rather stay down bottom where it's safe and easy to breathe. Safe is fear of investing in your dreams. It's safer to keep on dreaming about it than actually trying to live it out."

Boobie Salaam stares ahead with dreamy eyes. "You ever see when a fighter come out of nowhere? This your first time hearing of him, and he like twenty-five and O, all knockouts? Where the hell do you think he came from? Who did he fight? I will tell you who he fought! Nobody! Them nobody mufuckers took dives to help build a nigga's career. The same thing we are about to do, Lil bruh. I believe in you. Do you believe in you?"

"Of course," Darryl replies.

"Well, let's go for it," he says. "I'm going to leave you with this, and I'm gone. The best investment a man can make is an investment in himself. And I still got a spot for your man with one hand too. Maybe you can talk to him because I don't know him like that."

Coincidentally Lefty comes walking into the gym. Boobie Salaam quickly wraps up the meeting upon spotting Lefty. "Ay think on it, and talk to him," he whispers. He quickly shakes Darryl's hand and walks away, not once looking in Lefty's direction.

Lefty walks over with agitation on his face. The sight of Boobie Salaam always annoys him. He shakes Darryl's hand and looks over at Boobie Salaam, who is halfway across the room. "You can run, but you can't hide. One day you gone have to man up and dance with the devil."

Darryl shakes his head with a grin. He will never tell Lefty the slick comment Boobie Salaam has made about his one hand, and he's done it not once but twice. Darryl is sure that will be enough to set Lefty off. Darryl doesn't understand Lefty's hatred for Boobie Salaam. Darryl was humiliated by Boobie Salaam in the ring and he doesn't hate him. He sort of thanks Boobie Salaam for that day because that whole situation pushed him toward greatness and built character.

Lefty stares Darryl in the eyes. "I don't know what y'all was over here building so deep about, but whatever it is, don't trust him. I hate slick ass old-timers always trying to game motherfuckers," he says with hatred plastered on his face. "I told you, Baby Boy, you a good nigga and niggas like him can spot you a mile away. I wouldn't trust that old con-man as far as I can see him. With my bad eye," he says as he points at his dead eye.

Lefty gets angrier by the second. "Can't believe he got the nerve to tell you to tell me to come fight in that underground boxing bullshit he got going on. Like I'm some type of pit-bull in a dog fight. Or I'm one of his slaves fighting for the master's entertainment, like they used to do in the days of slavery. Every time I think of the time you asked me that, I feel like punching his head off."

"Man, later for him," Darryl says in attempt to calm Lefty down and keep the peace.

"Nah Baby Boy, I know his kind. One thing I don't do is eat with a snake. Before I eat with a snake, I would rather stay broke and fucked up. Baby Boy, a snake will eat off you, eat with you and then turn around and eat you, always remember that."

-20-

The Next Day

DARRYL HAS JUST EXPLAINED to Sunday the details of yesterday's conversation with Boobie Salaam. He now awaits her reply. He's so excited about it but wants to know what she thinks of the idea. "So, now you're gonna be a professional boxer?" she asks with sarcasm. "Uhm."

Darryl is speechless. He hates the fact that he expected any more from her than she's been giving him. Foolishly he thought she would be just as excited about the idea as he is. "Bitch, I'm tired of you!" he shouts as he stares at Sunday.

Sunday looks surprised. She realizes she must have really gotten under his skin because never before has he called her a bitch. At least not aloud to her face. "You so fucking negative! No matter what I try to do, if it don't consist of selling fucking drugs, buying cars, and giving you money to shop, it's stupid and a waste of time!" he shouts. She looks out the window, barely listening to him.

"Negative? How am I negative? I'm just a realist. All I asked was, you going to be a professional boxer now? You're the one acting all negative."

"Talking about hmmm!" he shouts. "Like you think I can't be a professional fighter. What, is that what you think? You think I can't box?"

"I never said you can't box," she says before turning her head back to her window.

"You better not because you never saw me fucking box!" he shouts with rage. "I can fucking box!" he shouts. Without even realizing it, he's trying to convince her because deep down inside, he believes she doesn't think he can fight. His self-esteem has been beaten up so badly by her that he constantly feels the need to prove himself. "I can fight, but you would never know because you never been to my fights. None of them!" he shouts.

"You know why? Because my fights don't mean shit to you! Don't nothing mean shit to you. Damn near three years we've been together or knowing each other, whatever the fuck you want to call it," he rambles. "You haven't supported me in shit! You just a negative ass bitch!" He slams the gear of the Acura into Park. "I'm tired of this shit!"

Sunday opens the door and steps out of the car. She's paying no mind to his rant. She slams the door shut and makes her way toward the entrance of Red Lobster. Thoughts of leaving her right here cross his mind as he watches her walk away. Instead, he gets out and slams the car door shut.

Darryl and Sunday sit across from each other in a booth-seat. She looks down, fiddling with her nails as he whispers angrily. "Just like the fucking tow truck company," he says with fury. "I couldn't even get yo' ass to answer the phone and send my man to jobs."

She looks up, finally ready to add her two cents. "You didn't have any jobs to send him on. You can waste your time if you want to, but you're not going to waste mine."

"Yeah, wasting time," he says a little louder. "You said it right. This whole relationship has been a waste of my fucking time."

A shadow over Darryl's shoulder tells him that someone is approaching the table. Sunday's eyes light up, and she spreads a fake smile across her face. "Hello," a sweet voice sounds off from over him. Darryl looks up, and his mouth drops wide open once he lays eyes on the waitress.

The waitress looks away with shame. She fumbles with her pen and pad to avoid looking into Darryl's eyes. "My name is Asia, and I will be your server this evening."

Darryl can't believe his eyes. He stares at Asia with surprise before he catches himself. *A fucking waitress, he thinks to himself. What the fuck is going on?* Darryl turns away from her not to raise Sunday's suspicion. This is the most awkward moment of his life. He can't believe this is happening. Dinner is about to be served by the love of his life to the woman he holds responsible for breaking up their true love.

"May I get your drinks, please?" Asia asks as she holds her pen against her pad.

Darryl peeks upward and notices that Asia has put on more than a few pounds. *Hold up, he thinks to himself. I know this ain't what I think. Say it ain't so, he says to himself. It's so, he says to himself with heartache.* The protruding of her belly tells him she's pregnant in the early stages. His heart sinks to his feet. He feels as if he could die right now.

"And what are you drinking, sir?" Asia asks as she stares into Darryl's eyes. Both of their eyes are glassy with tears. They stare at each other without blinking. Blinking will only cause both of them to cry right at the table.

Darryl looks away from her. His eyes set on the small diamond ring she wears on her left hand. The cloudy, single-stone diamond ring appears to be an engagement ring. *What the fuck is happening, he asks himself.*

"Sir, what would you like to drink?"

He shakes his head sadly. His heart is broken. "The hardest shit you got in the house," he replies. "This is the most fucked up day of my life," he says as he stares into Asia's eyes.

"You don't even drink," Sunday interjects.

He looks over to Sunday with hate before rolling his eyes. He looks back to Asia, and a tight-faced grin appears. "Whatever the hardest shit in the house is, give me a fucking double!"

-21-

DARRYL CRUISES THROUGH the intersection of 6th Street and 13th Avenue. He peeks through the rearview, and the car glued to his tailpipe has him alarmed. The grey unmarked police car trails him closely. He quickly straps his seatbelt across his chest.

He snatches his gun from his waist and slides it underneath his seat. As he cruises up the block, he stares straight ahead, but his hands are working. He opens the middle console and grabs hold of the half kilo, and he slides that underneath his seat as well. "Damn," he says nervously.

Just two blocks away from his destination and now this. He was on his way to make a weight sale. Something told him to take 8th Street, but he didn't. As soon as he passed through his block, the cop car parked on the corner jumped on him. The car has been tailing him for the past two blocks.

"Fuck this!" he says out loud. He has all of his paperwork, but something tells him the paperwork will not save him. These are not regular patrol cops looking to give out tickets. These are narcs looking for drugs. "Fuck that!" he shouts. "I can't take the risk of letting them pull me over," he says. "I'm about to take these pussies for a ride! As soon as I hit South Orange Avenue, it's over!"

As he approaches South Orange Avenue, he prepares himself to take the chase. He sits upright in his seat and braces himself. His heart pounds fast and hard. "Here we go," he says as he gets a few feet away from the corner. "Oh shit," he says as he's cut off by a black unmarked car. He's paralyzed with fear as he watches two suit and tie wearing detectives jump from the car in front of him.

Both detectives have their guns drawn and aimed at him. Darryl grabs hold of his wallet and holds it out of the window, high in the air. His door is snatched open, and he's dragged to the ground. He looks up, only to be surrounded by a total of five detectives.

"Here go my license! My insurance and registration is in the glove compartment!"

The detectives ignore him as they rip through his car hastily. No time passes before one detective steps out of the vehicle. "Cuff him!" he shouts with joy. He holds the kilo in one hand and the gun in the other.

Thirty Minutes Later

Darryl sits at the table inside of the dark and lonely room. He's been sitting for the past half hour without anyone coming into the room. He can't believe he's here again. He's sure this time he has earned himself a trip to prison.

He believes even the best attorney in the world won't save him this time. "Damn, I fucked up," he whispers. "Come the fuck on!" he shouts as he bangs on the desk. "I gotta get the fuck outta here." He bangs on the desk harder. *The longer they make me wait, the longer it will take for me to make bail. Bail, he thinks.*

He hates to tell his Nana, but he has no choice. She's the only one he trusts to tell where his money is to come and get him. Damn, he says to himself as he thinks of all she's going to say to him.

The creaking of the door causes him to look over his shoulder. Two detectives step into the room. The one in the back holds a stack of papers in his hand. The first detective walks past Darryl without saying a word. He walks to the window and stares out of it. "Darryl Lowe," the detective sings with a bright smile on his face.

Here we go, Darryl thinks to himself. Good cop, bad cop. "D, Lowe," he sings once again. "Before we start, is there anything you would like to tell us?"

"Tell you about what?" Darryl wears a straight face. "Y'all already know everything. I ain't got nothing to say," he says with a rebellious demeanor.

"No," the detective says. "Actually, there's so much more to say. We just hope that you say it, and we don't have to hear it in the street."

"Hear what in the street?" he asks. "Look, man, take me to the county, and let's get this over with. I don't have anything else to say." He closes his mouth and his eyes. He leans back in the chair, letting them know he has no plans of cooperating.

"Darryl Lowe, how is your girlfriend, Passion doing?" the officer at the window asks.

This catches Darryl by surprise. "What? What you mean?" He wonders how they know about her.

"I mean, how is she doing? How are y'all doing?"

"I don't know who y'all talking about," he lies. "I don't know no Passion."

"Of course you do," he says with certainty. "You were just with her last night at the Fifty Ball Motel in Irvington."

"Fifty Ball?" He laughs loudly. "I've never been to the filthy Fifty Ball in my life."

"Well, when was the last time you were with her?"

"I told you, I don't know no Passion. Anyway, what the fuck is this about?"

"What's it about?" the detective asks. "You don't know?" He smiles before adjusting the folder he holds. "Here...this is what it's about," he says as he lays the open folder on the desk.

Darryl stares at the most hideous sight he's ever seen. His throat swells to the point that he can't speak. As hideous as the picture is, he can't seem to remove his eyes from it. Passion lays sprawled out on the motel room carpet, butt naked. Her eyes are wide open, and blood drips from her mouth. An extension cord is wrapped tightly around her neck, and red bruises cover her body.

He finally musters up the ability to turn away from the photo. He attempts to keep his game face on, but the detectives see right through it. "Are you ready to talk to us?"

"Talk to you about what?" he asks in a squeaky high-pitched voice.

"Your voice just cracked, so I'm sure you must know her."

"I know her," he admits.

"That we know. A close friend of hers gave us your license plate number. Dancers at the bar say you came and picked her up. Supposedly you and her hang out regularly. They told us if anybody knows anything, it would be you."

"What is it that you want to know?" he asks.

"Let's start by you telling us why you did this to her."

"What?" he asks in complete shock.

"You paid her for sex, and it didn't go as planned, so you raped her and killed her so she couldn't testify on you?"

"Raped? Man, I ain't no fucking rapist, and I didn't kill her. What the fuck do I look like?"

"A trick, based on what the dancers are saying," the detective says with a grin.

"Man, fuck what them bitches saying. They don't know me and I didn't kill her."

"Well, tell us who did, or else you will wear a homicide along with that gun and kilo charge."

"Hell no! Oh, this is some straight bullshit right here! I need to call my lawyer."

-22-

Hours Later

DARRYL LIES BACK UNCOMFORTABLY on the hard cot inside of the County Jail. All of this is playing like one bad dream. As real as it is, he wishes it wasn't true. To find out that Passion has been raped and murdered makes his situation with the gun, and the cocaine seem minute.

He can't shake the vision of her from his mind. He wonders who could have done this to her and why. A part of him feels guilty this has happened. He feels he could have prevented this. That night she had called him a few times, but it was one of those nights he was caught up with Sunday.

Despite her line of business, he had so much love for her. The fact that she never denied who she was and laid everything on the table with him gave him no choice but to respect her. He often thought about crossing the line with her and making her his leading lady. Despite the many partners she's had, he's sure he could have built a solid and trusting relationship with her. Out of all of the sexual partners, she may have had, only one stuck out in Darryl's head. His used to

94

be best friend, Sheed, had her is why he never crossed that line with her. He could never have her as his lady, knowing that Sheed had her.

What he loved most about her was she had proved she would do anything in the world for him. All he had to do was state what he needed from her, and she was there to supply him with it, no questions asked. He feels like he never was there for her the same way. He thinks with all she's done for him, there's no way she still should have to dance and trick for a living. He's sure that guilt will haunt him for the rest of his life.

For a quick second, he's able to shake Passion from his mind. Thoughts of Sunday creep in slowly. He hasn't heard from her since a little while before his arrest. He wonders if she even notices he's not around. He wonders where she is at this very moment.

Meanwhile

Sunday climbs the fire escape as carefully as she can. Her wet, bare feet slip with each step. The rain, accompanied by the tears in her eyes, makes it difficult to see. "Sunday!" Roselyn shouts from the ground underneath the fire escape. "Stop, Sunday! Fuck him!" she exclaims. "He ain't worth all of this!"

"That's right," Sheila agrees. "Fuck him!"

Roselyn, Sheila, and Tasha stand on the ground, watching Sunday make a complete fool of herself. "Come down from there before you fall and hurt yourself!" Roselyn shouts. "Please," Roselyn begs. "Please?"

Sunday looks up and realizes how far she has to go to reach her destination. She becomes discouraged and stops. She holds on to the railing as she cries like a newborn baby. "Come down, Sunday!" Tasha demands.

Minutes pass, and Sunday is finally standing with her

girlfriends. They all hug her with compassion trying hard to console her. Roselyn grabs her by the shoulders and leads her to the front of the building. "You gotta stop putting yourself through this," Roselyn says. "He's shown you over and over what you mean to him. It's all a game to him. You have to stop letting him play you like this."

"I know," Sunday cries. "But-"

"But nothing," Roselyn snaps. "This nigga don't give a fuck about you, Sunday. Why can't you see this? You keep saying it's over, and your love for him is gone, but look at you. You're saying you're a big girl, and you can play the same game he's playing, but you can't. You have to cut him all the way off. No interaction, no gift accepting, and no sex," she says with emphasis. "You expect more than he's willing to give."

Sunday just listens as Roselyn lays the truth on her. Roselyn escorts her to the passenger seat of Darryl's BMW. She opens the passenger's door for her. "Get in," she demands. "I will drive. You're in no position to drive."

Sunday stops short. "Hold up," she says as she reaches into the car. She grabs hold of The Club. She walks hurriedly over toward the building with fury in her eyes. She stops at the back of the red Volkswagen Cabriolet. It's evident that this car belongs to whoever the woman is that Sal has in his house.

Sunday raises The Club high in the air, and with all her might, she swings it. The Club crashes into the back window, shattering it into tiny pieces. She doesn't stop there. She's not done until she's broken every window on the car.

She then walks over to Sal's Mercedes, parked in front of the Cabriolet. She immediately goes to work on the windows of that car as well. She swings recklessly until all his windows are shattered. None of this changes the fact, but it does make her feel a little better.

She walks over to Darryl's car and drops herself into the passenger's seat. Roselyn pulls off. She looks over to Roselyn. "Now I feel better."

-23-

Three Days Later

MINUTES AGO, Darryl was released from the County Jail by surprise. He had no clue of who he could call on to come to bail him out, but a miracle appeared. He now believes in miracles and bears witness that they can come from the strangest places. Never in a million years did he expect to find Boobie Salaam outside waiting for him. The fact that he paid the bail made him even more surprised.

Darryl wondered how Boobie Salaam even knew, but he informed him that the word had spread around the gym. As soon as Boobie Salaam got the word, he immediately put his people on it. Boobie Salaam tells Darryl that he wouldn't wish jail on his worst enemy, which is why he did what he did. Darryl is grateful for the favor but can't help but wonder what Boobie Salaam may want in return. He thinks of the words that Lefty repeatedly says about not trusting Boobie Salaam.

"You can take me right to my spot, and I can get that bread to you asap. I really appreciate you for this more than you know."

"Don't worry about it. This ain't nothing. I've been fucking with Scotty, Bail Bondsmen for years. It was just a phone call for me, nothing big. You can get that little change to me tomorrow in the gym, no pressure."

Darryl bangs his head against the headrest, thinking of all that he has in front of him at this time. "Fuck!" He's glad to hear that he hasn't been charged with Passion's murder. It was all a tactic to get him to tell what he knows. That's one thing off of his plate and now he has to figure out how he can clean the rest of his plate.

"Damn, Lil Bruh," Boobie Salaam sighs. "You got yourself into a pickle," he says as he shakes his head. "The trifecta. Drugs, money and a gun. I done seen dudes get 10 years for a little bit of drugs and very little cash, just because they got caught with all three. Now, you, a whole brick and over twenty-thousand in cash, I ain't gone lie, that's ugly."

"Shit, you telling me," Darryl sighs.

"Don't worry, though. I got a mean attorney for you. My man Ray Brown is the best in the business. He's like a magician and has the power to make shit disappear. I beat two homicides with him. I hired him and Richie Roberts. Together they worked on my case, and I walked away scot-free. He's costly but worth every dime of the money. He got me off my last beef, too. Yeah, I did a dime, but I was facing forty years," he adds.

"Ray Brown starts at a quarter. It ain't no price tag on your freedom, Lil' bruh. Don't worry, though. If you are short, I can help you. I got a couple of extra dollars to spare." He looks over to Darryl.

"Nah, the money ain't nothing," Darryl says arrogantly.

"I'm just saying that's how much I believe in you. Plus, I want to see you get through this. I need you with me. After we get you through this storm ain't

99

no turning back, though. You got the perfect situation right in front of your face. You have to reach for it. You follow me?"

Darryl nods his head up and down. "I follow you."

"Lil' Bruh, ain't nothing out here on these streets. Trust me when I tell you," he says with certainty. "The streets are for mufuckers who don't have a way out. You have a way out. You just have to want to get out of the way. Me, I'm out, and I ain't never going back. I made that promise to myself halfway through my bid. Them crackers taught me," he says with a smile.

"My advice to you is to take all that you have now and walk away before you can't walk away. All you have to do is give me the word, and I will start the engine for you. You got dreams, but it seems you're scared to chase them. You can keep dreaming those dreams, or you can bring those dreams to reality. Remember this, the same shit you dream about can turn out to be your worst nightmare if you don't reach for your dreams."

Boobie Salaam double-parks in front of Darryl's house. "Listen, Lil Bruh, your dreams are right there at your fingertips. You just have to reach for your dreams because your dreams will not reach for you."

Darryl nods his head up and down. "Understood."

-24-

Two Days Later

AFTER THINKING DEEPLY about all that Boobie Salaam said, Darryl has decided to take him up on his offer. After all, the plan sounds foolproof. He believes in himself. He also believes in Boobie Salaam because he seems to know what he's talking about.

After analyzing the situation, Darryl doesn't understand why he didn't jump on it the very first time Boobie Salaam propositioned him with it. He doesn't recognize how badly Sunday's negative mindset affects him. She constantly makes him question himself. He was all with it until Sunday made him feel like he didn't have what it takes to be a professional fighter.

Over the years he's been with her, she has managed to cripple his self-esteem. He identified Sunday as his problem a long time ago. He needs to find a solution to that problem now. For him, this seems to be a task that is easier said than done.

Darryl is in the gym for the first time in what seems like an eternity. He can't believe he's been away so long. At one time, this gym was his life, and now he feels like a foreigner here. He feels like a stranger in his own home with many new faces.

He stands in front of the heavy bag, pounding away at it. His clothes are drenched with sweat, and puddles of sweat are on the floor under his feet. He huffs and puffs, yet he continues to beat on the bag. He can't believe how out of shape he is.

"Gotta get this fucking money," he says to himself as he tries to psyche himself out to continue. Passion laying dead pops up in his head again. "Rrrooar," he growls as he tries to punch through the bag. He wishes he knew who did that to her so he could get revenge for taking away his rider. "Motherfucker," he barks as he beats on the bag.

He slows down the pace as fatigue kicks in. He allows his mind to return to Red Lobster, where he sees Asia. He envisions her standing there pregnant, and the rage builds up in him. He involuntarily pictures her having sex with another man, and it drives him crazy. "Motherfucker stole my lady," he says to himself as he imagines what he would do to this particular man if he could. He bangs the bag from top to bottom as hard as he can.

In a quick flash, Sunday's face pops up in his mind. At the sight of her face, a blast of fury rips through his gut. Mentally he places an image of her face on the bag. He bangs away at the idea of her. "You disrespectful bitch," he utters. "Fucked my life up," he whispers to himself with rage as he bangs and bangs and bangs. *Ding, ding!* The bell sounds, but Darryl continues to wail on the bag. "I'm tired of this ungrateful bitch," he whispers. "No matter what I do, this bitch ain't satisfied," he says as he fires an eight-piece combination at the bag.

"Hold, champ, hold!" Boobie Salaam says. "That's rest right there. You beating on that bag like a cheating bitch," he says with a smile.

Shit, if you only knew, Darryl thinks to himself. Darryl walks around the bag, trying to regulate his breathing. He's huffing and puffing uncontrollably. The bell rings, and Boobie Salaam stands beside Darryl, giving him instructions. He's so caught up in Boobie Salaam he hasn't even noticed his old trainer Charlie come into the gym. Charlie watches with jealousy as Boobie Salaam trains what he thinks to be his fighter.

After the fifth round, Boobie Salaam walks away, leaving Darryl alone with instructions. Charlie makes his way over to Darryl, and he stands right behind him. "Long time no see, champ," he whispers over Darryl's shoulder. Darryl looks over his shoulder and continues to bang away at the bag.

"What's up, Charlie? How you been?" he huffs from his dry mouth.

"I'm good. I see you got yourself a new trainer, huh?" he asks with sarcasm. "I guess we weren't good enough, huh?" he says with a cheesy smile. "After we took you from the Puerto Rican camp and taught you how to fight, you left us high and dry. On to the next," he says with evident attitude.

"But remember I told you this, I do this for the love of the sport. It was never about money. Sometimes dollar signs can impair your judgment. Everything ain't always about the money." He rubs his fingertips together like he's flicking through bills.

"A relationship that starts on money and develops around money will always be just that," he says with a grin. "All about money! Money is his motive. Open your eyes, and I'm sure you will see what I'm talking about. Stevie Wonder can see that. He's a hustler. He just ain't hustling drugs no more. He's hustling fighters," he says as he steps away from Darryl.

Darryl sits back for a second, pondering on Charlie's words. Charlie may have been speaking about Boobie Salaam, but he realizes those words could easily apply to Sunday as well. Boobie Salaam walks up. "What the hell is Charlie talking about?" he asks defensively.

Darryl shakes his head. "Nothing," he replies. "Nothing at all."

Three Days Later

DARRYL RIDES IN THE PASSENGER'S SEAT of Boobie Salaam's car. They just left the attorney's office a few minutes ago, and Darryl left a retainer fee of ten grand for the attorney to start on his case. Boobie Salaam offered to put up half of the money, but Darryl refused.

He would never take money from Boobie Salaam under any condition. Charlie's words keep ringing in his mind. Boobie Salaam isn't doing these things from the heart, and he's doing it all with hopes of gaining in the end. It's evident that Boobie Salaam looks at him as an investment, and one day he plans to get a return on his investment.

"Listen, Lil Bruh," Boobie Salaam says as he speeds up Raymond Boulevard. "You're going to be all right. You got a machine on your side. If anybody can get you through this, my man Ray Brown can. Look," Boobie Salaam says as he points in front of them. "Somebody just copped."

Darryl stares straight ahead at what he believes to be the most prestigious automobile ever made. The Forest Green Range Rover is the automobile of his dreams.

He's always wanted one back before he could afford one. Now that he can afford the truck, it doesn't mean much to him.

"Somebody chilling," Boobie Salaam says. "Look, temporary tag waving and the whole shit," he says as he catches up with the truck. Finally, the truck stops short at the corner of Norfolk Street. Boobie Salaam creeps past the truck and stops a few feet in front of it. "Damn, that shit looks good," Boobie Salaam says out the corner of his mouth as he stares straight ahead. The last thing he wants is to be seen admiring the truck.

Darryl sits up in his seat slightly and peeks over. Just as he looks over, the passenger happens to be looking over at them. The passenger and Darryl lock eyes. Darryl wants to look away, but his eyes are glued to the man sitting in the passenger's seat. Seeing the familiar face sends a chill up Darryl's spine. Rage fills Darryl's gut as he sees Sal laying low in the passenger's seat.

Sal turns his head, indicating he has no clue who Darryl is. Darryl slides forward in his seat, and immediately his heart stops beating. His face hardens like stone, and his body is frozen stiff. He is numb from shock as he sees Sunday sitting in the driver's seat as if she belongs there.

The light changes, and Sunday mashes the gas pedal. The truck speeds up the block smoothly. Boobie Salaam mashes his gas pedal as well. "Bitch, you don't want none of this," Boobie Salaam says as he trails behind the Rover.

Darryl's is tight-faced, trying hard to keep his emotions off his face. His belly feels like a wide-open pit. "Lying bitch," he mumbles to himself. His adrenaline races as he sits on the edge of the seat. He's beyond furious. He wants to get out and beat her to a pulp, but his respect for Boobie Salaam prevents him from doing so. He would never want Boobie Salaam to view him as a sucker for love. With his image on the line, he's forced to sit as if everything is all right.

Boobie Salaam pulls to the left of the Range Rover and speeds by it. "What I tell you?" he says as he looks over at Darryl. His face is covered with competitiveness, while Darryl's face is sour. Boobie Salaam mashes the gas pedal as hard as he can. "Yeah, that truck may be beautiful, but it ain't got enough horses, bitch," he says as he watches the truck in the rearview mirror. "Bitch trying to stay with me, though," he says. "Check her out!"

Boobie Salaam slams on the brakes at Bergen Street. A half a minute later, the Rover pulls to the right of them. Boobie Salaam looks to his right with a cocky smile. Sunday looks over and catches a glimpse of Darryl's face before turning away quickly.

Darryl keeps his eyes glued on her. Her discomfort is quite evident. She fidgets in her seat and keeps her back to them. She places her arm to the window, hand over her face to prevent Darryl from seeing her. She has no clue he's seen her long before she's seen him.

Darryl stares at her without blinking. He's afraid that if he blinks, he will miss the look on her face once she realizes he sees her. He watches her for the duration of the light. As soon as the light changes, Sunday busts an unexpected right and speeds along Bergen Street.

Darryl is crushed. Oh, how he wishes it wasn't true. He's surprised at how he isn't heartbroken right now. It's more rage that he feels for all the times she's lied to him. It's as if his heart has been frozen. *This is what I needed, he thinks to himself. I was right all the while. All this time. I knew the shit wasn't adding up, but I just couldn't prove it.* He pounds his fist on his thigh. "Lying bitch," he mumbles under his breath.

"*This is exactly what I needed to see. This bitch done disrespected me for the very last time. Now that I have witnessed it with my own eyes, I can move on and leave them two to live happily ever after.* The end," he mumbles. "For her, that is."

-26-

Hours Later

DARRYL STANDS IN FRONT of Sunday's house. He leans on the rail as she stands a few feet away from him. His demeanor is cold and distant. She cries as she's speaking. He stares over his shoulder as if she isn't speaking to him. Today none of her tactics are working.

"Could you please look at me when I talk to you?" she cries with desperation. "Look at me," she says as she grabs his face. He leans his head back and snatches her hand from his face, still looking away. He realizes the danger in looking into her eyes. Her tears could very well make him feel sorry for her, and feeling sorry for her could make him forgive her. "It wasn't what it looked like," she claims. "You gotta believe me."

He turns toward her, looking into her eyes for the very first time. "Tell me what it looked like," he says with his eyes squinted with agitation. He gets angry every time he replays that scene. "When I looked over, what do you think I saw?"

She pauses before replying. "You saw me driving Sal's truck." She lowers her eyes in shame. "I know it probably looked like me, and Sal was chilling, but it wasn't like that. I swear," she whines.

"So what was y'all doing if y'all wasn't chilling?"

She shakes her head sadly. "We had just come back from the car dealer. He traded his other car in and got that one. I told you his car was in my name. That's why I had to be there with him," she claims. "That's the only reason."

"Oh, so that's why you was driving the truck? Oh, I see," he says with sarcasm as he looks away once again.

"Darryl, you have to believe me when I tell you I don't want him. And he doesn't want me," she whispers sadly. Darryl thinks her tears are for him and this situation, and what he doesn't know is her tears are the reality sinking in. As much as she knows Sal is playing her, she can't seem to walk away from him. "It's about us." She steps closer to him. She presses her body against his.

The truth is it could never be about them as long as Sal is around. He's a distraction to her, and he stands in the way of her allowing herself to get fully into Darryl. Sunday is in a tough spot. She's stuck between a man who loves her and a man she loves but knows he couldn't care less about her.

Darryl pushes her off with force. He turns around to the street where his car is double-parked. He waves his hand high in the air giving the signal to Zak, who gets out of the car and walks over. "Sunday, there is no more us," he says as he stares deep into her eyes. "Give me the keys to my car."

"No," she denies as she pulls away and hides the keys behind her back. Darryl steps toward Sunday with a rage in his eyes she's never seen.

"Give me my fucking keys," he spits from his mouth.

She backpedals away from him. Darryl corners her in, grabs her wrist, and squeezes it tight. Sunday grunts with pain. "Get off me before you break my wrist." Darryl tries to crush the bone in her wrist. He squeezes it until she's forced to open her hand. He snatches the keys and turns away from her.

"Zak!" he shouts as he tosses the keys in the air. Darryl floats across the street toward his Acura. He feels like a weight has been lifted from his shoulders.

"Darryl!" Sunday shouts at the top of her lungs. He ignores her. "Darryl!" she cries out again. He hops into the car and slams the gear into Drive. Sunday runs over tapping on the window. Not once does he look in her direction. He mashes the gas pedal as if she isn't standing at the window.

He watches the rearview mirror as Sunday stands at the curb with her face buried in her hands. She sits on the curb and hangs her head in between her legs. He watches with no compassion at all. It feels good to finally see her enduring the pain she has been putting him through all this time. He nods his head up and down. "The score is finally tied," he says. "But the game is over!"

-27-

One Week Later/May 25, 1993

A WHOLE WEEK HAS PASSED, and Darryl has been able to stand firm against Sunday. He's proud of himself. This is the longest they have been apart during his years with her. It's like the hardest thing he's ever had to do, but still, he's been able to remain strong in his spot. She calls him at least twice every hour, every single day. She leaves messages sobbing and crying before she finally hangs up. He's never seen her perform like this. For the first time, it seems as if she really cares. Strangely he misses her dearly. At times he's tempted to answer the phone. When he gets the urge to answer her call or even initiate a call, he visualizes her driving Sal's truck, and that vision deters him from picking up the phone.

He can't help but wonder why Sunday isn't satisfied with him. In the beginning, he always felt like he wasn't on the level of the hustlers she was used to dealing with. Foolishly he accepted her disrespect because he believed he was lucky to have her. Now he no longer feels like that. He's confident in who he is. The man that everyone thought he was back then, he has finally become.

What baffles him the most is that she still has no respect for him with all the money, power, and respect he has earned over the years. It's as if she doesn't think he is even worthy of her respect. Even with who he has become, she still manages to make him feel less than any other man she's dealt with. It's like in her eyes, he's still a *nobody, non-descript.*

His self-esteem has been bruised. Without even realizing it, he's constantly in competition. Not with any man in particular, but with every man Sunday may believe is a better or bigger than him. It's him against mankind.

Today Darryl has allowed his competitive edge to make yet another decision for him. He now races along Route 46, leaving Zakar Motors. He's doing more than ninety miles an hour in his brand spanking new automobile. Seeing Sunday driving Sal's new truck inspired him to get something new of his own. He needed some retail therapy to help him get over it.

The craftsmanship of this vehicle makes Darryl's Acura feel like a taxi cab. The butter-soft leather upholstery melts as he sits in it. The windows are airtight, and no outside noise can be heard. Sitting in the driver's seat, Darryl feels like a pilot in an airplane cockpit. The car doesn't ride over the road; it glides. There's more wood trimming inside the car than a log cabin.

He peeks into the third lane. He barely gives the Honda to his left time to get past him before he makes his cut. He cuts a Nissan off, causing it to barely miss his bumper. He mashes the gas pedal as hard as possible while mashing the horn. The Honda dips over to the middle lane, and Darryl mashes the gas pedal harder. Cars pull alongside him just to get a look at the beauty of an automobile that's gracing the highway.

He blasts the volume of his stereo and bops his head to the crazy drum line that pounds through the speakers. "Bitches ain't shit but hoes and tricks!" he shouts over rapper Snoop Dogg's voice. Every time he thinks of Sunday and becomes the slightest bit sad, he turns on this song to keep him going.

"Lick on deez nuts and suck the dick! Gets the fuck out after you're done! And I hops in my ride to make a quick run!" he shouts. Hearing this song erases all sadness. Darryl has made a vow to himself that he's done with love, and from now on, it's all about him and his money.

"Fucking hoes, clocking dough, up to no good," he raps along with Daz. "We flip flop and serve hoes like flapjacks," Snoop interjects. "But we don't love them hoes," he sings. "Bitch, and it's like that!" Darryl shouts with passion.

He stares into his eyes in his rearview mirror as he raps along. "How could you trust a hoe?" he shouts over Snoop Dogg's voice. "Because a hoe's a trick!" he shouts, nodding his head up and down. "We don't love them tricks! Why? 'Cause, a trick's a bitch! And my dick is constantly in her mouth!" he shouts before pressing repeat.

Eleven song replays later, Darryl finally arrives at the block. He can't wait to see the look on their faces when they see him pull up. One block away, he looks up the block and notices it's packed just like he hoped it would be. He hits the power window buttons, and both windows roll down slowly. He hits the roof button, and that opens up as well. He's now halfway through the block. He presses repeat once again before blasting the stereo to the maximum. He steps on the gas, pushing the car to the limit. He gets to the corner, and all eyes are on him before crossing the intersection.

114

He watches them as they all watch him with great admiration, not even knowing it's him inside. He crosses the intersection and zips over to the curb with recklessness. "Oh, shits" and "what the fucks" are shouted from every direction. Darryl hops out of the car like this is his movie. He slams the door shut and walks over to the curb, where they all stand lined up.

They look the car over from bottom to top. The SC 400 Lexus Coupe sits perfectly on the chrome Harding rims. The black gut on the black body gives the car a mean but classy look.

"Got damn, nigga!" Zak shouts. "You on some next-level shit!" he shouts as he shakes his head. "Look around, nigga. Everything else around us is square."

He points to the cars in the area. "You in a Lex bubble. Like a spaceship! Nigga, you Elroy Jetson!" Darryl smiles modestly as they all laugh at Zak's comment. Even though the smiles are on their faces, he can sense something that bothers him. He sees jealousy and hatred in their eyes.

All the laughter comes to a halt. Deep tension creeps into the air. Darryl glances across the street, and as he lays eyes on who is there, his face distorts with anger. He pokes his chest out as he backs up against the wall.

Sheed crosses the street toward them. He's dressed in state-issued pants, shirt, and boots. The look on his sweaty face is agitated. As he approaches the curb, a smile pops onto his face. "What's up, niggas? Y'all act like y'all seen a ghost," he says with a bigger and more phony smile. "At least act like y'all happy to see a nigga."

They all stand, hesitant to embrace Sheed. Sheed may have been their leader before he went away, but that's behind them now. Darryl has taken them to a level that Sheed could never. Hungry dogs are not loyal. They will eat with anyone who has food. Darryl has provided the food for them all of these years, and it's been a hefty plate at that. Because of that, they stand with Darryl on this matter, even though they have no beef with Sheed. Slowly but surely, they all embrace Sheed. Although they are happy to see Sheed, they don't overtly express it out of respect for Darryl.

Darryl stands against the wall with a detached aura. Sheed steps toward Darryl, who is not even looking in his direction. Sheed stops short, leaving two feet of uncertainty between them. He extends his hand for a handshake. "D, what's up?" he asks with confusion.

Darryl turns his head toward Sheed slowly. The look in Darryl's eyes burn through Sheed's soul. Darryl looks him up and down angrily before staring at his hand in midair. He looks away, leaving Sheed's hand dangling in the air. "You tell me what's up?" He looks back into Sheed's eyes.

The tension is now even thicker. Sheed and Darryl stand like two stubborn rams ready to butt heads. Everyone knew this day would come, and they all have wondered how it would play out. Now it's finally time to find out.

Sheed draws his hand back with confusion on his face. "Let me talk to you over here," he says as he nods his head. He takes the lead, and Darryl follows. They walk a few feet away from the crowd. They stand face to face. "Like, what's the deal? What's going on?" Sheed asks. "Where did this tension come from?"

Darryl smirks. "Oh, you don't know?"

"Nah, I don't," Sheed replies. "I've been trying to figure it out the whole two, and a half years I've been away. It's like you was with me the first few months, then it was like, fuck me," he says with sadness. "Dukes telling me she was reaching out to you and you were not answering. It threw me off because I'm like, he

116

ain't that type of nigga. He would never turn his back on me. I'm down that bitch fucked up. Look at me, nigga, state down," he says as he points to his clothes.

"Dukes out here struggling without me. She can barely pay the bills, so you know she can't do much for me. I was a state baby down that motherfucker." Darryl still shows no sign of compassion.

"Then as niggas coming in, I'm hearing how you out here blowing up. That's when I really got confused. Like you blew up and just said fuck everybody. I'm writing these niggas," he says as he points to the crew. "And they all saying you on some selfish shit and you changed. Like, what the fuck?"

"I said fuck everybody? On some selfish shit?" Darryl asks as he points across the street and up the block. On both sides of the street are luxury cars. An Infiniti Q45, a Lexus ES, a Nissan 280 Zx, and a BMW 325 are spread out before them.

All these cars belong to the first-generation, as Darryl calls them, the original block members. Their old cars have been passed down to the second-generation, and all of them are spread out all over the block as well. None of the vehicles may be of the current year, nor do they hold the value that Darryl's car does, but it's clearly understood that everybody on this block is eating. Sheed was the father of the block, but Darryl is more like the grandfather of the block. He has two tiers under him. His runners have runners. He's upgraded all of their lives.

"Do it look like I said fuck everybody, nigga? Do it look like any of these niggas are missing meals around here, nigga? Do it look like I have starved anybody, nigga? These niggas never ate like they eating with me. But yeah, I have changed. I only give a fuck about niggas who give a fuck about me. That's how I changed. "

Darryl continues. "These niggas out here never had my back. They never wanted me out here. I made these niggas accept and respect me. Shit was going down, and niggas was just letting it go down. They go home and run for cover when shit get crazy. Then when the smoke clears, they come back out here and make a killing.

I'm the only nigga popping off defending the crown, repping the block that everybody is eating off. Then it hit me; if I'm the only nigga putting my life on the line, then I should be getting the most of the money. I changed the game. I ain't splitting equal money with no fucking punks who are not willing to split the beef and drama that comes with this shit! If you scared of other motherfuckers then you gone be just as fucking scared of me," he says with a killer look in his eyes. "At that point, I made a decision; either you gone rock with me or you ain't gone rock. Ain't no selfishness in that. I'm still letting them eat. They just not going to get full while I'm risking my life for it. And they making more money and living better this way than they ever did on their own."

"I feel you," Sheed says in total agreeance. "But you have created a lot of secret enemies for yourself out here. Not just on this block but all over the city. I heard all kind of shit down the way about you."

"I'm sure you did," Darryl replies. "Trust me when I tell you, I know a lot of niggas ain't feeling me, but ask them why they ain't feeling me. If a nigga ain't feeling me, it's because somewhere down the line he crossed me, and I didn't let him get away with it. In two and a half years, I haven't taken no Ls. Anybody that stepped out of pocket, I punished them accordingly. They are scared to come at me, so they hate me secretly. But I tell you one fucking thing, they better continue to keep it a secret because if I find out what they truly feel, I will make sure they don't feel nothing else. Ever," he concludes.

Sheed stands speechless. He can't believe the words coming out of Darryl's mouth. He's heard so many stories about Darryl, but he couldn't believe them. Now hearing this directly from his lips, it all fits. Still, he doesn't understand how Darryl has become like this. He's quite baffled.

"Like you said, though, you only give a fuck about niggas who give a fuck about you," Sheed says before pausing. "I'm one of the niggas that give a fuck about you. What about me? What about us? How did we get here?"

"How we get here?" Darryl asks over a sarcastic grin. "We got here when you decided to give your cousin, the sucker ass nigga Dre," Darryl says with no respect at all, "the green light to get money out here. Out here where I'm putting it down. That nigga ain't from here. And the only reason I didn't murder the sucker ass nigga is because he left before I could get my gun."

Sheed stands with confusion spelled out on his face. "Gave him the green light? When? I haven't heard from Dre the whole time I've been down. On my dead father, I ain't give him no green light. Why the fuck would I tell him he could come out here and get money? Like you said, he ain't from the Location.

"The North Pole," Darryl clarifies with emphasis. Sheed is clueless. "It ain't The Location no more. It's the North Pole now."

Sheed quickly brushes that off with no real thought put into it. "Anyway, do you know how many times he asked me could he come out here? And I always told him no. Do you know why? Because he ain't from around here, and I know how that shit goes. First, he around here getting money, and the next thing you know, he brings the whole projects up here. I would never tell him that."

Darryl is confused, and he believes every word Sheed just spat out. "Well, that's what he said," Darryl says defensively.

"And you believed him? A motherfucker you barely know said I said some shit, and you go off of that? Damn. I thought we were bigger than that. We got too much time in, nigga. You was supposed to hear me out. One phone call and I could have told you it was a lie, and everything would have been cool. Instead, he told you something, you believed him and turned your back on me."

Darryl has not a word to say in his defense. Sheed is right. He should have at least brought it to Sheed to see what he had to say about it instead of taking Dre's word as law. He didn't, and now two and a half years have passed them both by.

Darryl feels horrible. "Hmph.," he sighs. "You right," he says, nodding his head up and down. "My bad," he says as he reaches for Sheed's hand. Sheed returns the handshake.

The sound of a horn blowing breaks up their sentimental moment. Darryl looks to the street where Sheed's mother is double-parked. Sheed looks over. "One minute, Dukes!"

"Hey, Ma!" Darryl shouts. She rolls her eyes with disgust at the sound of Darryl's voice.

Sheed cracks a smirk. "Dukes pissed off with you, but don't worry about that. I will explain it all to her and let her know it was all just one big misunderstanding."

"Yeah, do that, please."

Sheed stands with discomfort on his face. He lowers his eyes shamefully. "Yo, you got a couple of dollars on you? I'm broke as hell," he whispers with embarrassment.

This breaks Darryl's heart to hear. "What you need?" he asks as he digs into his pocket.

"Nigga, I need everything," Sheed replies with a shameful grin. "I don't have shit. I walked all the way up here from the halfway house on Frelinghuysen. It took me a whole fucking hour. I was hoping somebody was out here just to give me a couple of dollars," he admits.

This breaks Darryl's heart into smaller pieces. To see his main man at the most vulnerable state of his life hurts him tremendously. Darryl digs into his right pocket and hands Sheed every dollar in it. He then digs into his left pocket and hands him every bill there as well. "I didn't count it," he says. "But I'm sure it's at least twenty-six or twenty-seven hundred. Help Dukes catch up. We going to get this thing back right," Darryl says.

"Thanks," Sheed says with a light of joy in his eyes. He takes off toward his mother's van. He snatches the door open wide. As he stands holding the door open, he speaks. "We got a lot of catching up to do." He points to the Lexus. He nods his head up and down. He winks his eye. "A lotta, lotta catching up to do," he says as he points across the intersection.

The intersection is fluttered with customers going to and coming from the apartment building. The foot traffic is equal to a busy train station, just all walking dead zombies. Inside the building is where all the work is being pitched from. The second generation, as Darryl refers to them, are all in the hallway serving the customers while the first generation directs the traffic.

Darryl came up with the idea of pumping out of the apartment building to keep the traffic off the street corner and make the block hot. With the astronomical amount of customers coming through, he felt it was disrespectful to the police and a slap in the face to have all that going on in the wide opening. Ever since he turned the apartment building into the pitcher's mound, they have been getting less heat from the police, which means they can make more money.

"A whole lotta catching up to do," Sheed says with emphasis. He looks at the flow and can't believe his eyes. He's ready to get back to the action!

-28-

Two Days Later

DARRYL SPEEDS ALONG the highway in the Lex Bubble. The words of Naughty By Nature's "Hip Hop Anthem" bangs through the speakers. Sheed has been sitting in silence the entire ride. He's just happy to be back in the world, and his being away makes him feel as if he's missed so much.

Today marks the second time Darryl and Sheed have been together. Darryl picked him up from the halfway house early this morning. They started the day off with Darryl taking him shopping. Darryl feels terrible he allowed Dre to make him turn his back on Sheed. Whenever Sheed mentions how broke he was while in jail Darryl is crushed. He plans to make it up to Sheed in a big way.

Darryl can feel Sheed staring at him from the passenger's seat. He looks over to find Sheed with a smirk on his face. "What's up?" Darryl asks.

"Nothing," Sheed replies. "Just checking you out. It's like the roles are reversed. I'm used to being over there in the driver's seat while you over here in the passenger's seat watching me do me," he says with arrogance. Hearing this come out of Sheed's mouth irks Darryl, but he manages to keep the signs off of his face. "How does it feel?"

"It feels like it's my turn," Darryl snaps. "Every man gets his turn, and it's up to him what he does with it," he adds with sarcasm.

Sheed senses the sarcasm in that statement and decides to change the subject. "Nigga, I've been gone for two and a half years. Bring me up to speed. Talk to me. I need to know everything."

Darryl hesitates before replying. "Shit. It's been a long two and a half years, and I don't even know where to start."

Twenty Minutes Later

Darryl parks along the quiet one-way street. He grabs a shopping bag from the back seat before climbing out of the car. Sheed gets out as well, and he follows close behind as he continues his conversation. "You're saying she's driving you crazy, but really you're driving yourself crazy," Sheed says.

"She proved to you what she's about, but you don't want to believe her. It's like you on some Captain Save a Hoe shit. When a motherfucker shows you their hand, you have to play them accordingly. She's all about money. You knew this before you got with her, and you should have never took her personal." Sheed is pouring it on thick.

"If I was home, you wouldn't be going through this. I would have never let you get fucked up over her like this." Darryl believes this to be true. Sheed always had a way of keeping him grounded and on point.

"I know what the problem is," Sheed claims. "You can't control her, and it's driving you nuts. You wonder why no matter what you do for her, she's never satisfied. You wonder why she doesn't respect you like she respects all these other niggas, right?"

Darryl nods. "Right," he agrees.

"I know I'm right. The fact that you can't control her keeps you there. It's in our nature to conquer and control, and because you can't, you can't walk away. You will not be able to walk away until you have conquered your mission, and that is if you ever conquer it."

"Fuck conquer," Darryl says as he presses the doorbell. "I'm done with her." The buzzer sounds, and Darryl snatches the door wide open.

"Yeah, right, nigga. Tell me anything," he teases. "You gonna fuck back with her."

"Shit, no, I'm not. I'm done with her. Today makes ten days I've been clean," Darryl says with a smile as he steps into the elevator. "She's been like a dope habit for me. Yeah, I kicked for a couple of days, and I even have the urge to take a hit every other night, but overall I'm getting over her."

"We will see," Sheed replies in mockery.

Minutes pass, and Darryl and Sheed sit side by side on the loveseat while Barbara walks back and forth throughout the living room. "Damn," Sheed says as she exits the room. He grabs the crotch area of his jeans. "Damn. Mommy got a fat lil' ass," he says with lust in his eyes. "I would love to catch that lil' bitch in the mommy house," he says with a perverted smile. "I will do her lil' ass filthy! Poppy, poppy, no doggy," he smiles.

"As a matter of fact, is a mommy house around here?" he asks. "I need to unload some shit," he smiles. "My nuts in the sand."

Darryl falls into laughter. "I don't know about no fucking mommy houses. I haven't been to one of them since you left," he says as the lock of the door is opened.

Their attention is diverted to the door. They both sit quietly on alert as they wait to see who is about to enter. The Big Boss steps into the apartment and eases both of their worries.

Darryl's face brightens up. "My man," he says with a huge smile.

Big Boss reciprocates with a warm smile. "What's up?" he says as he walks over to the loveseat. He reaches over Sheed to shake Darryl's hand.

"Que pasa?" Darryl smiles.

"Ah, asi, asi," he replies as he walks away.

A look of agitation pops up onto Sheed's face. "Yo," Darryl calls out. "You don't remember him?" he asks as he points to Sheed.

Big Boss looks at Sheed. "Maybe," he says as he studies Sheed's face.

"This my main man, really my brother. He is the one who brought me to you in the first place. Remember he bought the BMW off of you."

"Ok, ok," he replies with joy in his eyes. "Long time. Three years maybe?" he asks, reaching over to shake Sheed's hand.

Sheed is caught up in his feelings. Instead of shaking the Big Boss's hand, he puts his fist up. They bang their fists together. "How soon we forget," he replies as he stares into the man's eyes with hatred.

Big Boss senses the tension but is not clear on why. He quickly looks over to Darryl. Darryl decides to ease the moment. "He go away, but he's back now."

"Oh, ok. He go bacation," Big Boss replies with a smile. "Welcome home." Sheed nods in reply. Big Boss turns his attention back to Darryl. "So, Barbara, say you have a problem. What is the problem?" he asks as he peeks out of the corner of his eye at Sheed, who is looking him up and down.

"Nah, not a problem like that," Darryl replies. "I just need to talk to you about some things that I want to do," he whispers.

"Dimelo, talk to me," he replies.

Darryl has been doing a lot of thinking lately about everything. He feels he's been running in place for some months now. Every week he buys seven kilos of the raw and four kilos of the cheapy-choppa, faithfully. Although the profit he makes is hefty, he still feels like he could be doing more.

With this new case now over his head, he feels he must turn the volume all the way up. As many times as Boobie Salaam expresses that he will be all right, he still recognizes the ultimate decision belongs to the judge. He understands that it could easily go against his favor. With that thought in mind, he's decided to go as hard as he can just so his Nana and him will be ok regardless. The last thing he wants is to be locked up depending on people as Sheed was.

He's been evaluating some things and has come up with the theory that a man only grows as big as his connect. He will never be able to exceed the magnitude of the connect. A hustler's future depends on the capacity of his connect. The more work a connect has, the higher the possibility of growth.

Today, he plans to find out just how much room there is for him to grow. He's never asked anyone for a handout, but today he will. He isn't asking for the handout because he needs it. He's asking because he realizes intelligent people don't spend their own money. Intelligent people save their money and work off of others. Also, by asking the Big Boss what he plans to ask him, he will find out just where they stand. In all the years they have been doing business, Darryl has spent millions with him. It's now time to find out just how grateful he is and how much he really means to him.

"Talk to me," he repeats. "What is it?" he asks as he waits impatiently. Sheed sits impatiently. He wants to know what it's about as well.

"I need a favor," Darryl whispers. He pauses before speaking. He's not sure how the Big Boss will reply to his proposition. He doesn't feel comfortable asking for a handout. If the Big Boss rejects his proposal, he's sure their business relationship will change from here. But there's only one way to find out. "I'm trying to take this thing to another level," he says as he stares Big Boss in the eyes. "My business is growing, but I feel like I'm at a standstill."

"How can I help?" Big Boss interjects.

"I never ask for handouts, but I need consignment." He pauses, waiting for some type of reaction, but he shows none. Darryl continues. "I got a buck ninety in here." Darryl points to the shopping bag.

Sheed is flabbergasted. He believes his ears are deceiving him. He can't be speaking of a hundred and ninety grand. This he didn't expect.

"That's money for ten joints," Darryl says. "I need a lil boost."

Ten kilos, Sheed thinks to himself. What the fuck? His mind races crazily. Sheed never even thought of reaching ten kilos, not even in his wildest dreams. Whenever he thought of a drug dealer at the very height of their career, he thought of a kilo. It's like his mind wouldn't allow him to see past that. Sitting here now, Darryl forces him to look further.

"What kind of boost?" Big Boss asks.

"I wanna buy ten keys of the raw, right? I need you to front me ten keys of the cheapy-choppa," he says. "That's only a hundred and forty grand."

"No problem," Big Boss whispers.

"I will get that right to you the next time I come over here," Darryl says as he tries to convince him. "We're business partners, and you gotta trust me."

"No problem," Big Boss says again. Darryl is so busy talking that he doesn't hear him.

"I ain't going nowhere. You have to trust me on this one. I'm trying to turn this shit up. If you ain't willing to give me the push I need, then I'm going to have to take my money somewhere else where it's appreciated."

Big Boss interjects again. "No problem, no problem." He flashes a big smile. "No problem. I say it five times already. Whatever you want," he says with a smile. "I expected you to come for your normal order, so I'm not prepared today. I have half of the order here already. Give me," he says as he takes a glance at his watch, "one hour, and I will have it all here ready for you."

Darryl stares at him with bewilderment. He's surprised. "Ok, cool," Darryl says as he drops the bag on the table. "Load the car up and call me. I will send my man over right after."

"Deal."

Sheed's head is spinning at the numbers that were thrown around so loosely. If he weren't witnessing it for himself, he would never believe it. It's all playing out like a scene from the Scarface movie. The bad part is, he's not the star of the film. Shit, he's not even the co-star. Right now, all he has is a small cameo role.

Sheed and Darryl walk back to the car in silence. Through the silence, thoughts rip through Sheed's mind non-stop. He would never believe that three years could be so good to a person. He wonders what it is that Darryl has done in three years that he hasn't done in the eight years he's been hustling. Sheed started selling drugs when he was eleven years old, and he stands at twenty-two years old with nothing but the few dollars Darryl put in his pocket the other day. He's been on the bench three of those eleven years, sitting in prison, but still, he feels like he should have something to show for those eight years.

Darryl starts the engine. Sheed sits down and slams the door shut. He has a million questions for Darryl but doesn't know which one, to begin with. He ponders for a second before finally speaking. "Damn, I see you've been working, huh?"

"What do you mean?" Darryl asks. He knows exactly what he means.

"I mean, you got a hundred and ninety buy money. That ain't no duck walk," he admits. "You must have been working your ass off these past two and a half years? When I left, you was trying to scrape up the money to buy half a joint. You remember?"

"Like it was yesterday," Darryl replies.

"Now you buying ten. You blew the fuck up! Like I said, you must have been working your ass off. Like, how the fuck you blow it up like that, though?"

"I mean, I'm focused," Darryl replies. "For me, it's all about stacking. I don't do it for the bright lights and the fame. Yeah, I buy a car here and there, but I look at them like trophies for me to celebrate my accomplishments. I don't do nothing for the validation of the people. But to answer your last question, how I blow it up like that," he says as he stares into Sheed's eyes.

"After you left, I realized that without respect, you can't get no real money. Block getting robbed, stashes getting hit, profit just getting ate away, loss after loss. That's when I decided to put that pistol in my hand. I watched your game all those years, and you're a hell of a hustler. But that gunplay was all you was missing. That was holding you back. Me, I refused to let that hold me back."

Darryl pulls his gun from his waistband. "This the key to any success I've found out here on the streets. Niggas wasn't gone let me eat in peace, so I had to go to war!"

Sheed looks at Darryl in awe. It's strange to see Darryl in this form. A dude that was under his wing when he left has blossomed into someone altogether different. "But where the hell are you gonna move all that work?" Sheed asks, disregarding all Darryl has just said. "Twenty birds? That's a lot of coke."

"I'm going to move it the same place or places that I've been moving it."

"How long do you think that will take you to move? Months?"

Darryl laughs in his face. "Months? Hell no! Try a week and a half to two weeks, tops.

Sheed sits in disbelief. "Yeah, right?"

"Listen, man, it's not a game. You know how much money comes through the strip in a day?"

"Nah," Sheed replies.

"An average of fifty to sixty-thousand dollars comes through a day. All dime jugs," he adds. "Damn near two birds a day. Ten birds a week on the ground. A hundred grand profit a week, easy without me stepping foot out on the block. The other part of my business is selling weight. I buy that other coke for four dollars cheaper and wholesale it for eighteen to twenty a gram. I rip through five of those a week. Add that up at five dollars profit a gram. Yeah, twenty-five thousand a week," he barks with arrogance.

Sheed is dizzy from the enormous amounts of money Darryl speaks about. "So, you like a half a million profit a month?" Sheed questions with great surprise.

"Something like that," Darryl replies. "Give or take a few thousand," he says with a smile.

Sheed sits back, doing the calculations. "That's six million dollars a year. Do that for two and a half years, and you got what? About fifteen million?" he asks as he impatiently awaits an answer.

"Come on, man," Darryl says with a smile. "You looking into it too deep. You know this shit, don't go like that. Shit happens. One month you up, and the next two or three months you down. It's hustling, baby! Nothing is promised."

"Yeah, I know, but you should at least have about seven and a half million sitting around, right?" Darryl doesn't reply. He just smiles. "Five million?" Sheed asks. Darryl looks straight ahead, keeping his eyes on the road.

The silence is making Sheed even more curious. "I know you at least got a few million tucked away." Darryl looks at him with a smile. "I know you, D!" he shouts cheerfully. "You a cheap motherfucker!" He smiles. "You try to save every dime you get your hands on. I bet you still got the very first dollar you made working that summer job you had. You probably got that bitch framed and hanging in your room. Tell me, you a millionaire, right?"

Darryl blasts the volume of the stereo. "Damn, you really gonna ignore me?" Sheed asks with a smile. "You on some secret squirrel shit now? Alright, fuck it," he smiles. "That's your business. All I need to know is how can I get some millions under my belt? How can I be down?"

Darryl looks at him without saying a word. He lowers the volume. "You're already down. Just fall back for a minute and watch how this shit is done. When the time is right, all you gotta do is just jump right on in."

"When the time right? The time right, right now! I'm broke as hell! I need to eat."

Darryl shakes his head from side to side. "Slow down. Right now, just concentrate on getting out of that halfway house."

"Out the halfway house? Nigga, I'm going to be in there for fourteen months! I'm hungry right now!"

"Well, I will feed you right now. Anything you need, I got you. When you're done with the halfway house, you can feed yourself! I got my brother back, and I ain't trying to see you get violated and sent back. I need you out here with me like it was from the beginning. Me and you," he says genuinely. "I just need you to chill and don't do nothing to get sent back. Deal?" asks.

Sheed nods his head up and down. "Deal!"

One Week Later

DARRYL HAS HIS ARMS wrapped underneath his opponent's arm, with his hands clasped behind the opponent's neck. The only thing on his mind right now is victory, and he plans to win the title and make this the most memorable bout ever. He wants his opponent to recognize him as the grand champion when he walks away from this match.

"Oh, oh!" Sunday screams at the top of her lungs as Darryl holds her butt naked in the Cobra Clutch wrestling move. She lies on her belly, ass up, while Darryl rabbit fucks her with rapid speed. The short, fast strokes snatch her breath away. He grabs her by her chin, lifting her as he pounds away at her box. "Oh my God! Oh my God," she cries.

He unloosens his hands from her face. As soon as she buries her face into the pillow, he sits upright. He watches her ass roll after each stroke. Overlooking the beautiful sight hardens his manhood even more. He spreads her cheeks wide as he slowly strokes her. In and out, he slides. Suddenly he changes his rhythm by twirling his waist in a circular motion. Around and around, he goes.

Darryl was doing well with avoiding her phone calls. Each day he was getting better with it. He went from thinking about her all day to thinking about her only a few times a day. He felt he was totally over her until she came to the block. It was then that he realized it's easier to avoid her call than to avoid her in person.

He didn't want to hear a word of what she had to say until she started speaking his language. She told him she hadn't been fucked since the last time they were together. She claimed all she wanted from him was a fuck with no strings attached. She told him her mother was out of town. She said to him, "If you're down, meet me at the house at eleven on the dot with a bottle of Moet." He arrived fifteen minutes later, with a hard dick and no Moet. At his arrival, she dropped to the floor and gave him the oral pleasure he had been begging her for more than two years. Although she wasn't as good at it as he hoped, he was pleased with the gesture alone.

He lifts himself from the bed and gets on his knees. He taps Sunday on the ass, signaling her to assume the doggy-style position. As soon as she does, he grabs her by the waist and thrusts deep inside her with force. He long strokes slowly. "Right there, right there," she moans. "Right there, baby. Do that shit."

He quickly switches his flow. He begins pounding as hard as he can. "Oh, no!" she cries as she attempts to escape his grip. He holds her waist tightly as he pounds away. She wiggles in an attempt to get away from him, but he continues to hold her down. "I can't take it. You're going to make me cum."

The more she attempts to wiggle away from him, the harder he pounds. "You better stop running from me," he threatens. "If I chase you, I'm gonna make you pay." Finally, she manages to get away from him. She crawls

135

a few inches away before she finds her head banging onto the headboard. Darryl has her trapped in between the headboard and his rock hardness.

"What I tell you?" he asks as he crashes inside of her. "What the fuck I tell you?" he barks. He draws back as far as his length allows him to before slamming into her. He bangs her walls from every angle.

"Oh, oh!" she screams with pleasure. As he bangs away at her, a vision of Sal's face pops into his mind. He wonders if Sal has ever fucked her like this. He wonders if sex is why she can't let Sal go. He wants to be the best fuck she's ever had. These thoughts tap into his competitive side. His ego kicks in, forcing him to pound harder and harder. "Oh, oh, oh!" she cries out at the top of her lungs.

She has a way of making him feel less than a great lover. He believes she never reached an orgasm with him their entire relationship, making him feel inadequate. He's done everything he could think of but to no avail. At least he thinks it's to no avail. The truth is Sunday reaches orgasm after orgasm with him, but she has yet to admit it to him. She feels that a woman is at her most vulnerable state during that time. She refuses to let him see her weak side or even allow him to think he can ever have that much control over her.

"You ever been fucked like this?" he asks as he pulls her by her waist, slamming her ass against his thighs. "Huh? Have you ever been fucked like this?" he asks once again. "Answer me!"

"No," she cries. "No!"

He slows down his pace, going in and out as deep as he can. He hunches over parallel to her body. He whispers in her ear. "Tell me you never been fucked like this before." She doesn't reply fast enough, making him think that maybe she has. Again he starts pounding away at her. "Tell me!" he shouts. "Tell me nobody ever fucked you like this!"

Finally, she speaks. "I've never been fucked like this in my life," she moans.

He lifts himself and spreads her cheeks as wide as they can go. Barely inserting himself, he slides in and out slowly. "Never?" he asks.

"Never, ever," she whines.

He props himself on top of her. He slides in and out of her slowly as he sits propped on her back. He mashes her face into the pillow, and he damn near suffocates her as he rides her back. He digs with slow, passionate strokes.

"Oh my God," she cries. "What the fuck are you doing to me?"

I'm turning you the fuck out, he thinks to himself.

In the two years they have been together, their sex has never been this intense. He's always made love to her. After finding out about her and Sal, the rage that has grown in him has brought out hatred. With the amount of hate he has for her, in no way can he make love to her. All he can do is fuck her with hopes of being the best fuck she's ever had. He now realizes where he was going wrong with her. All the while, he was making love to her and getting no natural reaction from her. Today he's smutting her out, and now she's reacting.

He changes positions. He backs away from her, planting one foot flat on the bed. He rests on his other leg, which is flat on the bed. He grips her waist and drives himself into her with slow deep strokes.

After three minutes of intense stroking, he picks up his pace. He jackhammers her as hard as he can. She attempts to get away from him, but he just holds her that much tighter. The more she tries to get away, the harder he bangs her. "Oh!" she shouts. "Oh my God! I'm cumming, baby! Baby, cum with me," she cries. She loses all control of herself as her body trembles uncontrollably. "Cum with me, please?" she begs.

Yes, Darryl cheers to himself. Finally, he thinks. Sunday lies shaking like a person with epilepsy. He stops pounding in the middle of her convulsions and snatches himself out of her. He slides off of the bed, leaving her enjoying her orgasmic moment. As she lays there with her legs shaking uncontrollably, he exits the room, making his way toward the bathroom.

He comes out to find Sunday knocked out of sleep. She's snoring like a bear. "Yo," he says as he nudges her. "Sunday!" he shouts.

Sunday's eyes open slightly. She's shocked to find him standing fully clothed. "Huh?" she asks.

"Lock the door," he says rather nonchalantly. "I'm out."

She sits up with a saddened expression. "You out? Where are you going? What you mean you out?"

"Yeah, I'm out," he replies as he starts making his way to the door. For once, he has the ball in his court. Now he's leaving her, feeling inadequate by not allowing her to have the satisfaction of him reaching an orgasm. "You asked me to come over and fuck you, and I did. Later!"

-30-

One Week Later

I N DARRYL'S PASSENGER SEAT sits one of the most beautiful women he's met in a long time. He met her in Harlem some days ago. Something about this woman is different. She has the heart and the sweet innocence of Asia, but the fashion sense of Sunday. In his eyes, she's just the perfect balance that he needs in a woman. What he likes the most about her is that she knows nothing about the streets, and her life consists of work and home. The woman is almost six years his senior and a paralegal at one of New York City's top law firms.

He owes all thanks to his Lexus Coupe. The quality of women he's had the privilege of meeting since he's gotten the car has been unimaginable to him. It amazes him how a particular vehicle attracts a certain quality of women. The BMW attracted mainly young street girls, and this Lexus attracts street girls and mature, corporate women. Darryl considers this car the best of both worlds, the equalizer.

Their first date started perfectly. After lunch, Darryl cruised around with no destination, just giving her a tour of the city. That is when all hell broke loose. He and Sunday locked eyes at a traffic light from across the street.

That's the very first time they've seen each other since their last sexual adventure. She calls him every day, all day, but he doesn't answer. She couldn't understand why, but after seeing the girl in the passenger's seat, it all became clear to her. She assumes someone has taken her place.

What started as a slow-paced tour has turned into a high-speed three-city chase throughout the city. Sunday and her crew have been tailing him at high speed as he's raced through not only Newark but East Orange and Irvington as well. They chase behind him relentlessly as he attempts to escape them. No matter how fast he drives, he can't seem to lose them.

"Can you please tell me what's going on?" Yasmine asks as she sits on the edge of the seat. "Why are you driving like a maniac?"

He peeks back and forth into his rearview mirror as he speeds up South Orange Avenue. He hates to say this, but he has no choice. "It's my ex," he says with shame. To think he's on a date with a mature woman and brings her into this type of immature nonsense embarrasses him deeply.

He speeds up South Orange Avenue recklessly. He dips between cars without fear of crashing. He looks at his rearview mirror and is disappointed to see Roselyn's BMW is not even two car lengths behind. As he approaches the corner, he turns on his left blinker. He watches as Roselyn falls for the bait. She dips over into the left lane recklessly. He reaches the corner and busts a quick right.

"Your ex?" she replies with fear. "Oh my God!" Darryl races up Tremont Avenue doing at least eighty.

Just when he thinks he's safe, he sees the nose of the BMW peeking around the corner. "Damn," he says as he makes the left turn at The Tremont Lounge. "But if it's your ex, why all of this?" she questions. "Listen, can you please tell me the truth? Are y'all still together?"

Darryl watches as the BMW makes the left onto the block. The BMW swerves uncontrollably as Roselyn tries to catch up with him. "Nah," he replies.

"Then why are you running from her? Owwww!" Yasmine shouts as she places her hands over her eyes. "Watch out!"

Darryl swerves around the van that's creeping through the intersection. Their bodies fling from side to side. "You're going to kill us. Let me out!" she shouts.

Shit. If I let you out, they're going to kill you, he thinks to himself.

"If she's only your ex, why are you going through all of this?" she asks again.

"Because I know them. They about to start some bullshit."

"They? Them who?" she asks with nervousness.

He senses the nervousness in her voice and understands she has reason to be nervous. "Her and all her friends," he says as he races up the one-way street. At the end of the block, he busts a wild left turn back onto South Orange Avenue.

"What kind of bullshit?" she asks with fear. "I know you're not talking about fighting, are you?" she asks, hoping he's not referring to that. "I hope you're not talking about fighting. I don't fight. Shit. I don't even know how to fight. I never had to!" she shouts frantically.

"Well, if by chance we get caught, you will learn today," Darryl mumbles to himself. "Calm down. It's not going to come to that." He hopes that he's right.

He sits at the corner impatiently as the oncoming traffic pours up the block heavily. "Come on!" he shouts as he peeks back and forth into the rearview mirror. They're gaining on him quickly. He spots a tiny gap in between two cars, and he mashes the gas pedal as hard as he can. He slams on the brakes to prevent hitting the back of the car in front of him.

"I don't believe this," she whines. "I'm over here in God knows where, in a high-speed chase running from the ex of a man I just met," she rambles. "No one even knows where I am," she whines. "This is the worst," she cries.

"Go, go, go! Damn," he barks as he runs into a traffic light. Both lanes are three cars deep. There's nowhere for him to turn. The BMW is approaching, and he has no choice. He cuts the wheel to the left and goes around the cars. He speeds down South Orange Avenue against the traffic.

He's surprised when he looks in his mirror, and the BMW is coming right behind him. He takes the straight away as fast as possible, and Roselyn is not far behind. He's attempting to drive with some safety in mind, while it seems that Roselyn is using no safety at all. He realizes they can't continue to go on like this. Either he's going to jail, or somebody will die in a car crash.

"I'm not giving up yet," he says to himself. He makes the slight right at Vailsburg Park, and so does Roselyn. A few feet ahead, he makes a quick left followed by another sharp left. Roselyn is now almost glued to his bumper. "I gotta think fast," he says to himself. As he races up the highway doing a hundred miles an hour, he sees a State Trooper on the other side of the highway. That is when reality sets in. He thinks of the fully-loaded semi-automatic he has on his waist and asks himself if this is worth him going to jail.

He starts to slow the car down. He flicks his right blinker on as he steers to his right. He rides half a mile before turning onto the shoulder. "Wait, what are you doing?" Yasmine asks in a terrified state.

Darryl slams the gear into Park. Roselyn pulls up close to his bumper before stopping. All the doors pop open. Sunday and Roselyn race toward the driver's side while the other two girls make their way toward the passenger's side.

Just when they get right up on the car, he slams the car into drive and takes off like a bat out of hell. "Oh my God," Yasmine cries. "Take me home, please," she shouts.

Darryl speeds up the highway. He's almost a mile away before they have even gotten back into the car. He merges off the highway at the Central Avenue exit, and he speeds right through the toll and bears left onto Route 280. He peeks in his rearview mirror and is happy to see no sign of the BMW.

Harlem World, here he comes!

-31-

Hours Later

DARRYL HAS JUST RETURNED TO JERSEY. All the way to New York, he begged Yasmin to forgive him. She was so livid with him she didn't say a word the whole ride. She said three words upon her exit, and that was 'lose my number.' He hates himself for blowing a good possible situation, making him hate Sunday even more. For the life of him, he can't understand her. It baffles him that even after getting caught with Sal, she still feels as if she has the right to run up on him when she sees him with a woman.

Hours have passed, and he hasn't gotten one phone call from her since the car chase. That surprises him. He's glad she saw him with Yasmin, so she knows how it feels to see the one you care for with another. He needs her to feel the pressure of knowing she messed up. He just hopes Sunday got a good enough glimpse of her to see how beautiful she is. He knows for sure how jealous Sunday is of other beautiful women, especially women who are more beautiful than her.

Every time he replays today's situation, goosebumps pop up all over his body. He thinks of the danger he put himself in, racing through the city recklessly with a gun. He can't believe he put his life and freedom on the line like that. This confirms that Sunday is terrible news for him all around the board, and she brings the worse out of him.

He's happy to be home after such a long day because it could have easily ended up with him spending another night in the County Jail. He parks the car in front of the house and gets out quickly. He exhales happily to have made it home. As he walks up the small staircase leading to his apartment, he notices something strange.

"What the fuck?" he blurts out as he stares directly into his apartment. He has a clear view straight from the living room to the kitchen from where he stands. The huge picture window and all the surrounding windows are shattered. His heart pounds with fear. He assumes someone has broken in.

"No, please, God," he whines as he thinks of the work he has stashed inside. He sticks the key into the door, but there's no need. The door parts as soon as he touches it. He steps inside, expecting to see the house ransacked. To his surprise, everything is in the proper place. He races to the kitchen and snatches open the door to the cupboard. He reaches to the top shelf and fumbles around clumsily. He exhales a deep sigh of relief to find the shopping bag containing six kilos.

He quickly checks all his spots where he hides his money, and he's happy to find every hiding place intact. He runs to the bedroom and notices this is the first room out of whack. The bedroom floor is flooded with enough water to fill a small pool. His water bed mattress has been cut up in huge criss-cross slices. His attention is drawn to the mirror where the words 'Fuck you and your ugly ass bitch' are written in red lipstick.

"Fucking dumb ass bitch," he mumbles as he stares at the mirror. What if someone would have come inside and stolen the work and his money. Even worse, the neighbors could have called the police, and they would have come in thinking it was a break-in. Queasiness fills his gut as he considers both situations. He shakes his head with despair. He realizes he has to get away from her before she fucks up the rest of his life. And quick!

-32-

One Week Later

SHEED SITS BEHIND THE DESK in the garage. In front of him is a stack of paperwork. On the other side of the desk sits a middle-aged Caucasian man. He stares at Sheed over his oval spectacles. His face shows no emotion at all.

"Ok, Mr. Jackson, I will be leaving now," he says as he gets up from the seat.

"Ok, Mr. Pomp," Sheed says with a cheerful look on his face. "I will see you at the spot."

"Yep, and not a minute late," he says sternly.

Mr. Pomponio is from the halfway house, and he's come to check on Sheed and make sure he is where he's supposed to be. Between 8 a.m. and 4 p.m., Sheed is assigned to be here.

After a frustrating job search, Sheed came up with the idea of Darryl hiring him as a dispatcher. Sheed doesn't do any work because there's no work for him to do. This job is just a way for him to get out of the halfway house every day. Half the time, he's not even here. Luckily for him, he was this morning because he could have easily gotten sent back to prison if not.

Darryl has the halfway house believing Sheed earns three hundred dollars a week, but Darryl gives Sheed a total of fifteen hundred a week. Sheed doesn't do a thing to earn the money except ride around with Darryl all day. This is the easiest money he's ever made.

Just as the man leaves, Darryl comes walking in. Darryl locks the door behind him. He walks over toward Sheed. Darryl drops a shopping bag on the desk.

"Yo, that was a close call," Sheed says with a scared look on his face. "If I would have got here ten minutes later, I would have been back down old dusty. I gotta be more careful."

"For sure," Darryl agrees as he dumps stacks and stacks of money on the desk. Sheed's mouth waters as he eyes the desk full of money. "Help me count this," he demands.

"Yo," Sheed blurts out. "You know something?"

"What's that?" Darryl asks, not even looking up from the stack of bills he holds in his hands.

"You have brought me up to speed about everything that has gone on out here since I been gone. You told me how you took the block over and turned it all the way up. Step by step," he adds. "You have told me about the shit you been going through with Sunday, and you even have told me about all the bitches you met the past couple of years." He stares into Darryl's eyes. "But not one time have you mentioned Asia."

Darryl stops flicking through the bills. He sits just staring in the face of Benjamin Franklin. He's at a loss for words. He didn't realize he hadn't told Sheed the story. He understands his reason for not bringing her up, though. Deep down inside, he wishes he could forget it all.

"What's up with her?" Sheed asks. "Is she still in school? How is she doing? How are y'all doing?"

Darryl wants to tell Sheed, but he's too embarrassed. He's ashamed to admit he blew their relationship behind Sunday. He knows how Sheed will look at him if he tells him that. And the fact that Asia has moved on with her life and gotten pregnant by another man still hurts him. In no way is he ready to talk about that. He sheds a tear whenever he thinks of it. He can see it now, him crying like a baby as he tells the story and that he will never do.

Darryl starts flicking through the bills again. He looks up for a quick second. "She's good."

-33-

"**B**UT DAMN, WHAT ABOUT your promise to me?" Darryl asks. "You went down there and got pregnant on me?" He hates how the words sound leaving his lips. "And engaged?" He looks up at Asia, who stands without saying a word in reply. Tears drip from her eyes as well. "Say something, Asia. Don't just look at me with that stupid look on your face," he says with rage. "Tell me something. Damn," he cries.

Boom, boom, boom! Boom, boom, boom! Darryl pops up in the bed. He looks around, confused, realizing he was only dreaming about talking to Asia.

Since Sheed questioned him about Asia, he hasn't been able to get her off his mind. Before then, he had gotten so much better with it. He doesn't think about her nearly as much as he used to, but still, she crosses his mind. He tries hard to block her from his thoughts. Still, he thinks about her so much that he dreams about her.

He looks over at the nude woman lying, ass up next to him. Her name, he couldn't remember if his life depended on it. This is just one of the many women in which the Lex Bubble has reeled. A few hours ago, as Club Bogies was letting out, Darryl was cruising around the area, and he met her. He never has to go inside the clubs. He just waits for the let-out so he can parking lot pimp. He pulls something every time. Tonight it took him all of ten minutes of slick talk to reel this woman in the car. A Big Mac, small fries, and a milkshake later, they ended up in his bed rolling around in hot and steamy sex.

Boom, boom, boom! "What the fuck?" Darryl mumbles to himself as he sits as still as a statue.

The naked woman sits up as well. Nervousness covers her face. "What's up?" she asks.

"Shhh," Darryl whispers as he places his finger over his lips. He quietly plants his feet on the floor. He tiptoes over to the window and peeps through the peephole. What he sees causes his heart to skip a beat. Sunday stands in front of the door. It appears as if she's staring right into his eye through the peephole.

Ding, dong! Boom, boom, boom! Darryl looks back at his guest as he shakes his head.

Sunday had been calling him for hours from her home but he never answered. He received a call from her at about 2 and that proved she was still home. While he had this woman in the car he took a quick ride past her house and he can see the light from the television playing. Also, there was no car was in front of the house which made Darryl assume his house would be safe for a few hours. Without a car there he figured she had no way to get here. He had planned for them to be out by seven in the morning.

"Fuck," he whispers. Thinking with his little head instead of the big head has him in a bad spot.

"Who is that your girl?" she asks.

He tiptoes back over to the bed. "Nah, my ex," he whispers. "Don't mind her, though. If I don't answer the door, she will go away." He hopes he's correct.

The woman puckers her lips with sassiness. "I don't mind at all. You don't owe me nothing. She's your girl, not me."

Ten slow minutes creep by, and Sunday hasn't gotten the hint. "Open this fucking door!" She shouts as she presses the bell continuously. *Boom, boom, boom!* "Motherfucker, I know you in there! You might as well come out. I'm not leaving!" *Ding, dong! Boom, boom, boom!*

Now instead of ringing the bell, she's leaning on it. She's no longer knocking on the door; she's kicking it. She's also incorporated window banging into the regimen. The noise she's creating is unbearable.

Darryl wonders what the neighbors must be thinking of all the noise at four in the morning. He becomes fearful that someone may call the police. The last thing he needs is the police to come, especially with all the unlawful things he has lying around. This is all confirmation to him that he has to switch some things around and quickly. He can't keep allowing her to bring heat to his home. He understands this could very well end badly for him.

He debates about going out to quiet her down. "Nah," he mumbles to himself. He knows how erratic she can be. He knows if he opens the door, she will try to force her way inside, and if she does that, all hell will break loose. He also understands he can't allow her to stay out there, creating a spectacle.

He sighs with frustration as he grabs hold of his pants. He puts them on quickly.

"What's up? You letting her in?" the girl asks.

"Nah, I ain't letting her in, but I can't let her keep banging on the door like that," he says with frustration. "Wait right here," he says, grabbing hold of his keys.

"Wait, hold up." She bounces off the bed and quickly slides her dress over her naked body. She then grabs her purse from the floor. He watches as she retrieves her razor blade. She sits on the edge of the bed as if she's ready for whatever Sunday can bring.

"Put that up," Darryl says. "Ain't no need for no razors and shit. I'm going to go and calm her down. You just stay right here."

"Ok, motherfucker!" Sunday shouts. "You don't want to open the door? I got something for you."

Darryl runs to the peephole and watches as Sunday steps off the porch. "Good," he says to himself. He watches Sunday walk over to Roselyn's car, and she snatches the door open. "Finally," he yells out.

"What?" the woman asks. "She leaving?"

"Oh shit!" Darryl shouts as Sunday steps out of the car, holding a golf club. She strides across the street toward his car. "This bitch is about to bust my windows," he shouts as he looks around for his sneakers. After locating them, he puts them on and heads for the door.

"Too late," the woman says as she peeks through the curtains. "She just busted all your windows."

As Darryl peeks through the curtains, Roselyn's car speeds up the block. His face shows that he's had enough. "What you done to that bitch? She crrrraaazzzyy," the girl says with a smile on her face. "She must be dick whipped! Go on out there and secure your vehicle. After that, come back in here, and whatever the fuck you done to her," she says as she stares into his eyes. "Do it the fuck to me!"

Three Days Later

THROUGHOUT ALL OF THE CHAOS Darryl has going on in his life, he still can't get Asia off of his mind. Right now his life is one big fast paced, ball of confusion that he can't seem to catch up with and get in front of. It all seems to be spiraling out of control and he has to regain control of it all and quickly.

After doing some real deep soul searching, he's come to some understanding about himself. Financially he's at the best place of his entire life. He no longer has money problems and hasn't had any money problems in the past three years. He realizes all of his problems revolve around women. It all started with Asia, and things just seemed to have snowballed from there. One thing led to another. He also realizes that instead of solving his problems, he tends to try and ignore them, hoping they will go away.

He attempted to act as if the problem with Asia never happened, and all he did was pile the problems he had with Sunday on top of that. Then he lost Passion, a woman who meant a great deal to him. Instead of dealing with her death, he found it easier to block her out as if she meant nothing to him. While going through problems with Sunday, instead of finding a solution, he refused to even attempt. He just brought other women into his life, hoping that would be the solution.

He realizes he can't go on this way. He must face his problems one by one. It all started with Asia, so he should solve that issue first. He will need clarity on the matter to put it all behind him. He is here for his moment of clarity.

"Hello, my name is Dan," the man says as he stares into Darryl's eyes. "I will be your server for today."

"Uh, excuse me, but is Asia Davis working today?" Darryl asks.

"Yes, she is," the man replies.

"Well, can I request her as my server?"

"No problem," the man replies with a smile. "I will get her for you right now. May I ask your name?"

"Nah, nah," he stutters. "I want to surprise her."

"Ok, no problem." The waiter walks away from the table.

Darryl sits back with nervousness in his gut. He can't even believe he's here. All the things he planned to say are no longer locked in his head. It's been so long, and so many things have changed that he feels he no longer even knows her. "What the fuck am I going to say," he mumbles to himself.

His thoughts are interrupted by the shadow that appears over his shoulder. "Hello, sir, my name is Asia," she says as she stands in front of him. She's reading from her pad. "I will be your server today." She looks up.

Darryl looks up, and they lock eyes. Asia's face becomes red with embarrassment. Darryl's eyes drop to her swollen belly. The small package that she carries is now ready to be delivered. Asia turns and shuffles away from the table.

He gets up and chases behind her. He grabs her hand and pulls her toward him. "A, wait," he demands. "I just need to talk to you."

She turns around with her eyes fixed on the floor. "I'm working," she whispers.

"Well, what time do you go to lunch? I just need to talk to you. I need to clarify some things, and I need clarity on some things," he says as he looks down at her belly. "It won't take long. I promise."

"I don't go to lunch for another four hours."

"Well, I will wait. I've been waiting for three years. Four hours will be a duck walk for me."

Asia shakes her head. "Just go. Please?" she begs.

"Asia, you know I'm persistent and patient. I will wait here for as long as it takes. I'm not walking away from here until I have clarity."

She peeks around nervously before speaking. "Clarity on what?" she asks with signs of agitation on her face. "What we had, has been over for three years now. You don't owe me nothing, and I don't owe you not-" she says before she stops. "Well, what I do owe you, I will pay you back as soon as I can."

"Later for that bread. As far as I'm concerned, we are even. What you owe me is to hear me out, and that's all I ask." She looks into his eyes and melts away. "After I hear you out, will you leave me alone?" she asks.

Darryl nods his head up and down. "Yep."

"Forever?" she asks.

"Forever," he says slowly.

"Go back to the table. I'm going to clock out for a break and come right to you."

Darryl and Asia sit face to face for the first time in years. So many emotions are brewing in both of them. She looks at her watch. "You got twelve minutes."

"Well, I guess it's showtime, huh?" He flashes a grin. *Damn, he thinks to himself. It's been three long years. How can I squeeze it all into twelve minutes? Where do I start? he asks himself as he stares into her doll baby eyes.*

"Eleven minutes," she says as she glances at her watch.

Fuck it, here it goes, Darryl says to himself. "I don't even know where to start," he admits. "I'm just going to freestyle from the heart. First, I want to tell you that I made the biggest mistake of my life. Every day since that day, I've been paying for that mistake. Not a day passes that I don't think of you.

A lot of things have changed in both of our lives," he says as he points to the engagement ring on her finger. "I know you're living your life, and in no way am I trying to remove you from your situation. I just want you to know how I feel about all of this. Seeing you pregnant crushed me that day, and I wanted to die."

"Eight minutes," she interjects.

"It was like my world was over. I mean, I'm not even going to sit here and lie to you, telling you that I'm happy for you and congratulate you because I'm not happy for you. I mean, I wish you well in life, but never will I be happy about it. You pregnant by a motherfucker," he says with disgust. "What the fuck happened to our pact? You promised me that you would never leave me for one of those smart college geeks. Since when did you start breaking promises?"

"You breached first, so the promise was void after that," Asia replies with sassiness. "You're the one who had a relationship on me while I was away at school, remember?" she asks with sarcasm. "And technically, I didn't break my promise because you asked me to promise you I wouldn't leave you for one of those smart college geeks, and he wasn't in college. And he wasn't a geek.

Darryl gets irritated. "Wow, so, you're defending him against me?" He becomes jealous at the thought of her standing up for another man.

Asia doesn't even entertain him. "And as far as you seeing me here pregnant," she says before pausing. "How the hell you think I felt not just seeing you here with the gold-digging bitch but having to serve y'all on top of that? Hawk spitting in y'all food didn't make up for the way I felt," she says with a devilish grin.

"As far as you not congratulating me, I don't expect you to. But the difference between you and me is I genuinely care about you. No matter if we are together or not, I still want the best for you. You have always been in my prayers. It hurts when I hear all the negative things that I have heard about you. How the streets view you, I can't see that."

Darryl interrupts. "How the streets view me? How do you know how the streets view me?"

"Darryl, you know for a fact that the streets have no secrets. I can guarantee you that I know about almost every move you have made. And I'm not even a street girl," she adds. "When you got arrested again, it hurt my heart. I thought you learned your lesson the last time, but it's obvious that you didn't. Then how do you think it felt to hear how the man I loved more than life was running around acting like a fool over a girl who doesn't even want him?"

This remark cuts like a knife. "What? Acting like a fool?"

"Yes, a fool," she replies. "You heard me correctly. She's spending all your money, driving your cars, and driving you crazy," she says with a smirk on her face. "You spoil her rotten, giving her any and everything, and still she doesn't want you. You're stalking not only her house but all her friends' houses as well. Embarrassing yourself, arguing and fighting men over her for what? For a bitch that doesn't even want you. That's so sad," she says brokenheartedly.

"I could have easily laughed at you as everybody else does. Like, good for him. He cheated on me, and that's what he gets," she says with a slight grin. "But I didn't. In fact, I felt sorry for you.

You said it yourself. You got caught up. You were a little boy playing a grown man game. A game that you were not ready to play. You thought you were ready to play with the sharks, and guess what?" she asks as she stares into his eyes. "The shark ate you alive. Or is she still eating you alive?" she asks as she awaits an answer.

Darryl sits dumbfounded. He had no idea that Asia was so in tune with his life. He guesses she is right about the streets having no secrets. He's embarrassed about the things she stated about Sunday playing him. As mad as it made him, he refuses to defend it because he knows it's the truth.

"So, since you know all about my life for the past three years, bring me up to speed with yours," he suggests. "So, tell me, who is he? What is he into? How long y'all been together?"

Asia looks down at her watch. "Uh," she utters as she gets up from her seat. "My break is over, and time is up," she says. "Nice talking with you," she says, turning around and walking away from the table. "I hope you clarified all the things that you wanted to clarify."

"Asia!" She continues to step as if she doesn't hear him. "Asia!" She disappears in the back of the dining area. "Asia!"

-35-

NANA STANDS AT THE STOVE. The hot grease is popping like gunfire. She bobs and weaves, just not to get hit by the grease pellets. Darryl sneaks up behind her and kisses her on the cheek. "Fried chicken. I'm right on time."

Nana turns to look at him. "I didn't hear you come in."

Darryl sticks his hand in the bowl and grabs a chicken breast. "Ah-ah! Don't go in my food without washing your hands."

Darryl ignores her. He takes a bite of the chicken as he sits at the kitchen table. He sits there with thoughts bouncing around in his mind. He's so deep in thought that he doesn't notice Nana looking at him. He looks up, and their eyes lock.

"Butter Baby, you ok?"

"Yeah, Nana, I'm good," he says.

Nana sees differently, though. "Butter, I know you, and something is weighing heavy on you." She studies him closer. She walks over to him and lifts his head to examine his eyes. He tries to turn away from her, but she holds his head tighter and zooms in closer. "Butter, something don't look right. It's your eyes. You using dope?"

Darryl laughs hysterically. "Using dope, Nana? I don't get high. I don't even drink."

"Well, something isn't right."

"Well, it ain't that." Darryl is tempted to tell Nana about his case and the possibility of going away to prison, but he would hate to break her heart right now. He doesn't want to blindside her with it if the time comes but it seems to be no easy way to tell her this. She's finally accepted the fact that he's a drug dealer but still it hurts her gravely. He's sure him going to prison she will never be able to accept and may possibly do more than hurt her.

"Butter, the look in your eyes is empty. Like you got no soul left in you. Ever since you were a little boy, I have told you that money doesn't guarantee you happiness. You didn't believe me, though. You got a whole lot of money now. Are you happy?"

"Nana, not right now, please," he says. "I'm trying to enjoy this delicious chicken breast," he says with a smile. "Nana, did you put your foot in this chicken?"

"Uhmm, hmm," she sighs, playing along with him.

"How's Asia doing?" Nana asks as she walks away. Darryl hesitates before replying. He knows his Nana well, and he knows she's reaching right now. "I guess she's good. I haven't heard from her."

"Well, I hope you ain't hearing from that other girl either. What's her name, Monday?"

Darryl falls out in laughter. "Sunday, Nana, Sunday."

"Well, you should've left her last Saturday," Nana says with no sign of a smile. She's dead serious.

"You crazy, Nana."

"Nah, I ain't crazy. That girl don't mean you no good. I told you that when you pulled up with the busted car windows. I told you before, and I'm telling you again to be careful with that girl."

Nana sits across from Darryl. "I'm going to tell you something that I never told you before. Your Pop -Pop, I loved him to death, but he was a street runner. He liked to run the streets and hang in them bars at all times of the night. Streets had a hold on him so tight that he didn't come home for days, sometimes a week. He was a great provider, but he couldn't stay out of them streets. He lived on them streets, and he died on them streets. You know how he died?"

"Yes, of course, Nana. He got murdered in a bar fight over a drink."

Nana shakes her head. "No Butter Baby. He died in a bar fight but not over no drink."

Darryl is perplexed right now. His Pop-Pop was murdered when he was four years old, and this is the story he's been told. He's eager to hear what she's about to say.

"He was stabbed to death by his girlfriend," Nana says.
"His girlfriend?"

"Yes, Butter, his mistress. Ol' Jezebel," she says with disgust.

Darryl is saddened, and he doesn't know what to say. He hates that his Nana had to endure this. "But, how were you able to move on knowing that? Like a whole funeral and everything knowing his mistress murdered him? How did you stomach that?"

"It was tough, but I had no choice. He was my husband, and I loved him. The women of my day were taught to let a man be a man. A man comes and goes as he pleases. A man made sure to handle his house before he left to run the streets. He did that. He always handled his house before going to be in them streets. He just never made it back home to me."

Darryl fights back the tears. It hurts him that his grandmother has been through so much. A good, god-fearing woman, but it seems, she never had a chance at a happy life. All her children strung out on drugs, and now to hear this story about her husband, a man that she lost her virginity to. He's the only man she's ever been with and she lost him to the hands of his side-piece. This makes the case he has over his head even worse now. He feels this could be the straw that breaks the camel's back.

And your daddy's father, I know you don't know much about that side, but you know how he died, right?"

Darryl shrugs his shoulders with no interest at all. His father was never in his life, and he has no connection with his side of the family. All he does know is his dad's father was a minister.

"His wife murdered him."

Darryl is astonished. "His wife?"

"Yes, married to an old crazy woman from my hometown in Virginia. Everybody knew she was crazy as a bedbug, even yo' grandaddy. Nobody knows what they were arguing about. The neighbors say it was lots of yelling for hours before he left out that morning for work. He left out and got in his car. Before he could pull off, she got in front of him with a shotgun. She blew his head off through the front windshield."

Darryl is speechless. "Yo' granddaddies on both sides, murdered by crazy women." Darryl sits back, thinking. No one would ever believe this.

"Y'all got a thing for crazy women," Nana says. "I don't know if y'all find them already crazy or if y'all make them crazy. But I do know you better be real careful with them crazy women.

Darryl is in belief. Hearing this leaves too much for thought. Is this why he has so much trouble with women? Is it in his bloodline from both sides? Whether it is or not, he realizes he must get away from Sunday before he ends up like both of his grandfathers.

Two Weeks Later

SHEED RIDES SHOTGUN in the Lexus. He and Darryl both ride without saying a word. Darryl is enjoying the music while Sheed barely hears the music at all. Something is weighing heavy on his mind.

He lowers the volume. "D," he says as his eyes drop onto his lap. "I know we agreed on me waiting until I get out of the halfway house before I get back to work, but that ain't going to work. I've been thinking long and hard about it, and I've come to the conclusion that that's a long-ass time. I mean, you've been looking out for me, and I'm grateful as hell, but I'm a grown-ass man. I can't keep standing in your face every Friday with my hands open, looking for a handout."

"Yo, Sheed, that ain't no handout," Darryl replies. He takes this as an insult. "I'm giving you your just due. You always took care of me when I didn't have shit. Don't look at it like that."

"Well, as a man, that is the only way I can look at it. Listen, man, Duke's bills are piling up, and things need to be done. Plus, there's shit that I need. You know me. I'm a flamboyant, flashy type of nigga. This fixed income shit ain't working for me. I need you to bring me in."

"Sheed, we already discussed this. You, my man, and I don't want to see you jam yourself up. Tell me what it is that you need, and I will take care of it."

"D, you ain't listening to me. I'm ready to do me. This sitting on the bench shit like a water boy shit, watching you play, that ain't me. I want to play too. I got some things of my own lined up," he claims. "Some niggas from the halfway house be trying to get with me. They got niggas on the outside that need work. None of them got no work to give nobody, though. That's where you come in at. All I need is the startup, and I can take it from there."

Darryl turns the stereo's volume to the maximum while Sheed is still talking. "Yo!" Sheed shouts as he lowers the volume. "Why the hell you turning the radio up while I'm talking? I'm pouring my motherfucking heart out to you, and you ain't even paying fucking attention."

"Because we already talked about this, not once, not twice, but three times already. This makes the fourth time, and my answer is still the same. Just like I told you the other three times when you're done with the halfway house, I will give you that start you need."

"Man, later for that shit! You talking about a year from now! I need shit, right now!"

"What, Sheed? Tell me what you need? You got money in your pocket, clothes on your back, and you drive around in a fifty-thousand dollar car all day long while in the halfway house. What is it that you need? Tell me."

"I will tell you what I need. I need to be my own man. It's like I'm losing my identity. I'm driving around in your car spending your money. I ain't no different than one of your bitches. The day you choose not to give me no money, I'm fucked. I feel like a bitch sitting around waiting on her allowance every Friday." Sheed has been holding onto this for a minute, and it feels good finally letting it out.

"A bitch is in a better place than me because she giving up that twat. She got more leverage. Niggas always need pussy, which means a bitch is always gone be in demand. At least she doing something to earn hers," he says with anger.

"Let me ask you something man to man," he says as he looks at Darryl. "Do you get a kick out of seeing niggas under you? Does that make you feel like a big man? Do you get a kick out of knowing mufuckers need you? Tell me? Is that what it is?"

Darryl turns toward Sheed slowly. He's stunned by Sheed's words, and it breaks his heart. Darryl pulls over and parks. "Yo, where the fuck all that come from? That's how you feel about me?" he asks. "Huh? Is that how you feel? Why the fuck would I get a kick out of seeing you under me?

First of all, I don't look at it like you under me, and I didn't know you looked at it like that either. If that's the case, all the years that I was *under you,* I had no problem with that because you, my man. You was driving big cars and spending money like it wasn't no tomorrow. You even bought me clothes and sneakers, and I never felt like you looked at it like I was *under you.* And I never felt like one of your bitches!

And now, because my man is still in the halfway house and I don't want him getting into trouble and getting sent back, I'm the bad guy? Because I'd rather just give my man whatever he needs just to keep him safe as long as I can, I'm doing something wrong? I'm sorry that you look at me like that. It breaks my heart to know you feel like that."

Sheed sits quietly with his lips puckered up, pouting. Darryl slams the car into drive and pulls off. "That's crazy, though," Darryl says angrily.

For twenty minutes, they ride in silence before Sheed speaks again. "Yo, D, I apologize," he whispers. "Forget that I said all that. I let my emotions get the best of me. It's just this regular shit is starting to take a toll on me. I ain't no regular fucking nigga. The difference between me and a regular nigga is the regular nigga don't mind being regular. I do," he adds. "And that ain't how I feel about you," he claims.

"Forgive me?" he asks as he extends his hand. Darryl stares Sheed in the eyes, looking for sincerity before he shakes his hand. "You forgive me?"

Darryl nods his head up and down slowly. One thing he knows for sure is that what comes out of a man's mouth is only a fraction of what he holds in his heart. "I forgive you," he says. *But I will never forget that you said this, he thinks to himself. Not ever.*

-37-

Days Later

A HALF-HOUR AGO, Darryl received a call from Boobie Salaam, which has led them both here. They sit in Boobie Salaam's car, parked in the back of the parking lot of Don's Diner. Boobie Salaam exhales a deep sigh. "Well, I got some good news, and I got some bad news. Which one do you want first?"

"Give me the bad news," Darryl replies as he takes a deep breath to prepare for it.

"You got indicted by the grand jury," he whispers. "I just left Ray's office."

Darryl shows no sign of emotion. He had already prepared himself for this. He expected to be indicted. "That's the bad news?" he asks.

"Yeah," Boobie Salaam replies. "But Ray said to tell you not to worry. He's got this. He also told me to tell you that he needs you to do something."

"And what's that?" Darryl questions.

"He said you must enroll in some type of school before the first court date."

"School?" Darryl repeats with attitude.

"Yeah, school. Take a trade or something. He said he doesn't care if it's computer school, nursing school, Essex County, or *porn star school*," he says with a smile. "He said that will work in our favor when you stand before the judge."

"I got you," Darryl says, brushing Boobie Salaam off.

"Nah, fuck that, I got you shit. Don't just say that to shut me up. If you want him to perform his magic, you have to do as he tells you to do. Now tell me you're going to enroll in school?"

Darryl shakes his head up and down. "I got you."

"Lil Bruh, listen to me. Your future depends on it. That's a small price to pay to stay out here on the streets. Look at it like this, enroll in school and remain free or don't enroll and go to prison. In there, you will end up going to school anyway, just to pass the day away. Look at it like that," he says sternly.

"What's the good news?" Darryl asks, trying to change the subject.

A smile appears on Boobie Salaam's face. "I told you I've been working hard, right?" he asks. Before Darryl can answer, he speaks again. "I've been busting my ass day and night, but now it's all coming together. Knock on wood," he says as he taps on the wood trimming along his door panel. "I might have set up your pro debut," he says with a spark in his eyes.

"Word?" Darryl asks in slight disbelief.

"Word," Boobie Salaam repeats.

"Dude is from Mississippi. He's thirty-six years old, and his record is twenty-five and eleven."

"Thirty-six fights? He got way too much ring experience for me. This will only be my first fight. I don't have no business in there with him."

"Exactly," Boobie Salaam says with his eyes stretched wide open. "And when you knock his ass out, you will shock the world."

"You sound real confident," Darryl says with a look of uncertainty on his face.

"Of course, I'm confident. I talked to his manager already. They're both hurting and down on their luck. He said his fighter would fall whatever round we need him to fall in for two grand. They have been beating my phone up for two days trying to put it together."

"Oh yeah?" Darryl asks.

"Yeah. So what do you think? Are you ready?"

Darryl nods his head up and down, but the look on his face is not that convincing. "I guess so."

"You can't guess, Lil Bruh. This isn't the guessing game. You have to know. Either you're ready, or you're not. I will give you a couple of hours to think about it all. If you are ready, meet me right here at nine tomorrow morning. We will go to Trenton and get your boxing license. When I get here in the morning, if you're not here, I will assume that you're not ready." He extends his hand for a handshake. "Later."

Darryl returns the handshake. "Later," he says as he forces the door open.

"Lil Bruh, you this close to your dream," he says, holding two fingers in the air. "Don't just dream about it. Wake up and bring it to reality."

-38-

Three Days Later

DARRYL SPEEDS UP THE BLOCK. Just as he reaches the garage, he slams on the brakes. He slams the gear into Park and forces the door open. He runs full speed ahead to the entrance.

He walks into the office where Sheed sits with his feet propped up on the desk. Darryl looks like a madman.

"What's up?" Sheed asks. "You all right?"

Darryl paces back and forth around the room for a few seconds. "Yo, I need you."

"Alright," Sheed replies as he gets up from the seat. "What's up?"

Darryl walks over to the closet and fumbles around on the top shelf. He holds the nine-millimeter in the air. He hits the lever on the side, and the clip drops from the bottom into his hand. He examines it to make sure it's fully loaded. He slams it back into the butt. *Cling, cling!* He slides one bullet into the chamber. "Let's go," he demands as he leads the way out of the room.

Sheed follows behind hesitantly. He has no clue what's going on, but he senses that it's serious. Once they're out of the garage, Darryl locks the door and tosses the car key to Sheed. "Drive," he instructs as he walks towards the passenger's side.

As Sheed is starting the car, he looks over to Darryl. "Where are we going?"

"Just go straight," he instructs.

Sheed drives in silence.   A million thoughts are running through his mind, and his curiosity is killing him.   All he can think of is getting caught doing whatever they are about to do and getting sent back to prison.   He can't believe Darryl is putting him in a situation like this.

"Yo, D, tell me something," Sheed whispers. "What's going on?"

"Make a left at the corner," Darryl replies.

"Yo, why are you ignoring me? What's the deal?"

"At the second light, make a right."

Sheed pulls onto a small block. Darryl sits on the edge of his seat as if he's in search of something. "Yep, he here. Good," he says with great satisfaction. "Park right here," he instructs.

"Yo, D, for the twentieth time," he says with anger. "What is going on?"

Darryl stares straight ahead as if Sheed hasn't said a word. His sole reason for ignoring Sheed is out of embarrassment.   It's times like this that he misses Passion the most. He never had to explain his reasons for anything he wanted to do, and she never questioned why he wanted to do this or what a person did. She just drove when he needed her to drive.

"Turn the car off," Darryl demands.

"Yo, you going to tell me something! You got me out here with a blindfold on. We are about to ride on some shit, and I don't have a clue what it's about! I'm in the fucking halfway house. I get caught out here, and I'm going back to prison."

Darryl snickers. "Oh, now you worried about going back to prison? Just days ago, you were begging me to give you something to get back in the game with. Prison wasn't one of your fears then. Was it?"

"Yeah, and days ago, you said you was protecting me from going back to prison. You protecting me today, too?" he asks with sarcasm.

"You know what? Pull off. I will handle this on my own like I always do. You never rode on nothing, so why should I think you would ride with me now? When it's time to ride, fuck all of them questions. What they do? What they say? What happened? You think today is the right time? You acting off of emotions," he says sarcastically. "Fuck all that excuse shit. When it's time to ride, it's time to ride!"

Sheed sits back feeling disrespected. "You think I make excuses? Of course, I'm going to question you. You strapping up and asking me to drive without telling me shit."

Darryl stares straight ahead and focused. "Bingo!" he shouts with joy. "Yo, there goes my target. I got one question for you," he says as the anxiety bubbles in his gut. "Are you with me or not?"

Sheed shakes his head slowly. "Don't ask me no dumb ass shit like that. Of course, I'm with you."

"Cool!" Darryl shouts as he snatches his gun from his waistband and tucks it inside his jacket pocket. He pulls his cap down over his eyes. "I will be right back!" He pushes the door open, steps foot onto the concrete, and slams the door shut.

Darryl walks hurriedly with his head hanging low. His prey, Sal, strolls down the stairs, and Darryl puts a little more pep in his step. Just as Sal steps off the porch, Darryl makes it two houses away from him. Sal cuts in front of Darryl as he steps toward the curb.

Darryl unrolls his mask over his face before reaching out and grabbing the back of Sal's coat. With his right hand, he draws his gun. Sal turns around fearfully. The element of surprise is against him. His eyes stretch wide with terror as he stares into the eyes of the masked man. Darryl pulls Sal closer to him and plants the gun against Sal's side. *Boc! Boc!* Darryl lets Sal go, and he stumbles backward clumsily. He trips over the curb and falls onto his back. He lies there, back on the asphalt, while his legs are on the sidewalk. "Please, please?" he begs. "Don't kill me, please? Take everything!" he cries.

"Shut the fuck up," Darryl snarls. Suddenly the vision of Sal and his man stomping on him plays in his mind. Darryl aims at Sal's leg, and he squeezes. *Boc!* He replays the argument they had at the skating rink. He aims at the other leg and squeezes. *Boc!* The vision of Sunday driving the Range Rover while Sal sits in the passenger seat comes to mind, and Darryl aims at his chest. He fires *Boc!*

Sal grabs hold of his chest and screams like a child. Darryl peeks around quickly before aiming and firing again at his chest. *Boc!* Darryl backpedals away from Sal with his gun still aimed. Once he gets a few feet away, he turns around and takes flight toward his car.

Darryl snatches the door open and falls onto the seat. "Go, go!" he shouts as he pulls the door shut. Sheed sits in shock. "Go, motherfucker!" Sheed drops the car into Drive and pulls off nervously. "Bust the U-turn!" Darryl says in a hyper tone.

Sheed makes a wild clumsy K-turn in the middle of the street, and he races up the wrong side of the street. "Slow down, slow down," Darryl says calmly. "Driving all crazy will just draw attention to us. Drive regular. The getaway is better than the take," he says with a nonchalant demeanor that is quite shocking to Sheed.

Back at the Scene of the Crime

Sunday jumps down the entire flight of stairs. She runs over to Sal, who is rolling around in blood and despair. She kneels over and lays his head on her lap. "Somebody call an ambulance!" she shouts in a frenzy. "Please, I need an ambulance! Somebody help!"

A Couple Miles Away

Complete silence fills the air as Sheed pulls into the garage. While Darryl takes this time to come down off his adrenaline high, Sheed is still in somewhat of a shock. While locked up, he heard several stories of how vicious Darryl had become. It was hard for him to believe it because he never saw that side of Darryl. Sheed was quite surprised to see Darryl gun the man down with such skill as if he's done this a million times. The fact that he still hasn't shown any sign of compassion tells Sheed how coldhearted the streets have made him. Seeing this firsthand makes Sheed bear witness to how ruthless he now is.

Sheed slams the gear into Park before leaning low in the seat. He had some things he wanted to say to Darryl for the entire ride, but he held onto them. Now he feels it's time to air those things out. "D," he whispers with nervousness. He's not even comfortable talking to Darryl right now. After seeing what he just saw, he feels he doesn't know him anymore.

"You my man, so I gotta keep it all the way real with you," he says before taking a deep breath. "In the two and a half years that I was away, you have accomplished a lot. I mean, I step back on the scene, and I see how you have grown. You turned up the volume on your hustle game. You went from Darryl to D-Low. You went from an eight ball, three and a half grams, to twenty keys. You went from buying my old car to buying brand new shit off the showroom straight cash! You damn near stepped up every area of your life, except one," he says as he stares Darryl in the eyes.

"Every area except for your pimp game. It's like when it comes to these bitches," he says. "You know what, I'm not even going to say these bitches because it's only one bitch. When it comes to Sunday, it's like you're running in place. You are doing the exact same shit you was doing when I left. Two and a half years ago, you wanted to shoot the nigga over the bitch. Now I'm back, and you just shot the nigga over the bitch. You was determined to do it."

"Here you go!" Darryl snaps. "I told you it wasn't over, no bitch! That nigga played me three years ago, and now he got his payback!"

"D, only a bitch can bring out those types of emotions that you are running off."

"I ain't running off no fucking emotions!" Darryl's phone rings, but he's so enraged he doesn't hear it. "I'm a man before anything! I think with my head!"

"Oh, yeah? Ok, let me ask you, would a man in his right mind jump out of his personal car and blast a motherfucker four times in broad daylight? That's some emotional shit right there! What if he lives and figures out that it was you?"

Darryl's phone begins ringing again. "Nigga, the motherfucker jumped me in front of my girl! What part you don't understand? I want the motherfucker to know I did it! And I don't give a fuck who else know that I did it!"

"And that's some emotional shit right there, too." Sheed shakes his head from side to side. "Ask yourself, without answering from an emotional standpoint, is she worth going to jail for?"

"Nah, she ain't worth going to jail for. But if I go to jail for slaughtering the nigga that jumped me in front of my girl, then it is what it is." Darryl's phone begins ringing for the third time, and he still doesn't answer it.

"You know what? You got all the answers, I see. You know what I need you to do, though? Ask yourself this question, and whatever the answer to the question is, keep it to yourself. I don't even want to know. Can you look yourself in the face and honestly say you did that because of him jumping you? If you can, it's all good," he says with a smile.

"But if by chance you shot that nigga over a bitch that wants to play with both of y'all, then know that you have just done some straight-up sucker shit. It ain't on him. It's on the bitch. No matter what you do, she's going to play with that nigga. She was playing with that nigga before you, and she's still going to play with the nigga after," he says sternly. "That is if the nigga still alive to play," he adds.

"I don't want that bitch no more!" Darryl claims. "Me and that bitch finished!"

"Then why you blast the nigga?" he asks sarcastically. "You should have just left them mufuckers alone. What it is, though, is it, you don't want the bitch no more, but you don't want to see her with him. That bothers you that they're going to be together forever. You can't handle it!" Sheed words just ripped through Darryl's heart.

The saying the truth hurts is true. Deep down inside, whether Darryl admits it or not, he knows that Sheed is telling God's honest truth. "So did you do it paying him back for jumping you three years ago? Oh, and if that is the case, why you not concerned with getting even with the nigga that helped him jump you?" he asks with a smile. "Never once have you ever mentioned him to me. Or did you blast him because he still fucking Sunday?"

Darryl stares down at his lap without saying a word. He has his answer ready to roll off his lips, but he's ashamed to let it out. His phone rings again, but he acts as if he doesn't hear it. He lets out a deep sigh. "Three years ago, when I wanted to shoot him, I swear to you it was over him jumping me," Darryl says.

"Today, I can't lie to you," he whispers. "I'm just doing my normal drive past her house, and I see the nigga pull up. That shit burned me the fuck up. It's like I'm over here barely able to sleep, thinking the bitch stressing out over me too, and she ain't," he says with embarrassment. "She still doing her. She doing the same shitty shit that she's been doing. But popping up at my crib fucking shit up with me and my bitches," Darryl says with anger.

"So, I guess you're right. Today it had nothing to do with them jumping me. It was all about him still fucking her," he says, lowering his eyes with shame. "I'm fucked up over this bitch." For the first time, he's admitting this. It's as if a weight has been lifted from his shoulders. "This bitch got me. I gotta shake this shit."

"That's all I wanted you to admit to yourself," Sheed says. "I just wanted you to stop hiding behind that bullshit. Ay, man, you got bit by the love bug. It happens to a lot of you motherfuckers," he says with a huge smile. "It's time to move on, though. You feel me?"

Darryl nods his head up and down. "I feel you!"

"Ain't no looking back from here. She don't owe you nothing, and he don't owe you nothing, no more. It's over."

"It's over!" Darryl agrees. His phone starts to ring again. "Damn, damn, damn!" he shouts. "Who the fuck is this?" he shouts as he looks at the number on the display. Seeing Sunday's number sends him into deep thought. He scrolls down and realizes that all the missed calls are from her. As he's looking at the call log, she calls again, and this alarms him.

"Who is it?" Sheed asks.

"It's Sunday," Darryl answers slowly. "She never calls back-to-back like this unless it's an emergency," he adds as he stares straight ahead. His mind wanders, causing him to become more nervous. "You think she saw me?"

-39-

Three Nights Later

DARRYL IS AWAKENED by banging on his front door. He pops up, sitting upright in his bed. His heart is pounding louder than the pounding on the door. *Boom, boom, boom!* This is his first night back here. He's been staying at the hotel ever since the day of the shooting. Ever since the shooting, he hasn't been able to sleep a wink, and just when he does, *Boom, boom, boom!*

He doesn't know if Sal is dead or alive, and it wears on him. He also wonders if anyone saw him. Sunday has been calling him nonstop since that day. As badly as he wants to answer, he hasn't. His purpose of wanting to answer has nothing to do with him missing her. It has everything to do with him wanting to know what she may know about the situation.

Boom, boom, boom! Darryl sits on the bed as still as can be. The only thing on his mind is that it could very well be the police on the other side of his door, and they could be here to bring him in on charges of murder.

He tiptoes to the door as quietly as he can. He slowly places his eye against the peephole. He sighs with relief. For the first time in a long time, he's happy to see Sunday. He doesn't want her here either, but he will take her on any given day if it's between the police and her.

Boom, boom, boom! She bangs louder and louder. He stands stiff as a statue, just hoping she will leave. For a quick second, he wants to open the door. He wonders what she knows. *Should I let her in? he asks himself. Nah, this could be a setup. Maybe Sal's boys put her up to coming here so they can bust in the door behind her.*

Boom, boom, boom! His mind is running wild. "Damn, I can't let this bitch keep bringing this attention to my place of rest," he mumbles.

Sunday knows just how much Darryl hates her causing a scene and she uses that to her advantage. He's working on changing that though. The past couple days he's been searching for a new apartment. Tonight, he parked his car around the corner so she would think he's not home, but he figures she must have seen it anyway.

Boom, boom, boom! Boom, boom! Boom! Boom! Boom! Boom, boom, boom, boom! Boom, boom! Boom! Boom! Boom! "Stupid bitch," he mumbles as he grabs the doorknob. Hold up, he thinks to himself. He runs over to his bed. He reaches underneath the pillow and grabs hold of his snub-nose .38. He tucks his hand down in his boxers. He runs over and snatches the door partly open.

"Open this fucking," Sunday manages to shout before Darryl grabs her by the collar and yanks her inside. He slams the door shut and locks the door quickly.

"What the fuck is wrong with you?" he barks. Without even realizing it, he's placed the gun against her throat. He quickly catches himself. "I didn't know who the fuck you was banging on my door like that. You almost caught a bad one." It's pissing him off that she's showing no sign of fear. It's as if she takes him as a joke. He nudges her with the nose of the gun. "You better stop playing with me and disrespecting my house like this."

Sunday isn't the least bit worried. She snatches his wrist, pulling the gun away from her neck. "Why the fuck you haven't you been answering your phone?" she slurs. The smell of alcohol smacks Darryl in the face and almost knocks him to the floor.

"Why the fuck do you keep coming here with this bullshit? It's over. What part of that don't you understand? Why do you keep bringing attention to my spot?"

Sunday staggers back and forth. "Why did you bring attention to my spot?" she asks with sarcasm.

"What? What the fuck are you talking about?" He holds a tight grip on her collar. He's so furious with her that he could shake the life out of her.

"You know what the fuck I'm talking about," she says with a sinister smile. "You coming around my house with bullshit. You don't give a fuck about bringing attention to my house," she says, rocking back and forth. "Why the fuck should I give a fuck about bringing attention to yours? You better hope that he pulls through because half the block saw the black Lexus leaving the scene of the crime. You don't have to worry about me. You better be worried about them."

Oh, so he is ok, Darryl thinks to himself. "Black Lexus?" Darryl asks as if he doesn't have a clue. "Hope who pulls through?"

"Ok," she smiles. "We both can play stupid. You don't know, and I don't know," she says as she takes a step toward the bed. She staggers like a drunkard.

Darryl walks over to the bed and takes a seat on the edge. "Yo, you're gonna have to leave my house and never come here again," he says sternly. He looks over at her, standing on the opposite side of the bed. "You hear me?"

She flashes a drunk but seductive smile before unbuttoning her trench coat. She opens her coat wide, exposing her nakedness. "I ain't trying to hear you," she says, allowing the coat to drop to the floor. "I'm horny," she slurs, "and I want to fuck right now."

Darryl looks her over from head to toe and becomes erect instantly. *I can't, he thinks to himself. Hell no!* "Sunday leave."

Sunday falls onto the bed and crawls over to him. "Daddy, can you fuck me?" she asks in a little girl's whining voice. "Please, daddy." She strokes him through his boxers. Darryl pushes her off of him.

"Ok," she slurs. "Since you won't fuck me, I will fuck myself." She lies back and spreads her legs as wide as she can. She licks her middle finger before sliding it deep inside of her. She grabs hold of her right breast and caresses it. She stares him in the eyes as she licks her nipple gently. She closes her eyes and legs tightly as she fingers herself. She opens her eyes halfway. "Daddy, come fuck me, please?" she begs as she spreads her legs again.

Darryl looks down at her juicy twat. The more she fingers herself, the juicier it gets. He can hear the juices simmering with every stroke of her finger. "Daddy, you got some dick for me?" she whines.

Darryl can no longer resist. He kicks his boxers off. He leans over to her. "Listen, Sunday, this doesn't mean that we are together. You want me to fuck you, and I'm going to do just that. We fucking," he says with emphasis. "You hear me?"

183

"Yes, daddy," she replies submissively. "I hear you," she slurs. "Now fuck me." Darryl hops on her. He wastes no time before entering her and starts banging away at her. "Yes, daddy, fuck me! Like that!" Darryl spreads her legs wide open as he bounces on the pussy like a trampoline. Sunday cries with pleasure. "Yes, yes!"

To soothe his pride Darryl tells himself he's only doing this to keep her close and to keep her sane. He feels he has to keep her near until he makes his move. "You gonna stop bringing this bullshit to my house, right?" he grunts as he bangs as hard as he can. "Right?"

"Yes, daddy!" she shouts.

"Say you not coming to my house no more with the bullshit!" he demands. Her silence makes him pound harder. "Say it!"

"Oh my God," she cries. "I won't come to your house with the bullshit no more," she says with her mouth, but her mind says something totally different.

"Promise me!" he grunts as he lifts her leg high in the air. He drills her as fast and hard as he can. "Promise me!"

"Right there, daddy!" she shouts. "Right there! I promise, I promise!" she screams. *Nigga, whatever, she thinks to herself. Just shut up and fuck this pussy.* "I promise, daddy!"

-40-

Three Weeks Later

JUST AS ATTORNEY RAY BROWN instructed, Darryl enrolled in school. As much as he hated to do so, he realized he had to in order to remain a free man. Two weeks ago, he enrolled in Essex County College. He didn't know how scholastically behind he was until he took the entrance exam. The only subject he excelled in was math. His ability to calculate numbers off the top of his head and figure out word problems came from calculating numbers all day in the underworld. The rest of the subjects he failed terribly. He failed so badly that he had to take many preliminary classes to catch up.

After another day of frustrating classes, Darryl's day has come to an end. He walks sluggishly through the building on his way out. He drags on with his head hanging low. He looks up for a quick second, and what he sees surprises him. Down the hall, ahead of him, he sees a short pregnant woman dragging along. *Asia? he says to himself. Nah, it can't be.* He squints his eyes to block the other people out. As the woman gets closer, he realizes that it is very much Asia.

He steps faster with his heart banging like a drum. In minutes they're a few feet away from each other. Asia looks up from the papers she holds in her hand, and they lock eyes. "Asia, what's up?"

She nods her head with agitation before rolling her eyes. He stops short while she continues, stepping right past him. "Asia," he calls out as he follows behind her. "Asia."

He walks with her.

"What are you doing here?" she asks. "You're not a college type of guy. Isn't that what you told me three years ago?"

"The question is, what are you doing here? In Essex County of all places?" he asks. He's puzzled to find her in a community college.

"I'm taking classes. That's what I'm doing here," she says with massive attitude.

"But why are you taking classes here in a community college when I gave you twenty grand for college? I mean, it's your life and none of my business, but I just need to know. Asia, just tell me what's going on, and I will leave you alone forever," he claims.

She stops short. "Forever?" she asks. "Promise me?"

He smiles brightly. "You asking me to promise you something? It's obvious that both of us have a problem keeping promises." She starts walking again. "Ok, ok. I promise."

She stops short again. "After I got pregnant, my mother thought it was best for me to come home. She wanted me close to her so she could help me out if need be. Ok, you happy now? Now you can leave me alone forever," she says as she starts walking again.

"But, what about your..." He can't even force himself to say the words. "Y, your," he stutters. "What about him?" he asks as he points to her swollen stomach.

"My child's father?" she asks.

"Yeah, him," he utters.

"What about him?" she asks with sarcasm.

"How does he feel about you coming back here? And why can't he help you?"

"He would help if he was around to help."

"What you mean?" he questions. "Why isn't he around to help? He's the one who got you in this mess," he says with frustration in his voice.

"Are you calling my baby a mess?" she asks with sorrow in her eyes. "Bye, Darryl," she says as she walks ahead of him. He chases behind her.

"I'm sorry, Asia. I apologize."

She storms away. She grabs hold of the door to the classroom. "Asia," he calls out as he grabs her by the hand. She snatches away as she steps inside the room. The door closes in his face as he stands deflated.

-41-

Days Later
The North Pole

"**A**WL SHIT," Darryl says as he steps into the doorway of the store. He peeks around the beam.

"Uh oh," Sheed teases. "Here go, your girl," he says as he keeps his eyes fixed on the red BMW that has just turned the corner.

"This bitch," Darryl whispers with anger. He keeps his focus straight ahead, acting as if he doesn't see the car double-parked in front of him. The last thing he wants is for Sunday to put him on blast. As far as Sheed knows, Darryl hasn't contacted her. He was too embarrassed to admit to Sheed they had sex after telling him he was done with her for good.

Darryl watches through his peripheral as Sunday gets out of the car. She stands with her hands on her hips without saying a word. "Darryl!" she shouts loud enough for the world to hear. Darryl looks over with a fake shocked expression as if he didn't know she was standing there. "Come here!" she demands.

"Oh shit," Sheed whispers. "You in big trouble," he teases.

"Yeah, right," Darryl says as he makes his way over to her. He adjusts his face to match the way he feels before getting to her. They stand face to face. "What's up?" he asks with agitation.

"Why the fuck do I have to keep calling you?"

As weird as it may sound, Darryl has gotten used to this level of toxicity that Sunday carries within her. Three years of this and it seems normal to him. It all adds to the adrenaline rush that he chases daily. The highs and the lows from her keeps his life full of adventure and that's another reason it's so hard for him to cut her loose. She supplies ups and down like a roller coaster but it's gotten to that point that he wants to jump off the ride. She just won't let him.

"Sunday, don't come around with that bullshit showing off," he whispers.

"Showing off! Who the fuck showing off? Who am I showing off for? Ain't nobody out here worth showing off for," she says with massive neck popping. "Nothing but a bunch of broke-ass niggas," she says as she looks around. "You're the one showing off for these no-frill ass niggas. They're nobody in my world."

"What?" Darryl says as he tries to cut her off. "What you want?"

Roselyn opens the driver's door. Sunday remains quiet, just waiting for Roselyn to leave. Roselyn gets out of the car and walks toward the store. She steps without saying a word. "We are on our way to People's Choice, and after it's over, I'm coming to your house."

"Nah," Darryl replies, shaking his head. "I ain't gone be home tonight."

"Where are you going to be?" she asks.

"What?" he says as he tries to fumble for an alibi. "Me and my man going over to New York tonight," he lies.

"Ok," she says. "And after that, I will be at your house."

"I ain't coming back until late."

"Well, I will be outside waiting for you. I will just drop Roz off and take her car."

Darryl is annoyed. "Sunday, I already told you it's over. Why we just can't stop this shit?" he asks in a calm voice.

Roselyn comes walking out of the store. All eyes are fixated on the white jeans she's wearing. The best way to describe it would be a donkey ass in white designer jeans. Her jeans are so tight they look like they've been painted on. "You ready?" she asks Sunday. "I gotta go and pick him up," she says as she gets into the car and slams the door shut.

"Alright, here I come," Sunday replies. She turns back to Darryl. "I will be there at 3:15," she says as she sits down. She closes the door. "Ok?"

"I ain't gone be there."

"Darryl, don't play with me," she says with a stern look on her face. "I know you tired of scenes, right?" she asks. "And I'm tired of causing scenes," she grins. "So, to avoid all of that, just be there when I get there," she says before rolling the window up in his face. Roselyn pulls off, leaving Darryl standing at the curb.

Since the shooting, Sunday has become even more demanding. She knows she has something over him, and she dangles it over his head to make him do whatever she wants. She plays him more like a puppet than she did before. Just when he has gotten his emotions intact and can now move on, she's found something to keep entangled in her web. She's used to controlling him and will do whatever it takes to keep that control.

"Got damn!" Sheed shouts. "Roz got that big ol' ass!" he says as he gropes himself through his jeans. "Yo put me on her."

"Hell no! I ain't doing no match-making. I'm done with that bitch. I just want her out of my life and away from me! I don't want nothing to do with her or nobody affiliated with her."

"Please?" he begs. "Come on, do that for me, please?" he pleads. "Let me just get some of that big ass, and you can do whatever you want with her after that," he smiles. "You owe me anyway. You ain't get me no pussy yet since I've been home. You ain't take me to the go-go bars, massage parlors, nothing," he says.

"Please, just put the word in for me so I can get some of that big ol' ass and we even for all the pussy I got for you when your nuts was in the sand. Just put the word in for me, and I will do the rest. Ok?"

Darryl nods his head up and down. "I will see, but I'm telling you now, I don't want no parts of neither one of them bitches!"

-42-

Days Later

DARRYL'S SPIRITS ARE LOW. He's been bending Lefty's ear for the last thirty minutes, just venting about the situation. He needed someone to vent to, and it couldn't be Sheed. He needs an ear of someone who is not familiar with the parties involved. Right now, he needs to vent without being judged.

Darryl sits on the bench with a towel draped over his head. He's pouring out his feelings so thick that he can't even look Lefty in the eye. "Shit is crazy. Like the bitch knows she got me by the balls, and she is using that to her advantage. The other night she just started naming a bunch of different things she knows, stash houses, my transporter, my operation, and even shootings and talking about she's sure the police would love to hear that. Like holding that shit over my head to box me in and get her way. I ain't trusting this bitch."

Darryl pulls the towel from over his head. "And it's crazy because that while talking to my Nana the other day, she tell me some crazy shit. Check this shit out," he says with his eyes wide. "My grandfather on my mother side was stabbed to death by his mistress and

192

my grandfather on my father side was shot to death by his wife." Lefty turns to Darryl with his full attention. "Like she told me, she don't know what it is with us and them crazy women."

Lefty nods his head like Darryl is onto something. "Like some shit in y'all DNA when it comes to attracting crazy women," Lefty says.

"Word," Darryl agrees

Lefty's face goes stone. "Baby Boy, with all due respect, that's the dumbest shit I ever heard in my life. Because both your grand-pops were murdered by broads, you gone use that to justify your weakness for a bitch? I ain't gone let you do that. Nana put a pacifier in your mouth when she told you that story. Baby Boy, take that pacifier out your mouth when you talking to me."

Darryl really doesn't know what to say at this point. He wishes he didn't say that. He looks up to Lefty who is shadow boxing, throwing punches in the air. He turns around to face Darryl. "Chick fucking with you and fucking with the old head, playing the middle with both of y'all. Chick knows you shot the nigga she's been fucking with for years and not even telling him where the hit came from. She knew him longer than she's known you, and she don't have no loyalty for him. So you expect her to have some for you? Bitch a cross-artist," Lefty says rudely.

Darryl accepts it as the truth. Lefty shifts his waist from side to side before throwing more punches in the air. "Pardon me for calling her a bitch and forgive me for not understanding this love shit. But I didn't grow up with love and affection and all of that mushy shit. I don't deal with love. I deal with mind over matter," he says he bends over. He does consecutive toe touches.

He stands up, bopping from side to side. "Let me share something with you. I grew up with a mother who always put her niggas before me," Lefty says with no emotion. "My mother, a good woman, just caught up in the mix. My father, my enlightener, died when I was five years old."

Lefty's eye brightens with a light Darryl has never seen in it. "My father, my enlightener, the epitome of the word Man. Look man up in the dictionary, and my father's face should be there. Solid as a rock," he says with great pride. "Taught me so much at a young age, and I never met another man like my father." Lefty places his leg on the edge of the bench as he dazes into the past.

"My mother never met another man like him either... and she tried," he says, shaking his head sadly. "My pops had big shoes to fill, and no matter how many men she brought in and out of that house, none of them could fill his shoes. My father fucked her up for other men. He did everything for her as a man should. So after he was dead and gone, she was looking for men to lead as my pops led. But none of them could stand up to pops. She put so much into trying to find the perfect man that she broke her only son. She always put those losers before me," he says with a sinister smirk.

"Every few months, a new nigga that I'm playing second to. Finally, she found an old, good for nothing nigga with a whole lot of game. She moved him in, and that's when everything changed. Me, I'm five years old watching this nigga beat the blood out of my mother's face, and I'm standing there helpless," Lefty says with a smirk.

"He had instilled just as much fear in me as he did in her. My mother screaming to me to run and go outside and call the cops. I wanted to, but when I get to the door, he calls my name and gives me that look that scares me to death. I wasn't scared for me. I was scared for her because he told me if I left the house, he would kill her."

Lefty starts shadowboxing again. The punches are now more powerful, and he's firing them with anger. "So, I never ran out to the call the cops. To save her life, I stayed and watched him beat her damn near to death. He beat on my mother for breakfast, lunch, and dinner. And sometimes, he beat her for dessert. This went on for a year and a couple of months."

This story touches Darryl's heart. He can see the pain that Lefty so desperately tries to hide. Lefty stops all movement and just looks over Darryl's head. "And then my seventh birthday came. Let me tell you something about seven years of age. My father, my enlightener, always told me that one knows right from wrong at the age of seven. At seven, one becomes a God, and at seven, one is to take control over his universe." Lefty nods his head in a slight trance.

"So one night, he came in drunk and got right to his regularly scheduled program of beating on my mother. This time it seemed like it went on longer than usual. It seemed like my mother's screams were louder than before. It seemed like the blood coming out of my mother's face was thicker and even redder than ever before," he says as his voice cracks a little. It's evident that he's reliving the story as he tells it.

"I ran in the room and threw the pillow over my head. Again I had sat and just watched as he beat her damn near to death, and I didn't run and tell the neighbors because I wanted to save her life. I feared he would kill her the moment I left the house." Lefty nods his head, just staring at the floor.

"So, while I'm in my room, I hear her screams and cries piercing through the walls. All I could think of is my father, my enlightener, telling me that at seven years old, I become a God and it will be time for me to take control of my universe. I then walked to the hallway closet where I knew the good for nothing nigga used to hide a God Jewel. The jewel that a God needs to keep himself alive," he says with emphasis. "The jewel that a God needs to guard and protect his universe," he says with more emphasis.

"My Ole Earth at the age of seven is now a part of my universe, and it was my duty to guard and protect her." A glow of life sets in Lefty's eye. "I put the God Jewel in my hand and ran into my room. I had seen on television how to slide one into the chamber. I slide it in the chamber and cling," he says as he reenacts. "And it gets stuck.," he says as traces of worry cross his face.

"With force, I pull it back, and it won't budge. I pull harder, and finally, it slides forward, and BOOM. The kickback was too much for my weak, little wrist. The God's Jewel bangs into my eye before flying out of my hand.

Darryl sits on the edge of his seat like he's watching an action-packed movie. "I feel a bloody shower dripping down my face, blood dripping down my shirt, my pants, the floor. I look over and all my fingers on the floor." Sadness pastes his face as he looks on the floor to the left. The look on his face is as if he can still see his fingers lying there. Darryl listens with his mouth wide open. He's never heard a story so intriguing.

"The room becomes one big blur. As fast as I could wipe the blood from my eye, more blood would appear. It was like the whole inside of my head was draining through my eye socket—a throbbing, a pain that has yet to be matched up until this day. My mother comes running in, eyes black and blue, leaking blood," Lefty shakes his head with sadness.

"She loses her mind when she sees three-quarters of my hand blown the fuck off. Old good for nothing nigga comes in and sees his gun on the floor, and immediately he knows what I was up to. He realized I was going to put an end to it once and for all. Understanding that made him beat me worse than he had ever beat her. He did everything except Lynch me."

Lefty stops like it's the end of the story. Darryl sits in suspense. "So, what happened?"

"My Ole Earth chose him over me. Old good for nothing nigga talked her into shipping me to a Boy's Home. Said I was a problem child and had mental issues. The only mental issues I have are the ones he caused," he says with a crooked grin. "Shipped me off to a home, and him and my Earth relocated somewhere I don't know."

"You never seen them again?" Darryl asks curiously.

Lefty shakes his head. "Never. I wouldn't even know where to start."

"Damn," Darryl exhales sadly. "I'm sorry to hear all of that."

"Don't be. It's what my hands called for." He raises his hand and his nub high in the air. "I dealt myself this hand."

Darryl is speechless. Now he understands why Lefty is a loner and so cold-hearted. Lefty starts firing punches in the air again, shadow boxing. "So, as I said, pardon me for not understanding that love language. For me, it's mind over matter. I don't deal with matters of the heart. I deal solely with knowledge and understanding," he says sternly.

"The third letter of the alphabet is the letter C is Cee, with the letter C, is to understand clearly through the third eye, which is the mind. I Cee with the logic of understanding, which is why I'm not above busting a motherfucker's head open when they're begging to have their head bust open. And that goes for man and woman." He points in Darryl's face aggressively.

"Don't play with her, Baby Boy. I see you love hard, and some may even consider you soft for a bitch, but I don't judge you for it. I still see you solid and upright. You just got a weakness for the broads. Women are your kryptonite.

The prison is filled with men who have spared women, the same women that played both sides of the fence. Prison is filled with men who wish they would have, but they didn't, and now they have to live with that regret for the rest of their lives in prison. And then there are those who are lying in the graveyard because they didn't. Trust me, Baby Boy, I've seen this movie before."

His words send chills through Darryl's body. "Baby Boy, you a good nigga with a good heart, and I've seen what happens to good niggas out here in these streets. They get swallowed up. I tell my man this all the time. I tell him he needs to walk away while he can, just like I'm telling you. The game ain't for niggas like y'all." He shakes his head, sympathizing with Darryl for the very first time.

"And that's another reason I want y'all to get together. My man got a bunch of plays in motion. Big, big plays. I always talk to him about you, and he's been listening. He doesn't fool with everybody, but he really wants to sit down with you. I will set it up if that's ok with you?"

"Hell yeah," Darryl replies with no hesitation. He's heard so much about Money Dee from Lefty and from the streets, and he's sure anything he can do with him would be a come-up. Word on the street is he has the Midas Touch, and anything he touches turns to gold.

"Consider it done," Lefty says. "But as far as the girl, all you have to do is press the button, and I will *take her out of your misery.* Unless you wanna sit in prison for the rest of your life wishing you had?"

-43-

Three Days Later
Essex County College

DARRYL HAS HIS BACKPACK over his head to shield himself from the heavy downpour of rain. He's leaving school. He snatches his car door open and falls into the seat. He looks down at his clothes and becomes pissed once he sees how drenched he is. He starts the engine and pulls off.

The rain floods the windows. He sits on the edge of the seat, face close to the windshield as he drives so that he can see. He turns his wipers on as fast as they go as he pulls up to the red light. As he's sitting, his attention is diverted to the bus stop, where he sees a single person standing.

As he looks harder, he realizes that it's Asia. She stands there soaked with no umbrella. He honks the horn, but she doesn't even look in his direction. He rolls down the window. "Asia!" he shouts. She looks over with a joyous look on her face as if she's been rescued. Once she sees that it's him, she turns away, looking down the block. "Asia, come on!" he shouts. "Get out of the rain."

She shakes her head no. "I'm good, thanks!"

"You're not good," he says as he pulls over close to the curb. "Come on and get in out of the rain."

"I'm ok," she replies. "My bus will be here in a couple of minutes."

"Asia, stop the stubborn shit. It's just a ride, and we don't have to say a word to each other all the way to your house," he claims.

She stands stubbornly for a few seconds before walking toward the car. He pushes the door open for her, and she gets in and closes the door without saying a word. He turns the volume of the music up and pulls off slowly.

After a few minutes of silence, Darryl's voice breaks through. "Asia, I apologize for what I said to you that day," he says as he looks at her. "My feelings just got the best of me." She stares ahead, ignoring him. "You heard me?" Darryl asks.

She looks over at him. "I thought you said we won't say a word to each other? Hmph," she sighs. "Another broken promise."

"No, I said we don't have to. I didn't say I wouldn't try to. Come on, why do things have to be like this? We both know some things shouldn't have happened, but we can't take them back. If we could, I would be the first to take back a lot of shit. Why can't we just move on? I mean, we can at least be cordial, can't we? We don't have to be enemies."

"I'm not your enemy, and I'm not necessarily your friend either."

"Why we can't we be friends?"

"You don't know how to be a friend. You proved that to me already."

"Huh? What you mean? I'm a real friend," he claims.

"Friends don't hurt each other like you hurt me," Asia explains.

"Asia, as I told you, I pay for that mistake every day. I hate myself for that, and I will probably hate myself forever behind that mistake. I will never be able to live it down until I know that you forgive me for it."

"I forgave you two years ago," she claims. "I had to in order to move on with my life."

"Oh, two years," he says. "Is that how long you and him," he says as he points to her stomach, "been together?"

Asia lets out a long sigh. "Here we go."

"I can't help it. I need answers, and I won't stop until I get them. Just answer my questions so I can stop bothering you about it. There are just a few things that I need to know. Not about your relationship. I'm just wondering why you're here."

"Why is it any of your concern at this point?" she asks.

"I'm just concerned. What can I say?" he asks with a simple look on his face. "Like, why are you back here? Did he get you pregnant and leave you?"

She takes another long sigh while shaking her head. "You can say that in a sense."

"Oh yeah?" Darryl asks. His heart sinks just hearing that someone would do that to her.

"Yes, but not voluntarily. He would have never left me like this if it was up to him."

Darryl sits back, analyzing her words. "Why wasn't it up to him? What, he locked up?"

"No. He was murdered four weeks into my pregnancy."

His jaw drops. "What? Asia, I'm sorry to hear that," he says with sincerity.

"No need for you to be sorry," she replies. "This had nothing to do with you. I decided to date him, knowing what he was into. Now I have to live with the decision that I made."

Darryl sits back quietly. She claims that this has nothing to do with him, but he feels it has everything to do with him. If he had never done what he did, she wouldn't be going through this. What hurts him the most is that the woman he ruined their relationship over was not even worth it.

"Asia, you're a good girl. You got your head on right. You're about your business. You're not out here in the streets," he says with tears in his eyes. "This ain't supposed to be your life. I know this probably don't mean nothing to you right now, but for the zillionth time, I'm sorry. It's my fault that you're in this situation."

He plants his hand on her knee, and she quickly removes his hand. "A, the past three years, I've been selfishly sitting back, kind of hating you for the pain you caused in my life by leaving me. Not once did I even think about how my actions affected you. Will you ever be able to forgive me?"

She looks him in the eyes. "Honestly? Never. You say that this isn't supposed to be my life. I agree, but for every action, there's a reaction. What else can I say, but shit happens? It just so happens that it happened to me."

-44-

DARRYL SITS IN THE DRIVER'S seat of his car while Sheed lies back in the passenger's seat. Sheed just asked Darryl about Roselyn for the hundredth time since he saw her that day. Darryl attempted to put the word in for him as he begged, but the only thing that came out of it was some negativity that Darryl immediately charged off as gossip. As much as he wants to believe that it's gossip, it's hard to do so. Sunday spoke with so much confidence that he has to wonder if it's true or not.

Darryl defended him to the fullest, swearing that it was a lie. He knows that people gossip, but he wonders where a rumor of this magnitude started. There's only one way to find out, and that is to ask Sheed. Darryl has wanted to ask him about it since he first heard it, but he didn't know how to approach the situation. He decided to act as if he never heard the rumor, but he feels that as a lifetime friend, he owes it to Sheed to tell him what people are saying about him.

"Look," Sheed says. "All quiet and shit. All I asked you to do is put a word in for me, and you couldn't even do that for me," he says with a smile.

"I did put the word in for you."

"So, what's up?" he asks with a spark in his eyes. "What she say?" Darryl sits back quietly. This is what he was trying to avoid. He exhales. "What she say? Is I'm getting some of that big ol' ass or what?"

"Yo, do you know a girl named Fee? I think she's from 21st Street?"

"Fee, Fee, Fee?" Sheed says as he thinks quickly. "She dark skin with real big titties?"

"Yeah," Darryl replies.

"Yeah, yeah, I know her. She used to come down to Bordentown to see my man. She got two kids by him."

Damn, Darryl thinks to himself. Darryl figures that if the people and places match, there may be some validity to the story. He hopes not, though. "You and her all right?"

"Yeah, she's cool. We only kicked it a few times, though. Why, what's up?"

"That's Roselyn, little cousin. I guess she was around when Sunday told her about you wanting to meet her. Out of nowhere, she started throwing dirt on your name. She was saying some crazy shit. I defended it, but that bitch swore on her dead grandfather that she has proof for the bullshit she was talking."

"What she say?" Sheed asks with a carefree demeanor. Darryl hesitates before replying. It's difficult for him to even let the words out of his mouth.

Anxiety gets the best of Sheed. "What, what the bitch say?"

Darryl stares straight ahead. "She said that you sick," he whispers.

"What?" Sheed asks. "Speak up. I can't even hear you."

"She said you sick," Darryl utters as he stares out of the window. He's ashamed that he even repeated those words to him. "I defended it, but they act like they know some for sure shit. I was going to let it go. You

205

know I ain't with that gossip and rumor shit. Bitches are always going to talk. As your man, though, I just couldn't hear some shit like that and not tell you what mufuckers saying about you."

Darryl looks at Sheed, waiting for his reply, but he's yet to give one. He just stares straight ahead with no expression. "Where you think they got that shit from, though?" Darryl asks.

"Man, fuck them dumb ass bitches!" he says as he continues to look out of the window.

Darryl senses that something isn't right. The brush-off is in no way the proper defense for a rumor like that. He expected so much more. "But where does a rumor like that come from?"

Sheed sits back quietly and lowers his head with shame. "There's only one place that she could have got it from. She had to get it from the nigga, O," he whispers.

"Was y'all all right, though? Why would he dirty your name like that?"

Signs of distress cover Sheed's face. "I mean, I thought we was all right. It ain't like we knew each other for years. I met him down there."

"But why would a nigga make up something like that, though? That's some fucked up shit to put on a nigga."

Sheed's silence confirms the rumor. Darryl expected him to fly off the handle after hearing this. He has yet to say a word in his defense. "What's up?" Darryl whispers. "Is that true?" Sheed replies with a head nod. A single tear falls onto his lap. Darryl is caught off-guard by this. He peeks over at Sheed, whose face is now covered with embarrassment. A river of tears floods his eyelids, and Darryl has no clue what to say to him.

As they ride in silence, Darryl thinks of all the girls they have pulled a train on. His safety comes to mind. Anytime he went behind Sheed, he always wore a condom, but still, he's worried. He wonders how long he knew and if he purposely didn't tell him. His mind goes back to when people told him how Sheed never wore condoms. He wonders if that is the reason why he never wore them. Did he know all the while? Was he angry with his situation and taking it out on the world?

"But how?" Darryl asks. "When? When did you find out?"

"I found out when I got tested when I first got locked up. I never told nobody, but I guess the nurse must have told niggas. That has to be how the nigga O knew."

Darryl is uncomfortable with this whole conversation, but he has so many questions that he needs answers to. "Do you know who gave it to you?"

Sheed sighs. "Come on. You know I done fucked thousands of bitches. There is no way in the world I would be able to track down who gave it to me. I don't even wreck my brain and try. It could have been any one of those whores."

Darryl's heart is heavy. "Sheed, I'm sorry to hear this, man."

"Yeah, me too. I've been living with knowing this shit for three years now. When you think of AIDS, you think of filthy dope fiends!" he barks with rage. "You don't think of a fly motherfucker like me," he says as he shakes his head. "I've gotten a lot better with it, though. At first, I wanted to kill my fucking self," he says with disgust. "Now I learned just to charge it to the game."

Darryl's mind races rapidly. All the faces of women he's known Sheed to be with unprotected come into his mind. If he doesn't know when he contracted the disease, he could have infected many of them. Also, the faces of the new women that Sheed has just started dealing with since he's been home pops into Darryl's mind. He wonders if Sheed is telling them about his illness. He thinks it over and over until his curiosity takes over.

"Like," Darryl says with brief pausing afterward. "Like, now what?"

"What do you mean?" Sheed asks.

"I mean, now do you tell girls about that?"

"Hell no!" Sheed blurts out. "You crazy?"

"I mean, you don't think that's fucked up to put somebody life on the line with no warning?"

"Did the bitch who gave it to me give a fuck about putting my life on the line? Hell no, she didn't! Don't nobody out here give a fuck about me, man."

Darryl senses the bitterness in Sheed's voice. Darryl also realizes that before Sheed went to prison, he always said, 'don't nobody give a fuck about us out here.' Since he's been home, he says, 'don't nobody give a fuck about me.' Something about prison has changed his mindset. "Sheed, I give a fuck about you."

"I mean, outside of us," he revises.

"But that shit ain't right just to pass it on to a girl who has no clue."

"Man, fuck that shit. Life is one big gamble. This the game!"

-45-

One Month Later

Darryl is tossing and turning in the bed. He hasn't been able to sleep much for the past two weeks. Tomorrow starts Judgment Day. Bright and early, he has to stand before the judge and give his plea.

Things have been incredibly stressful for him. He often thinks of what life will be like for him if he's found guilty of the charges. He wonders what type of life he will have after coming home from doing a ten-year sentence. With his Nana being over seventy years old, he wonders whether she will even be alive when he comes home.

He wonders if she will be able to take care of herself without him around. He also wonders how he will break the news to her about going away for ten years. He's sure she will be heartbroken. He just hopes the broken heart doesn't lead to a heart attack.

Throughout all the stress of this case, Sunday's pressure just makes it worse. He's been doing an excellent job of staying away from her. Still, she pops up at his house some nights unexpectedly. She's been popping up less since Sal got out of the hospital.

The last time Darryl saw or talked to her was two days ago when she asked him for twenty-five hundred dollars to go shopping. Since the shooting of Sal, Sunday has doubled the amount she begs for. He knows she's trying to blackmail him, but still, he refuses to allow her to play him like that. He told her no, and all hell broke loose. He was all kinds of fronting ass niggas, and he was even invited to a meal at her private table when she told him to suck her pussy. Those were her last words to him before she hung up on him.

Lefty's words often come to mind as he thinks of the threats she continuously fires at him. Lefty has touched on that subject a couple more times. Darryl is at the point that he no longer vents about it for fear that he may make a move on his own. After hearing Lefty's life story, Darryl believes he could do something like that and not even miss a night of sleep afterward. On the other hand, he would probably never be able to sleep in peace again.

Last night as Darryl sulked in pity, he got the sudden urge to call Sunday. Deep down inside, he wanted nothing from her but mere sympathy. He called and called, but she failed to answer or return his calls. In his final message on her machine, he told her that tomorrow he starts trial and if she never sees him again, it's because he lost trial and won't be home for ten plus years.

Foolishly he expected her to return his call and show some compassion. He later realized he's a fool for even believing she would show compassion now when she's never shown any in all the years that he's known her. He realizes that he's wasted three years of his life with a woman who cares nothing about him. Now, as he stands at what could possibly be the end, he's standing all alone.

210

Darryl shakes his head as the grief settles in his heart. He throws the pillow over his face. "It's just me against the world." He sucks it up and charges it to the game.

-46-

The Next Day

THE HALL OF THE COURTHOUSE is busy. Darryl paces back and forth, a nervous wreck. Today has to be the scariest day of his life. He doesn't know exactly what an anxiety attack is, but he swears he's had at least two of them already.

Anger is coupled with his fear, making him a time bomb. His anger is a result of his foolishness. Foolishly he expected Sunday to call him this morning to accompany him. Even though he constantly tells her that they're not together, he expected her to still come and support him. She does everything that girlfriends do; come to the house unexpectedly and beg for money, but when it comes to him needing some support, she's nowhere to be found.

I can't believe this bitch didn't show up, thinks to himself. I took care of this bitch for three years, and this is what I get in return? This is some straight bullshit. But it's all good, though.

This is the all-time last draw for him. He understands that as much as he tells her they're not together, it hasn't sunk into either of their minds. He tells her

212

they're broken up, but she still comes to his house, preventing other girls from coming over. He tells her that they're no longer together, yet he still gets an attitude when she doesn't call, and he's forced to think that she's with Sal.

It's an outright mess that he has to sort out. He plans to sort it out sooner than later, though. He realizes there are a few steps he has to take to solve this problem. He figures the first step will be once he finds a new apartment. He figures if he's out of her sight, he will eventually be out of her mind. Then she will leave him alone to live his life.

The sound of the elevator interrupts the small conversation that he's having with himself. The elevator doors open up, but he continues to look out the window. The sound of footsteps behind him causes him to turn around. Boobie Salaam greets him. "What's up, Lil Bruh?" he says as he holds his hand high in the air.

Darryl's face lights up with joy. He had no clue that Boobie Salaam was coming, and seeing him makes Darryl believe that he really must care. "What's up?" Darryl asks as he returns the handshake. "Thanks for coming."

"Awl, man," Boobie Salaam replies. "No need for thanks. You, my Lil man. Why wouldn't I come through and show you some support?" He leans over and gives Darryl a reassuring thug hug. "Don't worry about it. We are going to be all right, Lil Bruh." He backs away from Darryl. "Where the hell is Ray at? You talked to him?"

"Yeah," Darryl replies. "He told me he would be here in five minutes, and that was a half-hour ago," he says with sarcasm.

"Let's go inside and wait for him," Boobie Salaam suggests. Darryl turns and stares at the double doors. Terror rumbles through his body as he thinks of what is on the other side of those doors. Although today is his first court date and nothing will happen today, he's still quite fearful. "Come on," Boobie Salaam says as he tugs at Darryl's suit jacket sleeve.

Darryl realizes today sets the tone for the rest of the court dates. He plans to make the best first impression he can. He looks down at his neatly pressed suit just to make sure everything is in order. He adjusts his tie and tucks his shirt in his pants before following behind Boobie Salaam.

Boobie Salaam holds the door open for Darryl to enter. He takes a long look at the old white-haired judge. The judge locks eyes with him and sends an arctic blast through his body. Darryl looks away from him nervously.

Before Darryl steps into the room, he takes a quick peek around. He notices that being in Superior Court is entirely different from Low court. The tension is so much thicker. He takes a deep breath as he steps into the room.

He peeks to his left, then his right. As he turns away, he does a double-take. He spots a familiar face sitting in the far corner of the room. Asia nods her head at him before lowering her head. He didn't even realize that she knew when his court date was. He figures he must have told her throughout the few conversations they've had over the weeks. How she knows doesn't matter to him, and what does matter is that she's here to support him.

He's surprised that she would come considering their standing is pretty much the same. The last heart-to-heart conversation they had was when he drove her home in the rain. Other than that, it has been basic hello and good-bye. Anytime he attempts to take it anywhere besides that, she finds a way to cut it short.

The double doors swing wide open, and Ray Brown enters the room. His aura demands respect, and his confident demeanor attracts the attention of everyone in the room. He struts over toward Darryl, causing everyone to now watch him. "Hey, son," he says, greeting Darryl. "You ready to play ball?"

An Hour Later

Darryl cruises up Market Street, leaving the downtown area. In his passenger's seat sits Asia. After pleading not guilty, another court date was assigned. Pleading not guilty to something he is guilty of wasn't that difficult to do with all that's on the line. He did it with a straight face that anyone would believe.

Darryl peeks over at Asia and as hard as it is to think of the love of his life pregnant by another man, it's even harder to actually view it. He's adjusted to it but it still is hard for him to look at her stomach and understand there's a baby inside. It's even harder for him to block out the thought of the act that put that baby inside her. He exhales a deep sigh of pain. "Like, what made you come, though?" Darryl asks.

"You didn't want me to?" Asia asks.

"Nah, it's not that. Don't get me wrong. I appreciate it. I just didn't expect it," he admits. "And how did you know it was today?"

"Didn't I tell you the streets don't have secrets? I can find out anything I want to know. Just like I found out all the things that I didn't want to know."

"I got you."

"I almost didn't show up," Asia says. "I didn't want to run into your gold-digging girlfriend. I figured laying back in the back of the courtroom, she wouldn't even notice lil' plain ol' me," she says as she looks away. "By the way, why didn't she come here with you?"

"Hmphh," he exhales loudly. "It ain't like you think," he claims.

"How is it then? Your freedom on the line, and she can't even come and support you? After all the money that you have spent on her?" she says with sarcasm.

"Come on, Asia. Knock it off," he says as he double parks in front of her house.

She pushes the door open. "The truth hurts, doesn't it?" she asks with a smile. "Do me a favor," she says as she gets out of the car. "Look back at all that has happened in the past three years and ask yourself was she worth it." She holds the door open. "It was supposed to be you and me until the end, but you ended our relationship to be in a relationship with a bitch that wasn't even relationship material. Later, Darryl!" she says as she closes the door in his face.

Darryl sits back, listening to her words echo in his head. How correct she is. It hurts that he allowed a woman to play him like this, and it hurts him more that Asia knows he allowed a woman to play him like this.

-47-

Two Weeks Later

IT'S EIGHT IN THE MORNING and Darryl walks out of his apartment with his eyes half-open from sleepiness. He's had a long night. The sun is blinding him. He tucks his hands in his sweatpants as he walks toward Boobie Salaam's car.

Darryl has just broken his number one rule inviting Boobie Salaam to his home. He regretted it the second after he gave him the address. He doesn't trust dudes knowing where he lives. The only reason he invited Boobie Salaam was because of his persistence.

Darryl explained that he would be out in an hour or so, but Boobie Salaam told him the news he had for him couldn't wait. He backed Darryl into the corner by not just asking his address but by accompanying that question with, 'What, you don't trust me? I thought we were bigger than that. I've invited you to my home several times.' Those statements left Darryl no alternative but to give up the address.

Darryl gets into the car with an angry look on his face. He hates to be awakened out of his sleep. He's so mad that he didn't even greet Boobie Salaam at his entrance. "What up to you too," Boobie Salaam says with sarcasm. "First and foremost, Lil Bruh, I understand you not wanting mufuckers to know where you rest and all," he says.

"But I ain't never going to be the one you got to worry about when it comes to shit like that. I'm a real mufucker all around the board. If you don't know, ask about me. Niggas vouch for me. My honor means everything to me. I never stole from nobody, and I don't owe nobody nothing. I'm a reputable dude. You ain't never gotta worry about me setting you up or no shit like that. I'm an earner. I work for mine, Lil Bruh."

"Nah, bro," Darryl says, covering his mouth. He doesn't want Boobie Salaam to enter the dragon and get a whiff of his morning breath. "It wasn't like that," he claims.

"Yeah, it was like that," he replies. "But no offense taken. Back to the subject at hand." His eyes light up with joy. "Lil Bruh, we on our way! We got our first fight coming up in six weeks."

"Word?" Darryl asks.

"Yeah, word! And guess what?" Boobie Salaam doesn't even give him time to ask what. "Guess where we fighting at? The fucking Garden!" he shouts.

"You bullshitting me?" Darryl asks.

"Now, don't go getting all excited like you going to be on television and shit. There are about ten fights on that card, with us being the least important. Unless every fight has a first-round knockout, and they have to put our fight on to kill time before the main event," he says, shaking his head, "then chances are we won't be seen."

For the first time throughout all of this, Darryl gets excited. He's dreamed of this day for many years. "It don't matter!" he shouts. "Just fighting at the Garden is enough for me, and I don't give a fuck if nobody is in the fucking audience."

"Now, ain't no real money involved. The fight ain't worth but four grand," he says with disappointment. "And twenty-five hundred of that is going to your opponent and his team. Six hundred is going to airfare for him, his trainer, and his cut man. Another four hundred and fifty go for hotels for them. By the time we feed them and send them on their way, we won't have a dime to split. But guess what? We will have our first win under our belt on a professional level."

"Hopefully," Darryl interjects.

"Hopefully, my ass. After giving this mufucker twenty-five hundred, if he's still standing after the first round, he won't make it back to Mississippi. I promise you that," he says with sincerity in his eyes.

"First round?" Darryl asks.

"Yep, first round. I told him I need him to fall no more than forty seconds into the first round. The crowd is going to be crazy over you. Knocking mufuckers out in the first round is going to create a hype for you that's out of this world."

"But that shit ain't gonna look phony?" he asks.

"Not at all. We are going to tell him what combination he is to fall after. Once he gets his cue, he knows what to do from there. Lil Bruh, we are there. We this close." He holds his fingers in the air. "Only you can fuck it up from here."

"What you mean?"

"You're walking on eggshells right now with that case over your head. That's a situation that we can't change right now, but we can make sure no new situations derive. At this point, I have to ask you to fall back from whatever it is that you're doing out there. I know that's a hard thing to do, but if boxing means to you what it means to me, I'm sure you can manage. I mean, shit may get tight for you after you spend the little money you got saved up," he says with arrogance. "If you got any savings," he adds.

Hearing this strikes Darryl's ego. "All that big-time talk, you can save that. I'm a quiet nigga, but I can make a lot of noise. Don't let my humble demeanor confuse you. I got real money. I can stop hustling today and still be all right for years to come."

"Nah, nah, I ain't saying you don't," Boobie Salaam replies.

"I can walk away from it all right now and still live comfortably."

"Then you should have no problem doing so. So, I got your word on it?"

"I can't give you my word on me stopping today, but I will give you my word on eventually trying to stop."

"Fair enough," Boobie Salaam replies. "So you got any questions?"

"As a matter of fact, I do. Since you are always speaking about integrity, honor, and loyalty, I'm sure you can understand where I'm coming from. I'm a loyal nigga myself, and Raheem and Charlie did teach me everything I know. You got a problem bringing them along with us?"

"Not at all," he replies immediately. "They can train you, and I will act as your promoter and your manager." He stares into Darryl's eyes. "You know, on the real. If you wouldn't have wanted to bring them along, I would have been forced to look at you other than honorable."

"And you know, if you would have had a problem with me bringing them along, I would have been forced to look at you other than honorable as well," says Darryl.

Boobie Salaam holds his hand in the air, and Darryl clasps it tightly. "We both know what the bottom feels like," Boobie Salaam says with a stern look in his eyes. "It's up from here!"

Darryl nods his head up and down. "For sure!"

-48-

A Taste of Texas Bar and Grill

MONEY DEE STANDS BEHIND the bar, pouring himself a drink. It's still abandoned, not even open for business. On the other side of the bar sits Darryl. He just followed Lefty here. Darryl is eager to get this meeting rolling. Lefty brought him here but excused himself. He told them he didn't want to be in the middle of business that didn't concern him. He's happy that he could finally connect the dots between the two of them.

"Lef told me a lot about you," Money Dee says. "It says a lot about you for him to bring you to me because he doesn't cosign nobody. Our relationship, our brotherhood is sacred, and for him to bring you into that, that's huge." He takes a sip of his drink. "To be honest with you, I never heard him speak so big about no man ever, except his father."

Darryl is honored to hear this. "It's crazy because he speaks highly of you as well."

"And that's why our bond or business relationship has to be valued and held as sacred because he has that trust and faith in the both of us," Money Dee says.

"I agree," Darryl replies.

"With all that out of the way, I just want to get right to the point. I ain't a man of much talking," he says before taking another sip. "I don't know how much you know of me, but when it comes to that snow, I control the forecast in this city. Most of the snow covering the streets in this Essex County comes from my hands. I'm Al Roker, the weatherman when it comes to that shit. I determine how much snow a city will get and what cities not gone get snow," he says with arrogance.

"With all that Lefty has told me about you, it's weird to me that me and you have never crossed paths until now. I heard you do well for yourself, but with me, you will do great. Them Dominicans you're dealing with, they are in the way. The only reason the Dominican even have a place in this game is because the Colombians are afraid to deal with us themselves.

They don't trust us and want no parts of us. They understand that the Dominican is safe. Safe enough for them to trust and close enough to us that they can deal with us. So, the Colombian puts the Dominican in the middle as the buffer. All they are, are point men, getting points in the middle and taxing us from the Colombians hands to theirs to ours."

They say when the student is ready, the teacher will appear. Right now, Darryl appreciates the tutorial. He always looked at the Dominican as the top of the food chain, but this lesson changed his perception.

"I've been in bed with the Mexicans the past ten years while everybody else been running to New York to get overcharged by the Dominicans. And that's why nobody can't touch me in this game. Mexicans are bringing everything through Texas. Remind me later, and I will show you pictures of my ranch house, better yet, my mansion down in Texas. Twenty-one bedrooms sitting on acres and acres," he brags. "I let my Mexicans crash there when they are in transit. Head of Cartels, and they are like brothers to me. I'm welcome in their home with their wife and children, and so are they to mine."

Money Dee paces circles behind the bar. He takes another swig of his drink. "It's only like three or four Dominicans who supply the whole Washington Heights, Spanish Harlem, and all four of them don't have access to the amount of coke I have access to. And mark my word, all that is about to change over there in the next couple of years. Mexicans have taken control of the cocaine marketplace. All them Dominicans who have been depending on Colombians will be done! The Mexicans used to be under the Colombians, the Colombians using them as mules and workers. They overturned the situation, and now they have their own franchises."

He takes another sip from his glass. "All that is neither here nor there right now," he says. "Lef brought you to me like his brother, so I will carry you like my brother. I get the joints for fourteen thousand a unit. I normally move the units for nineteen to twenty, but I will treat you like a brother since you were brought to me like a brother. I will give them to you for fifteen and a half, only scoring a point and a half in the middle."

Darryl listens, and his head is spinning. Getting pure coke straight from the cartel at the same numbers as the cheapy-choppa would take his game to another level. Excitement takes over him, yet he keeps his cool. He doesn't want to show his excitement and blow an opportunity.

"It doesn't hurt me none because it's obvious that our movements don't intertwine or collide in no way, no how. But," he says as he holds one finger in the air. "I have a required minimum of twenty units. I'm not above consignment either since you came in through family. But on the front, I got to put some grease on it. I got to add some more points on top.

"I'm keeping it real with you and letting you know why I'm willing to bring you in and only score a point and a half in the middle. For me, it's all about purchasing power. It's a few niggas I rock with who have their money in the bag. My money with your $300,000 and this nigga half a mill and that nigga seven hundred thousand put me in a position of power with my Mexicans. Now on the streets, due to the numbers we are getting it at, we all will be powerful in our own right," he explains.

"The benefit for me is making the connect value me and respect my worth. All of us together in collaboration makes me look stronger, which makes us stronger. It gives us more opportunities and more work. The more buy money I bring to the table, the more they are willing to dump on me. And that's the real deal," he says while shrugging his shoulders.

"I go to these people with five or six million cash they will throw me ten million worth of work on consignment."

Darryl's mind is working. Ignorantly, he had thought that he had arrived and was at the top floor of the drug game. And to find out now that there are a couple more floors up that he never even thought about. His mind never really went past the level that he's at. Arrogantly, he thought he was a big fish when in all reality, he's just a regular size fish in a tiny ass pond, and that's what makes him appear so big.

"And that's why I don't mind giving it to you for the price they give it to me plus transport cost. The larger my capacity, the more potential there is for your growth. At fifteen and a half, you can hit the poppy nigga who's been hitting you," he says coupled with a smile.

"You can give it to him for seventeen and beat the number he is getting it for. They're only dragging a point or two in the middle, that's it. They're nobody but point men. And trust me, they will be looking for work real soon because the Mexicans are on the rise, and they are about to ice the Dominicans out. When they had the ball, they didn't play fair, and now the Mexicans got the ball," he says with a smile.

Money Dee makes his way around the bar. "So, what you wanna do? Do you want to buy your way into this network, or do you want to keep getting pimped by the Dominican? All your hard work goes unnoticed while the Dominican gets all the perks and the accolades. The more coke you buy, the more the Colombian looks out for him. And the Dominican never reciprocates the love to you, and he just keeps his foot on your neck. Over here, it's nothing but opportunity, room for growth. With the Dominican, there's always that ceiling over your head."

Darryl thinks long and hard. All of this sounds like a dream come true. "I gotta tell you, I appreciate you for even sitting here and having this conversation with me," Darryl says. These are his first words. He's just been sitting quietly with his ears wide open. "Let alone the opportunity you are willing to give me."

Darryl sits quietly, just trying to choose the right words. "But as far as all of that, I'm cool with that. I came here looking for a way out." Darryl can't even believe that he just turned down the opportunity of a lifetime. Lately, the signs seem to have been coming to him from every direction. The walls seem to be closing in on him, and he feels he needs to stop while he can.

First, the cop tells him he's throwing rocks at the penitentiary. Then came Lefty's warnings. After that, Boobie Salaam comes and tells him how close they are.

He just feels like now is the time to take a step back before it's too late. All of that has him thinking that he needs to find an escape route. With this golden opportunity just presented to him, he knows he will only dig himself deeper in the quicksand. "I need an exit strategy."

Money Dee takes a seat right next to Darryl. "Well, in that case, I have one of those, actually quite a few of those too," he says as he plants his hand on Darryl's shoulder. "And actually, you're sitting in one of them. This spot right here is my newest project. I'm about to take this to the next level. Me and a couple of good men got our money in the bag together, and we're going to blow this thing up. It's the same mentality with this as it is with the other shit. You can invest with us on this."

Darryl exhales a sigh of relief. He was worried that by rejecting his proposal, he wouldn't be willing to deal with him on anything else. He's grateful that isn't the case. He's all ears.

"I'm more than willing to open up my whole hand to you," Money Dee says. "My whole layout, floor plans, blueprints, architectural designs, business strategy, marketing plans, shareholders percentages, and even the amount each investor has invested. I can't share the names because this is all confidential. At the end of the day, you know where we all come from, and nobody trying to open their hands for the world to see."

"I get it," Darryl says.

"I just need you to understand that this ain't no overnight success thing. I always like to explain because street niggas sometimes don't understand business. Unlike the coke and dope game, where you can get a return on your investment in a couple of days, this ain't that. The money you put in can take a couple of years to get a return on it. That's why I suggest if you don't really have it or if you need it to live off, don't even attempt to make this move."

Darryl's arrogance kicks in. He chuckles. "I hear you."

"But when this thing does blow, it's going to blow sky high. This is just the beginning, though. I've built an investment team, all good niggas like myself and you, and together we will take some shit over. "So, you're in or not?"

Darryl looks over. "I told you I came here looking for an exit strategy, and you just gave me one. Why wouldn't I be in?"

Money Dee reaches over, and they shake hands firmly. "Welcome to the next level of the game."

-49-

Three Days Later

SHEED SITS AT THE KITCHEN table inside Darryl's apartment. He can view the majority of the apartment right from where he's seated. Sheed watches each step Darryl makes closely, for he has no clue why he's been called here. Darryl has the cupboard doors stretched wide open as he fumbles around on the top shelf. He stacks a total of twelve kilos on the counter before shutting the cupboard's doors. Sheed watches as Darryl makes his way to the closet. He reaches inside and retrieves a small duffle bag.

After dumping the duffle bag on the kitchen table, he runs into his bedroom area. He opens the lid on his dirty clothes hamper and digs inside. He stands up, holding another small duffle bag. Darryl walks back over to Sheed and dumps this bag onto the table too.

He then walks over to the countertop and grabs the stack of kilos. He walks over and drops them on the table before taking a seat across from Sheed. He stares him square in the eyes for a few seconds before taking a deep breath. Darryl sticks his hands inside one of the duffle bags, and he lays a total of twenty-five stacks of money on top of the table.

"This twenty-five grand right there," he says as he digs into the other duffle bag. He dumps a total of six handguns on the table before dumping the big boy assault rifle.

Sheed becomes a tad bit nervous as he eyes the guns Darryl has laid out before him. As long as they have been friends, Sheed still feels a little uneasy around Darryl right now. When he witnessed Darryl gun Sal down, he saw a side of him that he had never before witnessed. It almost makes him feel as if he no longer knows Darryl and what he's capable of.

Darryl lays the AK-47 gently on the table. Sheed looks at the guns with amazement. "Nine millimeter," Darryl says as he slides the gun over to Sheed. "Three fifty-seven long," he says, sliding this gun over to him. "Thirty-eight special." He hands it to Sheed. "And my favorite, the forty-five Ruger, eleven shots. This my heart, right here," he says as he pulls it closer to him. "She stays right here."

"This right here is my big bitch," he says, grabbing the gun, which looks like a revolver on steroids. He admires the Desert Eagle from every angle before putting it down. "This my bottom bitch right here." He grabs the assault rifle from the table. He aims the AK-47 at the wall over Sheed's head. "When all these other bitches fail me, I know I can count on her to do the job. This bitch right here clears everything up," he says with a smile.

Darryl lays the AK and the Desert Eagle on the floor before dumping the other guns back into the duffle bag. He pushes the bag over to Sheed while staring into his eyes. He then grabs the top 2 kilos off the stack of twelve. He hands the kilos over to Sheed. He slides the money over, all twenty-five thousand. "Here," he says. "From me to you. A gift as a token of my appreciation for all the game you gave me," Darryl says sincerely.

"I know I said that I wanted you to wait until you got out of the halfway house, but there's been a change of plans. I don't plan on being around that long."

"Where are you going?" Sheed asks.

"Physically, nowhere," he replies. "But mentally, I have to get away. I've been doing some real thinking lately. You know, about this case and shit. If I'm found guilty, I can face ten years," he says with a look of sorrow on his face. "My lawyer said we got a good chance at beating it through technicalities, but there's always that chance that I may not. I just feel like I need to pump my brakes a little to avoid getting in any more trouble."

"So, you leaving the game?" Sheed asks. "Jail comes with this shit. When a nigga step out on them streets, he should know that there's a chance that he may go to prison."

"Yeah, true," Darryl agrees. "But when is enough? You have to know when to walk away. The game has been good to me. In three years, I gained more than most niggas get an entire lifetime out on those streets," he boasts. "I'm good!"

"But I ain't good. What about me? Or that don't matter to you?"

"Of course, it matters to me. That's why I'm setting you up with all the tools you need. The trifecta," he says with a smile. "You got money, and you got work to generate more money, and you got artillery to protect the money. And I'm leaving you the block. A goldmine with all the manpower in position. The whole North Pole is yours." Darryl catches himself and pauses for a second.

"Well, it was yours from the start. *The Location*, you're the pioneer of that." Sheed is the one who named the block The Location from the beginning of it. "It was built on your blood, sweat, and tears. It was your brainchild. I just cleaned up the reputation of it and gave it a face-lift. Now sixty grand come through there a day. A bird and a half fly through there on a bad day. Seventy-five to eighty grand profit a week," he says proudly.

Sheed's eyes widen with excitement. He likes the sound of what Darryl is saying, and all he can see in his future is his come-up. With the numbers Darryl is spitting at him, he figures he should be M'd up in ninety days, four months tops.

"I'm fading away into the backdrop," says Darryl. "I'm just going to serve my wholesale customers just to keep the bills paid. All touch and go shit with less risk. I'm focusing on this boxing game. I got something huge in motion too. In about three years, I figure I should be able to live off of boxing and my other play. I got enough bread to carry me through until then."

"Damn," Sheed replies. "You must be more than good if you can live off of your savings for three years. The game must have really been good to you."

Darryl shrugs his shoulders with a grin. "I gave you the blueprint. Play the game right, and it will be as good to you as it's been to me. You got the game in your hands," he says as he stands up and reaches for a handshake.

Sheed stands up and gives Darryl a firm handshake before hugging him. The hug is so tight Darryl can feel Sheed's gratefulness through it. "Yo, you have no idea how much I appreciate you for doing this and all that you have done for me since I been back," he says with sincerity spilling from his eyes. "I'm super proud of you and all that you have become, and I promise you I'm going to make you proud of me too. You just gave me all the tools to get to the top. Give me one year and I will meet you there."

-50-

Essex County College

DARRYL AND ASIA WALK SIDE by side down the school hallway. For the first time in a long time, Asia has cracked a smile for him. It's been so long that he forgot how beautiful a smile she has. Her smile to him is a good sign.

"You know," he says as he keeps his eyes on the floor ahead of him. "I've been thinking hard about something you said to me."

"And what is that something?" she asks curiously.

"You asked me what you're gonna tell your baby when the time comes that he or she asks you where their father is," he says with a nervousness written all over his face.

"And what is it that you're thinking about it?"

"What if you never have to answer that question?"

"Why wouldn't I have to answer the question? Every child wants to know who their father is."

"Yes," he agrees. "That is if they have reason to ask, meaning they don't know their father. With me around, the child would have no reason to ask that question," he whispers.

"I'm not getting what you're saying."

Darryl holds the door open for her to exit. She does, and he follows right behind her. "Asia, what I'm saying is if you just give me another chance, we will never have to explain to the child what happened to the father, and I will be all the father the child needs."

Asia walks in silence as the words play in her head repeatedly. She can't believe that he's even made a gesture like that, and she really can't believe that he would even be willing to do such a thing. "So, you think that lying to my child is the answer?" she asks with an agitated look on her face. "You think that's going to solve the problem?"

"It would be lying only if the truth ever came out. We may never have to face that problem. In the case that we do, we deal with it when the time comes," he says as he walks toward his car, which is parked directly at the end of the ramp. Asia just follows behind without saying a word.

A few Feet Away

"Roz, look!" Sheila shouts from the driver's seat of her Acura as she points across the street.

"What am I looking at?" Roselyn questions as her eyes scan the entire area.

"Right there." She points across the street. "That's Darryl walking with a pregnant bitch."

Roselyn's mouth drops wide open. She's speechless. "Yep, it sure is. Real pregnant, like any day pregnant. Uhmm hmm," she utters. "Hold up," she says. "Pull over right there. Let's see where they're going. Maybe he's just walking with her." Sheila pulls over and parks a few feet ahead. They both turn around in their seats, watching like police on a stake-out.

* * * * *

"So, what do you think about that idea?" Darryl asks as he opens the passenger's door for her.

"I'm not even considering it," Asia says as she sits down.

Darryl hops into the driver's seat, starts the engine, and pulls off without taking notice of Sheila and Roselyn watching his every move.

* * * * *

"Nah," Roselyn says. "A nigga just don't be driving another nigga's pregnant bitch around. They just don't do that," she insists. "Wait until Sunday hears this shit!"

Twenty Minutes Later

Darryl pulls up to the block. He just got an emergency call from Sheed. He tried to get him to wait until he dropped Asia off, but Sheed insisted he needed him this minute. He wouldn't take later as an answer.

Darryl spots Sheed standing at the corner. He stops at the end of the block. His purpose for parking so far away is because he doesn't want Sheed to see Asia. They haven't seen each other in years, and he's sure that Sheed will want to come and talk to her.

Darryl gets out and walks toward Sheed. As he gets closer to Sheed, he spots a goofy and playful look on his face. He knows when Sheed is in a playing mood, and right now, he's not in that type of mood. Sheed starts making his way to Darryl. "Why the fuck you park all the way back there?" Sheed asks with a smile. "What you up to, nigga?" he asks as he tries to pass by Darryl.

Darryl grabs him by the arm. "Cut it out. What's up? What was so important that it couldn't wait?"

"Oh," Sheed says with a big smile. "You got somebody in the car that you don't want me to see, huh?" He smiles. "Must be Sunday," he laughs. "Told you, you wasn't done with her." He takes big steps toward the car.

Darryl follows close behind, trying to pull Sheed back, but he snatches away from him and jogs toward the car. "Who that?" he asks. "Is that Asia? Oh shit!" he says as he picks up his pace. "Asia!" he yells through the closed window.

She flashes a smile as she hits the power window button. "What's up, girl!" he shouts as he sticks his head in the window. He kisses her on the cheek, happy to see her.

"Whoa," he says as his eyes land on her huge stomach. Confusion settles on his face. "Damn," he says with a smile. "I didn't know you was pregnant." He looks back at Darryl, and his facial expression goes from confused to sour-looking. "Damn, D, you didn't even tell me y'all was pregnant." He turns back toward Asia.

Darryl shakes his head from side to side, signaling her not to say a thing. The last thing he wants is to explain all of this to Sheed. Also, with him hoping that things are working out for him and Asia, he wouldn't want Sheed to look at him differently. He's sure he would look at him like a sucker to even be willing to pretend to be the father of another man's baby.

"Congrats, Asia!" he says as he walks away from the car. Sheed stands face to face with Darryl. "Damn, dog, how are you not going to tell me that? I'm your best friend, dog. At least I thought," he says with a saddened look on his face.

Darryl wishes he had a legitimate answer for Sheed, but he doesn't. He just stands with a silly look on his face. "What's up, though?" he asks as he attempts to change the subject.

Sheed shakes his head from side to side and sighs with disappointment. He doesn't understand how this conversation never came up. "My man got some niggas from Plainfield at his house, and they trying to buy three birds. I need you to grab that as soon as you can," he says as he walks away from Darryl.

Darryl watches Sheed walk away. He knows how crazy this all may seem to Sheed right now, but the sad part is he's not willing to tell the truth, to clear it up. Darryl turns around slowly, and with his head hanging low, he walks to his car. *There are just certain things that certain people will never understand, Darryl thinks to himself. And this just happens to be one of those things.*

-51-

Later That Night

AFTER RECEIVING BACK-TO-BACK calls from Sunday all day long, Darryl finally gets annoyed enough to answer. "What, what, what?" he barks in an agitated tone. "Why the fuck are you calling my phone like you crazy?"

"Crazy? You haven't seen crazy yet, you no good motherfucker! You done went and had a fucking baby on me?"

Darryl has no clue what she's talking about. "What the fuck are you talking about now?"

"Oh, you're playing stupid, huh? You know what the fuck I'm talking about! I saw you with your lil' midget, fat ass baby mother earlier. I should have jumped out and beat her ass!" she barks with rage.

He replays his day in his head and realizes that she must have seen him somewhere today with Asia. But where he can't figure out. He only drove from the school to her house, so he can't figure out how he was seen. "What the fuck are you talking about?" he asks again. These seem to be the only words that he has.

"You dumb ass nigga! You know what the fuck I'm talking about! You can play stupid if you want, though. Laugh now, cry later, bitch! I'm gone get the last laugh this time. I got something for yo' ass," she threatens.

"Do you realize that I'm the last bitch that you should ever cross? Do you, you dumb motherfucker? You don't cross a bitch that could ruin your life. I know shit that I'm sure the police and even the Feds would love to hear. I got enough information stored in my brain to get yo' ass the electric chair, you dumb motherfucker!"

"What?" Darryl asks. If only she could see the tight look on his face through the phone.

"Don't what me, motherfucker! Do you know why Italians don't believe in divorce, you dumb motherfucker? Let me tell yo' dumb ass why! Because their wives know too much. When a bitch knows all your deepest, darkest secrets, you don't ever let that bitch out of your sight. You would rather kill that bitch than have her go against you. If you weren't such a dumb ass nigga you would know better."

"Listen, you better stop threatening me," he says with fury in his voice. One thing he hates is to be threatened. He quickly thinks of Lefty, who has been telling him this all the while. "Threat? You dumb motherfucker, this ain't no threat." She chuckles. "This is a promise, bitch. I promise you if you think that you will live happily ever after, with your lil' fat ass baby mother, you got another thing coming. And you can take that how the fuck you want to take it. We are going to see who gets the last laugh, bitch! I got something for you and that bitch!" she says before ending the call.

-52-

One Week Later

DARRYL CRUISES ALONG Market Street with Asia in the passenger's seat. This is the first time she's been in the car with him since he was last spotted with her. He scans the area cautiously, just to see if he's being watched again. He feels like he and Asia are making so much progress. The last thing he needs right now is Sunday to pop out of nowhere and cause a scene, and that will set him so far back, if not blow his chances altogether.

"Where are you going?" Asia asks. She notices he's made a detour.

"Sit back and chill. I'm tired of you treating me like some stranger, too. Just be cool." He turns onto Central Avenue. Less than ten minutes later, he makes the right onto Mount Prospect.

"Darryl, I'm not playing with you. You were supposed to be taking me home. Where are you going?"

He makes a quick left in the middle of the block, and he parks directly in front of a tall building. "Come on," he says.

"Come on, where?" she questions.

"Just come on...damn," he barks as he pushes the door open. As he's getting out, the valet attendant runs to her door and opens it for her. She wiggles her way to the edge of the seat. The attendant reaches his hand inside and struggles to pull her out of the car.

As they walk into the building, she admires the scenery. Brass trimming and glass mirrors fill the lobby. The abundance of mirrors plays on her insecurities. She lowers her head so that she doesn't have to look at herself.

Darryl holds the elevator door open for her. The elevator begins to ascend, and her stomach bubbles with queasiness. The elevator stops, and the doors open on the twentieth floor. "Come on," Darryl says as he holds the door open for her to exit.

Directly across from the elevator, Darryl stops. He sticks the key inside, opens it, and holds the door wide open. He gives her a head nod signaling for her to go inside. She steps inside, and Darryl closes the door shut behind them.

Asia looks around in awe. She has never seen such a beautiful apartment. The hardwood floors and shiny new appliances are different from the raggedy home she grew up in. She looks upward, staring at the high ceilings.

This is Darryl's new apartment. After Sunday's threat to him, he could barely sleep in the old apartment. A part of him doesn't believe she would do anything, but he can't take any chances with her. One thing he knows is a scorned woman is a dangerous woman.

"What do you think?" he asks.

She hesitates before replying. "It's nice for you," she says as if she isn't the least bit impressed. "I guess."

"Nice for me? But is it nice for us?" he asks as he steps in front of her. He stares her in the eyes for seconds before she lowers her head bashfully. "I didn't get this just for me. I got this for us. This is our new apartment."

"No, Darryl, this is your apartment."

He grabs hold of her hands and clasps them firmly. "But you said you would think about us working on it. Didn't you say that?"

"Yes," she whispers. "But I haven't thought it out yet. It's a lot, Darryl. A lot has changed in both of our lives, and we aren't the same kids in love anymore."

"No, we're not. We're both adults who have been through some things, and those things we both have learned from. Now we are both mature and understand what this thing is about. All that we have been through will only make our bond tighter. Neither one of us will have the urge to fuck up because we both have fucked up making the wrong decisions in life. My choices are as vital to me as yours are to you. Neither one of us have any room to slip.

He places his finger under her chin and lifts her head. "Asia, don't blow this for us. Come here," he says as he drags her with him. They stop at a closed door at the end of the hall, and Darryl forces the door open. "Look," he says as he points into the room. "This could be the baby's room."

Tears drip from her eyes. "No, Darryl, no," she cries. "We can't do this. I can't do this," she says as she sobs.

"Do what, Asia?"

"I could never move in this apartment with you while I'm pregnant with another man's baby. How disrespectful is that to you and him?" she cries. "I'm not that kind of woman, and you know that," she sobs.

"That would make me feel like some type of slut or whore. Do you realize I can't even look you in the eyes out of embarrassment of you seeing me pregnant?

It feels crazy standing in your presence after all the years of dreaming of being pregnant by you. Now the vision is playing out, but you're not the father," she says. "If I can't even look you in the eyes, how can I sleep in the same bed with you? Me, carrying another man's baby and laying up next to you," she says. "How does that look?"

Tears fill his eyes as well. "I respect that, Asia," he says as he holds her hands. "Well, we can just wait to move in after you have the baby. You only got two more months to go, and I got three more months left on my lease. After you have the baby, we can both officially move in."

"Darryl, how the fuck do you even know that you can deal with that?" she spits from her mouth. "You're just saying things that you think I want to hear. This isn't a game that we're playing, Darryl. This is my life." She weeps. "How do you know that five years from now, you may come to your senses and realize that you don't want to play daddy to another man's child? How do you know for sure that you can handle that?" she asks as more tears well up in her eyes.

"You're making promises to me that you don't even know if you can keep. What if I jump out there and open myself up to you, and you hurt me again as you did three years ago? Only now, it won't be just me that you're hurting. It will be a baby that you told me to lie to and say you're the father. When you cheat on me the next time, I will be forced to tell my baby the truth. It's just too much for me to think about," she cries. "It's too much pressure."

He places his hands on her face, cradling her head. They stand face to face for seconds before he gets his voice together to speak. Both of their faces are covered with tears. "Asia, yeah, I fucked up three years ago. By me fucking up, a series of things came into play. You asked me how I can be sure that I'm ready to play daddy? You know I've never been a daddy. I will learn to be a daddy just like you have to learn to be a mother.

And I'm not going to lie to you, of course, it's going to play in my mind in the beginning that it's not my child, and I pray in time that I won't think about it at all. And you're right, I don't know if I can handle it. All I know is I'm willing to give it a shot to make this relationship work.

Asia, I fucked this relationship up, and I'm just grateful to be standing here with you hearing me out, and even considering giving me another shot. I fucked up then, but I promise you I will never fuck up again. I swear," he repeats.

"Not one of those teenage promises that mean nothing," he says. "This promise is from an adult who has been through some things and understands how real shit is out here. An adult who understands that when you have someone who truly loves you for you, you don't give that up for anything. I learned my lesson," he cries. "The hard way! We both fucked up by letting the love of our lives go. Now it's time to fix what we fucked up. Pick up from where we left off and live happily ever after."

He clasps her hands tightly. "Now, Asia, tell me, right here, right now," he says with piercing eyes. "Are you willing to work on our relationship? You got two months to finish out this pregnancy, and after that, we move into our apartment *together*. Are you willing?" he asks as he stares into her tear-filled eyes.

She buries her face into his chest and cries like a baby. He backs away from her and lifts her head once again. "Answer me. Are you?"

She nods her head up and down, with her eyes fixed on the floor. "Yes," she whispers. "As crazy as it may sound, Yes, I am."

-53-

Weeks Later

AFTER HOURS AT THE AUTO mechanic shop, all the workers are gone. Money Dee called Lefty over to come to meet with him. Money Dee paces as he usually does, just putting his thoughts together while Lefty leans back in a reclining office chair. He's known him forever, so he knows all about him and his thought process. He's a thinker who takes his time with every thought.

Finally, Money Dee speaks. "Threw the line out there about your Lil man, and I got the results back." Disappointment is plastered all over his face.

"And what were the results?"

"He's cased up right now and facing some time."

"Yeah, I told you all about that. A gun and some drugs."

"Yeah, but I didn't know it was that serious, though. Shit has been on my mind, crazy. I'm not feeling good about this," he says with signs of worry in his eyes. "He might be bad for the brand," he says as he walks off.

Lefty watches his every step, just waiting for him to speak again. "My concern comes from the fact that

I opened my whole hand up to him. I trusted you on this one and brought him in like family. I held no secrets from the kid. Now, I'm sitting here thinking that may have been a bad idea." Money Dee stares at the ceiling in deep concentration.

Finally, he turns around and looks back at Lefty. "I even took money from the kid, and it's kind of like too late for me to turn back. If by chance he's working, I'm fucked because I took the money. It was on a legitimate deal, but he can easily turn it around on me and say it was for illegal activity. Even if he doesn't, he could get me wrapped up in a money laundering case. Either way, as I said, it's bad for the brand."

"Oh no, hell no," Lefty snaps. "That kid is solid as a rock. You know I'm a good judge of character, and he don't have no greaseball shit in him. Honest Abe type of dude. Good nigga from the bottom of his heart."

"Good niggas go bad too, though, Lef."

"Ay bruh, listen, if I thought he had hoe in him, I would've never brought him your way. As a matter of fact, I would've never befriended him."

"I know for a fact you wouldn't do that to me," Money Dee says. "Just something in my heart is telling me that this one got past you."

Money Dee starts pacing again. Lefty has never seen his pacing session last this long, and he doesn't like it. The silence is giving him time to doubt his decision-making. Could he be right? Could Darryl have gotten one over on him and played victim just to reel him in? He gets angered for a second before he talks himself out of it. Then he rethinks it and gets angered again. Money Dee's silence is sending Lefty's mind on a roller coaster ride. Money Dee turns around slowly. "I should've gone with my first mind, but I trusted in you. Now, I know I won't be able to sleep until this isn't on my mind anymore."

Lefty doesn't like where this is going. "Money, listen."

"Nah, Lef, feel me on this. This can bring not just me down but a whole bunch of others. We can't let the trust I had in you and you making a bad decision cost everybody like that." He takes a seat against the hood of a car directly across from Lefty, and he looks Lefty in the eye without batting an eyelash. "Lef, great leaders don't make tough decisions because we want to. We make them because we have to." He exhales slowly. "I got fifty grand for you if you make this problem go away."

"Nah, Money, hell nah. This Lil kid has been none less than a little brother to me. I know he's solid, and I will put my life on him."

"Ok, it's obvious you have a soft spot for this kid. So soft that you can't do what you know needs to be done for the safety of this brand. I got fifty grand for you for turning your good eye, and I will get somebody else to do it. It won't be on your hands, and you still walk away with fifty grand. Lef, it's for the safety and the future of this brand. Fifty and you turn your good eye?"

-54-

Hall of Fame Boxing Club

Darryl is drained from the extreme two-hour workout. After a seven-round sparring match with a man from New York, Boobie Salaam gave Darryl six rounds of pad work. Darryl assumed that was the end of the workout, but Boobie Salaam had more work cut out for him. He instructed Darryl to get back into the ring. Darryl is just two days away from his professional debut fight, and Boobie Salaam wants him to look his absolute best.

Darryl stares at the heavy steel door, and he barely has the strength to open it. "Yo, Lil Bruh!" Boobie Salaam shouts out from the back of the gym. Darryl turns around toward him. "Make sure you get a lot of rest tomorrow! And remember, no sex!" he shouts with a stern look on his face. "For the next forty-eight hours, breathe easy! It's showtime!"

"Got you!" Darryl shouts back as he struggles to pull the door open. He struggles even more, to pull it closed behind him. He drags himself across the sidewalk. The huge duffle bag on his shoulder feels as if it weighs a ton.

He stands at the curb as the traffic passes him. Once the cars stop, he creeps across the street. He hits his alarm, and the lights brighten up the area. After dropping the gym bag into the trunk, he hops into the driver's seat.

He sighs with great relief. It feels so good sitting here that he doesn't feel like moving. He's sure he could sleep for hours right here. After a few minutes, he gets himself together and musters up enough energy to back out of the parking lot. He rolls the windows down to allow the wind to blow in his face, hoping it will keep him awake.

He blasts the volume of his stereo, and the voice of Tupac, rapping *Straight Ballin* rips through his eardrums. He sings along loudly as he races down Central Avenue. *"I'm up before the sunrise, first to hit the block. Little bad motherfucker with a pocket full of rocks. Learn to throw them thangs, got my lil skinny ass kicked. And niggas laugh, 'til the first motherfucker got blasted. I put that nigga in his casket. Now they are covering the bastard in plastic,"* he sings as the song gives him a burst of energy. This is one of his favorite songs, and he tells himself this song had to be made for him.

Up a few feet ahead, he spots the traffic light, which has just turned yellow. He would hate to get caught at the light and have to sit for three minutes. That's just enough time for him to fall asleep at the wheel. So instead of slowing down, he speeds up. The light turns red while he's a few feet away from the corner, but still, he mashes the gas pedal.

"Got a 45 screaming out survival!" he says while waving his free hand in the air. He busts a quick left onto First Street. *"And they say how do you survive weighing 165 in a city where the skinny niggas die?"* Heavy horn blowing sounds from the car in front of him that has just barely missed hitting the front of his car.

Darryl speeds along First Street like a NASCAR driver. *"Tell mama don't cry, cause even when they kill me, they can never take the game from a young G!"* He eats two more red lights. "I'm straight balling!" He makes a left onto Orange Street.

"Oh shit." he sighs as he studies his rearview mirror. The black Suburban with the police lights in the grill tells him that he's eaten one too many red lights. "Got damn! Fucking Auto Squad!" he says as he continues to make his way toward the ramp. "Damn, I could take these mufuckers for a ride," he says to himself as he thinks about it.

Nah, he thinks to himself as he analyzes the situation. This special force doesn't play fair. Their goal is to bring culprits in by any means necessary. You can come in willingly, or they will ram you into a building and take you in unwillingly. He would take them for a ride any other time, but he doesn't have the energy for it right now.

As he gets onto the 280 West ramp, the Suburban pulls up to his bumper with the lights flashing. "Psst, motherfuckers." he sighs as he steps on the brakes and lifts the gear into Park. He turns the stereo off, flips the middle console open, and quickly retrieves his paperwork. He throws both hands high in the air, out of the window, so they are visible.

He watches through his side mirror as the driver hops out of the truck. "Damn," he mumbles to himself as he sees the width of the man's shoulders. Standing at the height of about five feet, eleven inches, he's about the size of a standard doorway. They say that black makes you appear smaller than you are, but not in this case.

Even dressed in all black, his monstrous size still can't be camouflaged. He's dressed in a black army field jacket, black cargo pants, and black boots. A black skull cap covers his head. As the cop moves towards the car, his partner hops out behind him.

The policeman stands at Darryl's door. "License, registration, and insurance," the cop says in a demanding tone. Darryl stares into the man's eyes as he hands the paperwork over to him. The stern look the cop shoots Darryl is enough to freeze him.

To break the chill, he lowers his eyes to the badge that's dangling from the man's neck. Darryl's attention is diverted to the passenger's door, which is snatched open by the other cop. He doesn't say a word as he reaches over and grabs the key out of the ignition.

"Mr. Lowe," the officer says as he reads from the license. "You late for a wedding or a funeral?" he asks with sarcasm. "You had to be going at least ninety miles an hour. And you ran through three of my red lights with no regard."

Darryl looks away with a silly look on his face. There's nothing that he can say that will justify his actions. "You're right, sir. I'm not even going to insult you with a bullshit excuse. I was completely wrong." He watches the stone-cold look on the cop's face melt.

"Thank you," the cop says with sincerity in his eyes. "I appreciate that. Where are you coming from?"

"The gym, sir."

"What gym?" the cop asks.

"The gym on Roseville Avenue, Sir. I'm a boxer," he says as he looks into the cop's eyes. He hopes this will change the dynamics of this situation.

"A boxer? What, amateur?"

"No, sir. I'm a professional boxer, sir."

"Oh, ok, Mr. Lowe," he says as he reads from the license. "First and foremost, is there anything in this car that we should know about?" he questions. "Drugs or guns?"

"No, sir," Darryl replies without hesitation.

"Ok, since you didn't insult my intelligence, I will take your word for it. I'm going to go back here and run your license. If everything comes back clean, you will be free to go. You don't have no warrants, do you?"

"Nope," Darryl says with certainty.

"You got legitimate insurance, right? This ain't no fake card, right?"

"No, sir."

"You ever been locked up before?"

Darryl hesitates before replying. Telling the truth about this can change everything. "No, sir," he says with false confidence in his voice.

"Ok," he says as he walks back to the Suburban. Darryl watches as the man talks into his radio, and his partner stands next to him.

"God, please don't let my new charge show up," he begs. "Please?"

Both cops come walking back towards Darryl's car in no time at all. His heart is pounding, but still, he tries to keep calm. "Mr. Lowe," the cop says as he snatches the door open. "Please step out of the vehicle," he demands.

"Huh? For what?" Darryl asks as he's dragged out of the seat. The cop turns Darryl around with brutal force. He slams his hands on the roof of the car before clipping him at the ankles. He uses his foot to spread Darryl's feet apart. "What's the problem, sir?" Darryl asks with nervousness. The cop frisks him from head to toe without responding. "Sir, what's the problem?"

The sound of the handcuffs clinging together startles Darryl. He looks over his shoulder. "Sir, what did I do?" he asks.

The cop mashes Darryl's head against the roof of the car before cuffing his hands behind his back. "Darryl Lowe, you are under arrest, and you have the right to remain silent."

"Under arrest?" Darryl barks. "For what, running a red light?" The cop pushes Darryl toward the Suburban without answering him. "For what?" he asks again. "Yo, can I call my lawyer? My attorney is Ray Brown," he says, hoping that will instill some fear into the cop.

"You can call Ray when you get to the station," he says as if he knows him personally.

The other cop holds the door wide as Darryl is dragged with force. As Darryl stands at the door, he attempts to turn around, but the cop manhandles him to keep him facing forward. The more force the cop uses, the more unruly Darryl becomes. "Yo, what the fuck am I getting arrested for?" he barks with rage.

The cop tries to force Darryl into the back seat of the Suburban, but Darryl places his foot on the seat to prevent himself from being pushed inside. Both cops now attempt to push him into the truck, but Darryl is putting up the fight of his life. He flips and flops, making it almost impossible to get him inside until, *Thump.*

"Aghh," Darryl grunts after he's struck in the head. It feels as if a block of cement has been dropped on his head. He stops fidgeting and peeks over his shoulder to see what he's been hit with. His eyes land on the butt of the gun coming down toward his head again.

"Ok, ok," Darryl pleads before he's struck again and again and again. The second blow causes Darryl to see spots before his eyes, and the third blow causes his vision to blur. The fourth one causes Darryl to see nothing but darkness. Lights out!

Darryl is knocked out cold. The officer holds him tightly in his arms as he falls limp. The officer pushes Darryl in and lays his body stretched out across the backseat. His partner slams the door before trotting up to Darryl's Lexus. He hops into the driver's seat and pulls off. The Suburban tails the Lexus closely.

-55-

South Orange, New Jersey

T he cranberry Porsche 911 convertible with the Targa top pulls up to the beautiful one-family house. The garage opens slowly. The Porsche creeps into the garage. Lefty slips into the garage as the garage door closes behind the car. He kneels as he creeps up around the other side. Money Dee opens the driver's side door, and just as he gets out, he and Lefty meet face to face.

Money Dee's face goes stone as if he's just seen a ghost, better yet the Grim Reaper. "Lef, what up bro?" Money Dee asks with a nervous smile. "What the fuck you doing here? What's going on?" he asks as attempts to downplay the situation. He knows something is wrong with this picture yet he tries to talk Lefty down off the ledge. "Talk to me, bro."

"Shh," Lefty says as he shakes his head from side to side. Lefty snatches Money Dee closer to him and places him in a Full Nelson, the gun against his temple with one hand and his nub pressing against his Adam's Apple. He applies pressure.

"Come on, man," Money Dee gasps. Lefty squeezes tighter, making it harder for him to breathe and talk.

"We bigger than this," he says in a low whisper. He can barely speak.

"I didn't come to talk," Lefty says.

Money Dee points to the side door, which is the entrance to the basement. "My kids in the house, bro," he gasps. "Your nephew and your nieces," he says as he attempts to find a soft spot, even though he knows Lefty's heart is stone-cold. Lefty nudges him forward. Money Dee leads him into the next room, which is set up like an office.

"Bro, this me, bro," Money Dee says calmly. "Bro, this ain't for us right here. This is for other niggas. We are way bigger than this. What is it? Do you need something? Let me know what it is? Whatever you need, I got you."

"I need you to take me to it. That's what I need you to do."

Money Dee walks to a closet door and pulls it open. "Come on, bro. I know this ain't over no paper. Money is nothing compared to what we got. No amount of money ain't worth our friendship, our brotherhood."

"This ain't over no money," Lefty claims. "This is about principle." Lefty looks up and spots the built-in shelves on the closet's back wall. There are four fireproof safes in total, two to a rack. He's sure the safes are filled with money and maybe even drugs; enough money to set himself up for the rest of his life.

"I introduced you to a good friend of mine and introduced him as such, and I validated him just as I validated you," Lefty says as he pushes Money Dee in front of him. Money Dee turns around quickly, and Lefty aims at his head.

He raises his hands in the air. The nervous smile presents itself again. "That's what all of this is about? A new nigga? You going through all of this over a new nigga?"

"Nah, this ain't about no new nigga. This is about me keeping my word. I told both of you to handle each other as if I'm in the room even when I'm not in the room."

"Bro, listen. I changed my mind. I'm taking your word for it. If you say he good, he's good."

Lefty chuckles. "Nah bro, I can't go with that. This was never about you not trusting him. This was about you playing on the love I had for you. You wanted me to kill my Baby Boy so you could keep his money."

"Hell no bro," Money Dee says with another nervous smile. "You bugging, bro. I would never do that."

Lefty nods with a smile of his own. "You have done that."

"Look bro, I still got his bread right there, and I never touched it. Three hundred thousand," Money Dee says. "The same way he gave it to me," he says as he points to the duffel bag in the corner. "It's all right there. Take it, and let's forget all about this."

Lefty can see tears of fear building up in Money Dee's eyes. "Bro, this ain't for us."

"That's where you're wrong," Lefty snaps. "This is for anybody that goes against the code and breaks the trust and the loyalty. I had you down as honorable. You used me, bro. I had your back, and you used me like a stunt dummy."

Lefty cracks a devious smile. "Just like the old days, you always sent Big Dumb Lefty on a stunt dummy mission. Hype me up to do anything. Your own personal dummy. I see I'm still just Big Dumb Lefty to you after all these years."

This is Lefty's longest and only friend. Their friendship dates back to them being twelve years old. Lefty always protected him like a younger brother, and he always took care of Lefty like he was his younger brother.

"Bro, I always had your back," Money Dee says. "I never betrayed you."

"That's a lie, Bro," Lefty whispers angrily. "You betrayed me when you had me out here killing niggas for your gain. All the while, I thought they were playing on you, and you were playing on me." Lefty cracks a grin.

"Getting richer off my back and paying me peanuts. I never once asked you how much they beat you for or ran off with because I didn't care. I only cared that people were playing on my brother's good heart. When all the while." He smiles, but his anger is peeking through. "You were the one playing on everybody else, including me.

Giving me a measly thousand dollars to murder men that you had stolen hundreds of thousands from. I never did it for the money. I did it for the brotherhood. You conned them just like you conned me. A fucking con-man."

Lefty fights the urge to punch him in the face. "I never figured out that it was all a lie, and all these people weren't running off on you. Do you know why? Because in my heart, you were a good nigga. And you were my brother, so I had no reason to second guess you."

Lefty draws back the gun as if he's about to strike him in the head with it, but he doesn't. "It wasn't until this last move that I had to question it all. I figured out that it was all a lie. My Baby Boy did nothing to make you not trust him. The only thing he did wrong was giving you three hundred grand. You made up that lie because you knew I would take him off the map before I allowed him to fuck everything up for you," he says while shaking his head sadly.

"It was all a lie." Lefty feels like a complete idiot. "Just like all the other lies you told on men who did nothing wrong to you but give you their money in good faith to invest." He chuckles a hearty laugh. "And then you send Big Dumb Lefty out there to kill them so you can keep their money."

Money Dee realizes he has been figured out. Lefty has put it all together accurately. Money Dee has indeed built a name for himself selling coke and dope. Coke and dope made him ghetto rich. But then it hit him, and he realized that there's only one thing that sells faster than dope, and that's hope. He's made more money selling hope than he's ever made selling dope.

Hope is for the desperate ones looking for an answer, an escape, a bigger picture. He figured out that no one is more desperate than a man looking for a way out of the game. So he became a master at packaging the bigger picture. Once he packaged it correctly, he could sell it to hustlers that wanted out of the game. His reputation and even the cocaine network was his track record, and it was the bait that he needed to reel people in. His cocaine pipeline is actual, and it flourishes just as he says it does. And that's all the validation he needed to get men to invest in his brand. Only specific handpicked individuals get a return on their investment, and the others get killed before the investment matures.

Money Dee sees the viciousness in Lefty's eye. "Come on, Bro, how much can I give you to make this go away and get me back in good standing with my brother," he says in an attempt to try and soften Lefty's heart.

"Let's start with getting my man his money back."

"I told you it's all right there, not a dollar missing. But what do you need for yourself? You know I got plenty of it," he says as he points to one of the safes. "Let me open it, and you take whatever you need."

Lefty quickly thinks of the money that could be in the safe. He's sure millions are lying behind those fireproof walls. He would be set for life. Finally, he could change his circumstances for good but his reality sets in. "Bro, you know this ain't about money. You know I'm not money-driven. This is about morals, principles, and integrity for me. You can't pay me back with money. You can only repay me in blood."

He takes a deep breath, preparing himself for something he hates to do. Out of all the murders he has committed in life, this one is the hardest. But it has to be done. It's not just for the betrayal that he feels from Money Dee lying to him all this time. It's not even for the fact that he cosigned for Money Dee to Darryl. One of the biggest reasons he's doing this is to save Darryl. He's sure the next person he offers the money to knock Darryl off will.

Lefty steps closer, and Money Dee backs up against the wall. He crouches into a ball to protect himself. "Please, bro, my wife and kids upstairs. Don't let them wake up to my dead body, plea.." he says before the sound of gunfire drowns out his voice. *Boom!*

Money Dee's body drops to the floor. Lefty stands over him and aims at the back of his head. *Boom! Boom!*

-56-

Darryl sits on the floor. A blindfold covers his eyes. His feet are tied together with rope, and his hands are cuffed behind his back. He depends on his hearing as his sole sense. What he thought was Auto Squad is robbers pretending to be police.

More men have joined in. He can't be positive, but he does know he has heard at least three different voices. As he sits here, many thoughts occupy his mind. He wonders where this hit came from. With the way it all has gone down, he's sure it's an inside job.

The assailants have been taking turns beating on him. One by one and even two at a time, they have put hands and feet on him. Nothing seems to be getting through to him, and not even the pistol whippings make him cooperate. This frustrates the assailants, and they are tired of playing around with him.

"Listen to me, nigga," the man says before striking Darryl with the butt of the gun. Darryl absorbs the blow without a murmur. "You're going to get your baby mother on the phone." He strikes Darryl again. "And you gone tell the bitch we need a half a million, or you're a dead ass." He hits him once again.

"Yeah, call that bitch," says another voice. The man kneels on the other side of Darryl. "Call your baby mother," he grunts as he presses his gun against the back of Darryl's head.

My baby mother, Darryl, thinks to himself. It's now confirmed. Hearing this reassures him that this caper has been ordered by Sunday. *Got damn, Sunday, he thinks to himself. How could you?* Darryl becomes more fearful now as he realizes that Asia is also in danger.

The man snatches Darryl forward. "Listen, give me the number, and I'm gone dial it, and you're going to tell her to bring a half a million." The man leans closer. "What's the number, motherfucker!"

Darryl fears for his life, but he's terrified for Asia's life. As easy as it would be for him to make the call and have the money delivered to the doorstep, he refuses to do so and drag her into this mess. He feels that he is already responsible for destroying her life as it is. Without even realizing it, he shakes his head negatively. The words 'I'd rather die like a man than to live like a coward' replays in his head over and over again. He shakes his head harder and more reassuringly, letting the man know that he means what he's saying.

The man becomes even more angered. "No?" he barks. "No? You telling me fucking no?"

Darryl flinches after every word, expecting to hear the sound of the gun going off. Finally, he hears what he's been waiting for. *Boc!* His ears ring loudly. He closes his eyes tightly and tenses up, attempting to prepare himself for the unknown. The bullet crashes into the back of his skull, causing his neck to snap forward. He falls over onto his side.

In seconds the heat makes it feel like his head is on fire, and the burning sensation is nothing compared to the pain that accompanies it. He attempts to scream, but nothing comes out. He struggles to breathe, and each breath gets harder to take. He twists around in pain as he fights for his life. His windpipe is closing in, and each breath becomes more seconds apart than the last one. He takes a deep breath, but he can't hold onto the air, and it seeps out just as fast as he sucks it in. His lungs are closing up, causing his deep breaths to become shorter and shorter and shorter.

Boc! Boc! Boc! The first slug rips through his forehead while the other two melt into his face. His gasping and breathing stop immediately. His body stiffens, before collapsing onto the floor. His head tilts to the side and his body goes limp as the last bit of air he holds, escapes his body.

-57-

Twenty Minutes Later

EFTY RINGS DARRYL'S BELL AND REALIZES the door is partly open. He knocks on it twice before pushing it open slowly. "Baby Boy," he says as he peeks inside. He sees boots with the soles up, facing the door. He pushes the door slightly and looks closer. Through his good eye, it appears that someone is lying on the floor. He rushes inside, and to his surprise, he finds Darryl's dead body with his head in a pool of blood.

Darryl appears to be looking up at Lefty with his eyes stretched wide open. Lefty leans over and places his finger on the side of Darryl's neck. "Nah, Baby Boy, nah, hell nah," he says.

He puts the palm of his hand under Darryl's nose, hoping to feel him breathing but nothing. Lefty drops his head sadly. He can't believe he got to him too late. He assumes Money Dee already placed the hit on him, and somebody answered the call immediately. As he looks at Darryl's lifeless body, for the first time he feels something he has never felt before, and that is compassion. He also feels guilt that Darryl is dead because of him. Darryl trusted his word and his judgment, and now he's dead.

For the first time in over fifteen years, he sheds a tear. Lefty gently places his fingers over Darryl's eyes and closes his curtains. He drops his head with sadness. He weeps silently.

Meanwhile

The black Suburban pulls into the garage. As soon as the truck is parked, both doors swing open. The driver hops out and quickly makes his way to the back wall of the garage. He presses the keypad, and the garage door comes down slowly.

The back doors of the truck open up simultaneously. Both men get out, lugging garbage bags in their hands. They all stand together in a huddle in front of the truck. A fifth man walks over as the men are dropping the bags onto the truck's hood. "How we make out? What we got?" the man asks with anxiousness.

Sadness covers all of their faces. "Not too good," one man yells out. He pauses briefly before speaking again. "Bad news," he says as he lowers his eyes to the floor. "Shit didn't go as planned. He wasn't cooperating, so we had to leave him in there."

"Leave him?" the man asks. "Like leave him, leave him?" The man nods his head up and down slowly. Sadness plasters the man's face as he backpedals a few steps. He leans against the white Acura. He tilts his head back and stares at the ceiling for a few seconds.

"Sheed, we had no choice," the man claims. This man is Sheed's cousin Dre. "There wasn't shit in the house," Dre says with disappointment. "Not a dollar or a gram of coke. No matter how much we tortured and threatened him, he still wouldn't tell us shit!"

Rage covers Sheed's face. "I knew I should've gone the fuck in because I know for sure something was in there. Y'all didn't look good enough!" he barks.

"We turned the whole apartment upside down. There wasn't shit in there."

"Dre!" Sheed shouts. "You're not listening. I know for sure. How are you going to tell me something that I know for sure? Shit!" he shouts. "The come-up of a lifetime, and y'all blew it." He walks to the hood of the truck.

Sheed looks through the garbage bags. "What the fuck is this?" he asks. "Fucking sneakers and clothes? I don't believe this shit! That's why you couldn't find the money or the work because y'all busy in there packing up clothes and sneakers!" he shouts. "That's some straight feen shit!" Sheed stares into the faces of each one of them as they lower their eyes with disappointment.

He's more disappointed than all of them. He was sure this sting would set them all straight. He's sure there had to be something in there, and they just overlooked it. As much as he believes that he will never know the truth.

Sheed walks around the truck where the two police impersonators stand alone. Sheed stops in between them. He lowers his eyes before speaking. "Ay, man, all I can say is I apologize. I picked the wrong mufuckers for the job. I should have never fucked with those two dope feen mufuckers," he says as he points over his shoulder.

Sheed is bothered by the fact that he promised them this sting would put them in position. He met them both during his bid, and they were the only two inmates he cut into. Even though their hustles are the total opposite of his, he still took a liking to them. They were the first people who came to mind when he put this plan together. Because their profession is the robbery and home invasion field, he felt they were perfect for the job. He imported them from Trenton to come in and do the job. They covered their end of the bargain, but he didn't, and because of that, he feels as if he let them down.

Sheed digs into his pocket and starts counting through the bills. He hands a stack of bills to both men. "I dropped the ball, but I promise to make it up to y'all." He looks over to the other two men. "Pack all them dumb ass clothes and shit in the trunk!" he shouts with rage. He looks back to the other two. "That's twenty-five hundred apiece just to put a couple of dollars in your pocket and not waste your time. Give me a minute, and I promise I will be able to bring y'all in on something."

"Ay, man, shit happens," one man replies as he opens the truck door. "Sometimes you score. Sometimes you break even, and other times you come up blank. It's all a gamble," he says as he climbs into the truck. The other man follows his lead and gets into the passenger's seat. "Hit me up," he says as he starts the engine.

"No doubt," Sheed replies as he makes his way over to the garage opener. He presses the button before walking over to Darryl's Acura. "Let's go," he says to Dre. He opens the door and sits down. Once his passengers are seated, he backs out of the garage.

"Who pulled the trigger?" Sheed asks curiously.

"I did," Smitty says from the back seat. "I owed him that," he says with pride and satisfaction.

"Yo, Sheed, how you feeling, though?" Dre asks. "How do you feel about his death? I know how tight y'all was and shit."

"Yeah, how tight we was," he says with strong emphasis. "But sometimes best friends become strangers," he says with no compassion at all. "How I feel?" he asks.

"I don't feel like shit! How did he feel when I was sitting in prison starving while he was out here eating like the hog that he was?" he asks with venom in his voice.

"He didn't give a fuck about me, so why should I give a fuck about him?" He looks into Dre's eyes. "Don't nobody give a fuck about me. Nigga, that's the game!"

-58-

Days Later

Sheed sits inside the office of Churchman's Funeral Home. He watches as Darryl's Nana talks to the woman across the desk from her. She's been crying the entire time, barely able to contain herself. She feared this day would eventually come and begged him not to put her through this. She's just lost the last thing she had to hold onto. Darryl was her only reason for living. As she peeks over at Sheed, she feels no guilt wishing it was him and not Darryl.

Loud bursts of crying come from the hallway where Asia and her mother are. Asia is taking this badly. She hasn't stopped crying since she received the news. To be here making funeral arrangements for the true love of her life is something she never imagined doing. She knew there was always the possibility, but still, she never thought it would be something she would have to do.

The woman slides the paper across the desk to Darryl's Nana. Her eyes bulge as she looks at the total cost of the funeral. More tears run from her eyes as she accepts the fact that she's not able to afford to give her baby his proper burial. "And how much for a cremation?" she asks with a broken heart.

Sheed steps up. "No, Nana, don't worry," he says as he grabs hold of the paper. "This ain't your bill. It's mine. Darryl has always been a brother to me. However you want to send him off, I got it. Don't worry about the cost. Nothing is too much for my brother."

As much as she despises Sheed, this touches her heart. She gets up and hugs him tightly. She doesn't want to let go because, at this moment, this is the closest person that she has to Darryl. "Thank you, baby," she says as she wets his shoulder with tears.

One Hour Later

Sheed stands in the luxurious apartment, just looking around, appreciating the view. As much as he appreciates the view, it brings about more hatred. Being in this apartment justifies the resentment he still has for Darryl. Finding out that Darryl had a whole apartment that he never talked about confirms that their relationship had changed, and they were no longer the best friends he thought they were.

Asia steps through the corridor holding a duffle bag. As she approaches, she extends the bag toward Sheed. "Here," she says. "I know he would want me to give this to you."

"What is it," Sheed asks with his heart racing. He quickly unzips the bag. What lies before his eyes is the settlement to it all, and it's partially what he did all of this for in the first place. Satisfaction fills his heart as he counts through the six kilos that lie inside the bag. Also in the bag is a digital scale and a few guns.

Asia has given Sheed all the unlawful stuff except Darryl's money, which she has spoken to no one about.

She found so much money that she was afraid to talk to anyone about it, not even her mother. In the few days that he's been deceased, she still hasn't been able to count through all of the money. She stopped her count at a little over 1.3 million, and she still has a great deal of counting to do.

It's hard for her to believe what her, at one time, innocent high school love had become. She remembers the days of them walking home from school because he had no bus fare. He always told her that he was doing this for him and her. In the end, she has it all with no him. With her not being money-driven, this money means nothing to her without him.

She would give all the money up to have him back. She knows that's not possible, so she has to carry out what she knows would be his wishes. His fear was always leaving his Nana in the world alone. Asia plans to carry out what she knows he would want from her, and that is to take care of his Nana and make sure she's good until her time on this earth runs out.

Sheed's eyes are stuck in the bag. He already sees his come-up before his eyes. The 120-day deadline he gave himself to become a millionaire just got cut in half. He's beyond ecstatic, and he struggles to keep it concealed. Before he lifts his head, he focuses on keeping the fake sorrow on his face. "Asia, I want you to know that this call will not go unanswered. I already got my thoughts on who may be behind this. When I get the final word, they will pay for this shit, believe me," he says with convincing eyes.

Sheed stares at her with piercing eyes. "A, you ever heard bro speak of somebody name Lefty?"

Asia shakes her head. "Nah, not that I remember, why?"

"Nothing. Forget I even said it. I got this," he says while nodding his head. "But as far as y'all baby, don't worry because anything you or that baby need, I'm here for y'all. D was my brother, and I'm gone hold it down for him as I know he would hold it down for me." Asia rushes Sheed and buries her head in his chest. Her loud crying seeps out of the apartment and echoes throughout the hall.

Meanwhile

The train speeds along the track at 150 miles an hour. Lefty sits at the window seat, watching the scenery. On the floor under his feet are two duffle bags. One bag has his entire life inside, while the other holds his future. In one bag is all of his boxing equipment, his toiletries, his ID, Social Security card, his Birth Certificate, and any paperwork that he has accumulated over the years. In the other bag is the three hundred grand that belonged to Darryl.

His destination, he has not a clue. This train isn't the Path Train that he rode every night until he fell asleep. This train is an Amtrak Train headed far away. This situation with Darryl and Money Dee has beaten him down lower than he already was. It was the final straw and all the incentive he needed to pack it up and leave. He murdered his big brother for murdering his little brother, and that's something that he hopes he can one day forget. The guilt he feels for Darryl losing his life he's sure will never leave him.

The train slows down before making an abrupt stop. Lefty gets up and grabs the duffle bag full of money. He falls in line with the people making their exit off the train. Once he's off, he stands watching the train pull off with the bag of his past still on it.

As he always knew, a man can't change the conditions of his life until he changes the conditions of his heart.

Today he's changed the conditions of his heart by leaving his past behind him. He tightens the grip of the duffle bag that holds his future in it. He exits the train station with no prescribed destination. He takes a deep breath as he walks into his new life.

THE END

A FILM BASED ON THE NOVEL BY
AL-SAADIQ BANKS

Sincerely yours

IF HE CAN'T HAVE HER **HEART**... HE'LL SETTLE FOR HER **LIFE**

TRUE2LIFE AND SMASH FILMS PRESENTS "SINCERELY YOURS" BY AL-SAADIQ BANKS
STARRING HOPE BLACKSTOCK STYLES P. KAMEL GOFFIN EDMOND LARYEA AND KENISHIA GREEN
PRODUCED NAIM BANKS TYRONE ROBINSON AL-SAADIQ BANKS AND MANMAZZIN YODENIM
WRITTEN BY AL-SAADIQ BANKS & DUTCH DIRECTED BY AL-SAADIQ BANKS

BOOK ORDER FORM
Purchase Information

_____

_____

_____

Address: City: State: Zip Code:

Books are listed in the order they were written and published

$14.95 - **No Exit**

$14.95 - **Block Party** *1*

$14.95 - **Sincerely Yours**

$14.95 - **Caught em Slippin**

$14.95 - **Block Party** *2*

$14.95 - **Block Party** *3*

$14.95 - **Strapped**

$14.95 - **Back 2 Bizness (Block Party** *4)*

$14.95 - **Young Gunz**

$14.95 - **Outlaw Chick**

$14.95 - **Block Party 5k1** *Volume 1*

$14.95 - **Block Party 5k1** *Volume 2*

$14.95 - **Heartless**

$14.95 - **Block Party 666** *Volume 1*

$14.95 - **Block Party 666** *Volume 2*

Street Dreams and Nightmares the Duology *(2 Book series)*

$14.95 - **Street Dreams**

$14.95 - **And Nightmares**

Book Total: _____

Add $8.00 for shipping of 1-3 books
Free shipping for order of 4 or more books

Mailing Address:
True 2 Life Publications
PO Box 8722
Newark, NJ 07108

Make Checks/Money Orders payable to: ***True 2 Life Publications***